Scars Secrets & Scores

THE BEN & SELINA TRILOGY

KIRU TAYE

First Published in Great Britain in 2020 by
LOVE AFRICA PRESS
103 Reaver House, 12 East Street, Epsom KT17 1HX
www.loveafricapress.com

Text copyright © Kiru Taye, 2013

Scars
THE BEN & SELINA TRILOGY #1

Dedication

This story is dedicated to all the beautiful women and the fabulous people who love us, scars and all.

I want to give a special thank you to Doris, Michaela, Raven, Jennifer, Nana and Empi for reading the first raw draft and loving this story so much. Without your help I wouldn't have had the confidence to submit this story for publication.

To my readers, thank you for your support so far. I hope you'll continue to read as I explore the spicier and grittier parts of modern relationships in this new Passion Shields series. I love writing these stories. Enjoy reading them.

Love

Kiru

Blurb

She clutches at control to cover her flaws. He wants to strip her bare because she's beautiful.

Selina Moss hides a secret beneath her controlled happy exterior. Her body is covered in scars and she's never revealed them to anyone. However, it's her wedding night and husband, Benjamin Moss, is determined to strip down her barriers. Benjamin is not playing fair, not when he's deploying breath-stealing seduction as well as mind-melting sex toys. But will he still want her when she bares all?

"I look forward to having you naked in bed tonight."

Benjamin's rich voice whispered hotly against the skin on the back of her ears. The image of her bare body sprawled against the Egyptian cotton sheets of their five-star hotel bed loomed large in Selina's mind. Sparks of arousal travelled down her spine to her very core.

"All your beautiful chocolate skin on display for me."

His hand stroked her thigh—slow, purposeful strokes, igniting into flames of desire that licked her sex, melting it like wax.

She bit her lip, holding back a moan as she turned her head, needing to see his face, taste his lips.

"Congratulations to Mr and Mrs Moss." The strange voice cut through the spell that held her. She looked up, and a guest stood next to their high table, his short glass of what looked like brandy raised in salutation.

"Thank you," Selina smiled at the dark-haired, olive-skinned man she didn't recognise. He was probably one of Benjamin's colleagues or acquaintances.

"You made it, then, Juan." Her new husband stood. "Selina, this is Juan Roberto. He's part of Moss Star Security team."

Benjamin's words confirmed her thoughts.

"It's good to finally meet you." There was something of a knowing glint in Juan's eyes as he leaned in and gave her a brief kiss on both cheeks. With her senses heightened from wedding day excitement, his aftershave reminded her of sun-baked sandy shores and salty sea air.

"Same here." Cheeks smarting, she wondered if there were any members of his firm who didn't know about her.

The two men continued in conversation, something about Juan returning from a trip providing security for a pop star on a live tour in Europe. Selina relaxed back into her chair as the men talked shop.

Benjamin owned a security firm that supplied bodyguards to high profile executives and celebrities in the UK and internationally. As a result, their wedding guests were made of gorgeous hunks of men built like armoured tanks and their equally beautiful girlfriends or escorts. She'd met most of them during the six months she'd dated Benjamin and had gotten the impression they were a close family.

The private banquet room, though small, was tastefully decorated. White brocade covered chairs and tables, thin-stemmed centre-piece flower arrangements, the red and black theme she'd chosen reflected in the colours.

They'd catered for fifty guests, small by African wedding proportions.

Selina hadn't wanted a big wedding and would've done without a wedding at all. But under the circumstances this one was unavoidable.

Large crowds in enclosed spaces agitated her. So, the smaller the group invited, the better.

Having to deal with people was nothing in the scale of concern compared to what she had to face up to later tonight in the privacy of their hotel suite. There were things she'd held close to her chest, something she'd hidden from Benjamin. Secrets she was afraid to share.

All your beautiful chocolate skin on display for me. Benjamin's earlier words came back to mock her. How was she going to get through her wedding night without him finding out she wasn't as beautiful as he thought?

Wine glasses tinkled; cutlery clattered on crockery. Laughter rang out, the cacophony of voices and music overwhelming. Flashes of images of a celebration from a distant past merged with the present—joyous laughter and rhythmic dancing. General merriment.

The rat-tat-tat of gunfire. Pounding boots on the hard floor. Terrified shouts. Menacing mirth. Faces contorted with malevolence.

Selina's mouth dried out. Pins and needles pricking sensations travelled up her arm. Her body flushed with heat.

"Are you still with me?" Benjamin's sonorous voice drew Selina's attention back from her daydream.

Her chest constricted. Her corset felt as if it was cutting off her breathing.

"Breathe, Selina. Breathe."

The tone of his voice compelled her. She took a slow breath, drawing much-needed oxygen into her lungs, held it, and then let it out steadily. She repeated the process. There was no other way to breathe in this stiffened garment.

His hand covered the back of her neck, providing a cool respite from the suddenly elevated room temperature. Memories of the past had her in its grip, unpleasant recollections that had her heart pounding with fear.

She tilted her head up and gazed into her husband's grey eyes. His dark gaze seemed to see so much, know so much. Concern etched lines on his tanned rugged face, his neatly trimmed beard the colour of chestnut, the same as the hair on his head.

His hold on her neck turned into brush strokes on canvass, light and erotic, his Da Vinci to her Mona Lisa, making her catch her breath as delicious tingles shot down her spine.

This was Benjamin. The way he always seemed to have her in an erotic bind whenever he was close baffled her. The tightness of the outfit she wore didn't help as it meant her exposed skin was more sensitive than usual.

He raised one eyebrow, drawing a response from her.

"I was thinking of another time and place." Even when she didn't want to talk, Benjamin had a way of making her answer his queries, silent or otherwise.

"You don't have to worry anymore." He kept his voice low enough so that no one else could listen in over the din of the music and chatter of the guests.

"I know. But I can't help it." She paused and took a deep breath to quell the tears that threatened to burst free. "I feel so guilty. Meanwhile, I've been getting on with my life, and he's been without anyone."

She'd recently found out that the brother she'd thought had been killed was alive and living in Sierra Leone. Her only living relative. Another survivor of the war ten years ago.

"I think about all the things that could have happened to him..." Her shoulders shook as she shuddered in remembered terror.

Benjamin leaned in, his lips only inches from her right ear. "You're now my wife, and as I promised to take care of you and your brother, I will. Trust me."

That was precisely her problem—trusting people. Ten years ago, she'd lost her faith in humanity and had never entirely relied on anyone since.

Until she'd met Benjamin.

But it hadn't been easy. Initially, she'd rejected his advances, afraid to give in to the intense attraction she'd felt for him. Still, he'd been determined to prove to her that he was worthy of her confidence.

For her trust was a matter given in degrees, in increments of grey—neither white nor black. Never given wholeheartedly, not even to the man she now called her husband. But she'd granted him some commitment. Otherwise, she wouldn't have married him.

Still, it didn't mean she was ready to give up control of her life totally to him. It didn't stop her from worrying about stuff and making plans.

The grey of his eyes turned to slate, hard and yet somehow fragile.

Her lack of immediate response was all the answer he needed. He read her easily.

Discomfited, she rolled her tongue across her lower lip, tasting her cherry lip gloss.

"I'm sorry, Ben." She turned her gaze away, trying to avoid his. "Some things are easier said than done. I'll feel a lot more relaxed when Kaya is here with me."

She stared into the crowd. The guests were mainly his. She had invited only some close colleagues from the hospital where she worked as a pharmacist and the handful of friends she'd made since her arrival in the UK.

She'd struggled with the decision to get married. But she needed a safe and stable environment for her teenage brother. The authorities wanted to see it, too, before they would grant her the rights to adopt her own sibling. Ben had convinced her that marriage was the best option for realising it. Moreover, since he was a British citizen, it would make the process of bringing her brother to the UK easier.

Without another word, Benjamin stood. Christopher Star, his best man, approached him. "What's up?"

Ben leaned over and said something to his friend in a low voice that Selina couldn't hear.

"Right," Christopher said, his accent tinged with an Easter European drawl that had appealed to her the first time she'd met him.

"You're coming with me." Ben's fingers circled her upper arm, his grip rough and urgent, helping her up.

She glanced around, confused by his abrupt action. "What? We can't abandon our guests."

"We'll only be gone for a few minutes. Chris will cover for us if anyone asks."

He didn't wait for her response and tugged at her hand. Tottering on her stilettos, she followed him out into the foyer with the bank of lifts. When he pressed the button to call one, she had to ask, "Where are you taking me?"

"There's something I need to show you in our suite upstairs."

The corners of his mouth lifted in a boyish grin as the lift doors opened. Her gaze fixated on his lips—sensuously full, they were a mix of firmness on the edges and softness on the inside—and she wondered if he would kiss her.

Her pulse rate skyrocketed as they rode up, and he pulled her into the circle of his arms. He looked so handsome in his fitted charcoal suit, broad torso tapering at the hips. The taut muscles beneath the soft silk fabric offered protection as well as a glimpse of the possession to come. With her head on his shoulder, his all-male spice permeated her pores with every breath she took.

"You do know we can't leave our guests at the reception just for a quickie," she said. Tilting her head so she could see his face, she curled her lips in an I'd-like-you-to-take-me smile. Her core contracted in agreement.

Truth was, she needed to get laid—the hot, fast, sweaty kind. Since she agreed to marry Ben, they hadn't been together, not even for a hand job. The mad rush to organise a wedding ceremony in such a short period, his insistence for her to move her things into his waterside penthouse apartment in Chelsea, combined with a pretty hefty schedule at work for both of them had left little time for anything else.

"Who says we can't?"

He kissed her, a ruthless sweep of his tongue and demand of his lips. She clutched the lapels of his jacket, hanging on as sensation assaulted her.

Beneath her dress, her lacy thong got soaked as she squirmed against him. She'd worn the skimpy underwear to avoid panty-lines showing through her dress. Perhaps she should've chosen something sturdier like French knickers.

When he lifted his head, she was breathless, panting.

"Ben?" she asked when she finally got her voice back.

The dark colour of his suit emphasised the intensity of his eyes and complemented his tanned skin. With his South African heritage, his skin tone was always on the golden side, despite the recent bad weather and lack of sunshine.

"No. But I've got the next best thing for you."

They stepped out of the lift, and he opened the door to the bridal suite. She followed him in, heart pounding in excitement.

"Before the reception is over, you'll be begging me to fuck you."

Heat flared on her skin and sent darts of fire to her core. Speechless, she just stood there by the sofa in the living room, staring at him as he disappeared into the bedroom. Rose petals lined the floor from the main entrance leading into the other room. She recovered her composure and followed the red trail.

They led to the bed with white sheets covered in more petals. The light sweet aroma of roses filled the air, uplifting and soulful. Ben came out of the closet holding a brown leather overnight bag.

"Did you do this?" she asked as her heart jolted and warmth bloomed around her chest. She hadn't expected anything romantic. Their wedding was more of an arrangement than for amorous reason. Yet Ben continued to surprise her.

The glorious smile curling his lips reminded her of a benevolent Greek god.

"For the right price, you can get anything you want," he said. "Moreover, I wanted tonight to be special."

She nodded and swallowed a lump in her throat, blinking back tears. When her new husband was this thoughtful, how could she resist him?

She'd asked him to keep things simple. He had in his own way. But he'd spared no expense with a wedding reception in a five-star hotel in the most expensive part of London. And they would spend the weekend here since they didn't have time for a full week's honeymoon somewhere else.

He placed the bag on the bed, retrieving a white tube containing lube and a golden egg.

"What?" Her breath hitched, her eyes widening in recognition.

"Come," he said.

She went to him, her heart pounding against her ribs. He took her hand, pulled her to sit on the edge of the bed and squatted before her. Standing tall, he oozed strength and dominated any space he occupied, a leader among his peers. Yet, here he was stooped before her, his hands on her knees offering reassurance and safety.

Intuitively, he knew what she needed when she needed it. More than anything else about him, his on-the-mark intuition had attracted as well as scared her when she'd first met him. She curled her hands into fists on her lap. It still frightened her. He could see through her protective walls into the dark recesses of her soul like Superman with his x-ray vision.

"Selina, you know I hate watching you all wound up and worried. This afternoon I took a vow to take care of you no matter what. Your experience with me so far should tell you that I never break a promise, right?"

"Right." She nodded and licked her suddenly dry lips.

"Then, you know that I have to do something to ease your tension. I brought this." He picked up the egg and held it in his palm like an offering. "So, we could play during our honeymoon. But we're going to use it now."

"Is that what I think it is?"

"If you think it's a vibrator, then you're correct. You're going to wear it for the rest of the day."

"No way." She shook her head, but her body shivered in anticipation. She couldn't spend the evening wearing a sex toy, and more to the point, being sexually aroused. What would people think of her?

"Yes, way." The wolfish curl of his lips and the intense determination in his eyes told her more than his words that he wouldn't accept her rebuttal. "It's exactly what you need to relax you and take your mind off things."

"I don't know." She bit her lower lip. He was right. She needed to loosen up. She'd been so wound up earlier she'd had a panic attack. That wasn't good. But this?

"Do you trust me to do the right thing for you, for us?" His husky voice was cajoling, reassuring, telling her everything would be all right if only she would let go.

"Of course, but—"

"Then trust me now. Lift your dress up." His tone changed, brooking no challenge.

This is crazy. Still, she bunched her skirt, lifting 'til it pooled in a ruffle of black satin around her hips. It was easier, giving in to this. Some other things were more difficult to yield.

The hungry way he looked at her before his warm hands caressed her thighs had her heart hammering and her red lace thong getting wetter. He traced the pad of his fingers over the stockings and garter she wore—her bid at a traditional wedding outfit. The rest of her dress was hardly the customary white.

Whoever got married in red and black satin?

She did. In her own way, she marked the bloody tragedy that had ended her first marriage.

As if he could read where her mind was travelling to, Ben shoved her thighs apart, earning her attention once more. Any thought of objecting departed when his lips descended on the scrap of red lace covering her mound.

First, there was the scrape of teeth and then the suction of his mouth that had her whimpering in surrender.

"Oh..." Her body arched off the bed, her elbows supporting her weight. The touch of his full, firm lips drowned her in sensory overload. Sensitive all over, she shivered as her desire spiked to boiling point.

"I had thought of preparing you with the gel..." Ben hooked his fingers around the straps of her panties and pulled them down. He lifted her right leg and hooked it over his left shoulder.

"But this is more fun and sweeter, too."

His lips returned to her damp core, and he dragged a lick from her opening to her swollen bud. He repeated that twice, thrice, the short hairs on his cheeks scraping her thighs as if marking her. The next day her skin would be raw, undoubtedly, a reminder of this brief pleasurable interlude on their wedding day. For now, she would enjoy it. Her breath shortened and sped up as her body raced towards an orgasm.

A fever swept over her. She canted her hips, and he moved with her. She rolled to the side, but he held her still, unrelenting.

She'd never known a man like Benjamin. A man who could decipher her needs even before she could vocalise them. A man who could take charge of a sexual encounter with precision without her directing him to suck her or hold her. Usually, she was the one leading. It had been refreshing when she'd had her first encounter with him. He had seen her need instantly, the need to have a man take responsibility for her sexual pleasure. It was the only area she was willing to give up control.

His right hand travelled up her bodice and cupped a breast, squeezing through to her already puckered tip, zinging her body with electrical currents. The other hand cupped her round bottom. When his fingertip scraped her over-sensitised hole, the friction alone was enough to drive her over the edge.

Fuck! She mouthed in shock as the climax swept through her body, making her shudder spasmodically.

"Soon," Ben said as he rose and gripped her nape with the hand that had been pinching her nipple, tipping her up.

His eyes shone with a roguish glint, and she realised she'd said the F word aloud. There was no time to be mortified at her crudity as he then covered her lips with his glistening ones. She tasted her musky essence in his intense kiss. Twisting against him, frenzied cries bubbled in her throat as another orgasm ricocheted around her body.

Gosh, she wanted him. How she wanted him, between her legs, pinning her down, his body a piston, ramming into her, fast and hard until this mighty ache abated.

He withdrew from her and walked away. Still shaken, she tried to catch her breath and didn't look up to see where he went. He had a damp face towel when he returned. Without saying a word, he wiped her thighs and cleaned her up. Then he picked up the egg that had been abandoned beside her on the bed. He squeezed some of the lube on it.

"Spread your legs."

The order brought her back down to earth. She hesitated, biting her lower lip. What he wanted to do was a bit excessive. Her heart drummed against her ribs, with apprehension as well as anticipation.

She opened her lips and pursed them again. His facial expression did not welcome an argument although he said nothing. His grey eyes were hard, studying her as if he knew already what she was going to do and why.

"Lina, if you're worried about the people out there, don't be. This is very discreet and doesn't make a loud sound. No one will know you're wearing it apart from the two of us. I will control the vibrations with this remote control."

He lifted the controller that looked no bigger than a key ring. His other hand stroked down her thigh.

"I promise you it'll be worth your while."

The thought of the egg sitting inside her all evening with no one else aware appalled and excited her at the same time. They'd played with sex toys before, but she'd never used one outside the bedroom and certainly not in public. She was no exhibitionist. Or so she thought.

Still, being with Benjamin made her want to explore things she'd never tried before, fantasies lurking in her mind. He was making them real one encounter at a time.

How could she say no to him?

With resolve, she parted her legs.

His eyes sparkled with approval.

Her heart warmed at his pleasure.

He knelt on the bed before her. "Wider."

She did, and he pushed the oval vibrator in. When it was seated within her already wet channel, he let the little string dangle out. He picked up her thong, sniffed it briefly and pocketed it. Her core clenched just watching his arousing action. Then he helped her to her feet. She tottered on her stilettos as she adjusted her dress.

"Okay?"

"Yes." It felt strange having the egg inside her. She felt full. "I just need to get used to having it inside me."

"I'm going to turn it on now." Nodding, he pressed a button on the controller.

Unsure of what to expect, she stiffened.

Her stance didn't prepare her for the gentle throbbing sensation. Her inner walls clenched in reflex, her breath hitching.

"I'm going to keep it at a low setting for now. But I will vary it throughout the evening."

The thought of being aroused continuously set butterflies off in her stomach. "What if I ... you know."

"You can say the word, Lina. This is you and me. And life will be a lot easier if you hold nothing back from me. You can always tell me how you feel."

Easier said than done. Revealing her thoughts was not her strong point.

"What if I come? What if it's too much?"

"You're not allowed to remove it or to come." His eyes blazed with determination and desire.

Tilting her chin, he caressed her lips with his thumb in a gentle sensual way that was just Benjamin. He was skilled at combining romantic and erotic gestures. His hand slid to her collarbone in feather-light touches. Beneath his fingers, her pulse jumped in recognition of his mastery.

"You look stunning. The sexy way this inflexible corset holds your body, the way it cinches your waist that I can almost span my hands around." He gripped her waist as if to prove his point.

"Even now, your skin is flushed, your breast threatening to spill out of the top. The gems on your black skirt catch the light and shimmer like fireflies against the dark night. But I will enjoy watching you tonight, knowing you're fighting not to come, knowing you're deferring to me."

The fluttering of butterflies in her stomach increased along with her heart rate. How was she going to cope? Though the vibrations were low, she already wanted to pull her dress up and get herself off. Worse, grind herself against the elegant bulge curving his fly. Yet all she could do was nod.

"Later tonight, I'll give you all the release you need. Your orgasms are mine. Just as you are now mine."

That statement more than anything else he'd said today sent shivers of anxiety down her spine.

*****

I don't know why I agreed to this.

Selina fought another wave of pleasure rippling within her core, drawing in a slow breath and blowing it out steadily to quell the orgasm that was just within reach.

It had been the same all night long. How she'd managed to get through the cake cutting and first dance without disgracing herself in front of the guests still astounded her. Though, Benjamin had known when to reduce the vibrations, muting the sharp sensations when she was close to the edge.

Now seated back at their table, the setting was back to a low, even vibration, although each time she shifted her clit pulsed, which was why she sat so straight in her chair.

"I love the way you're sitting there, looking beautiful and elegant. The corset moulds your body, your skin flushed, which I know is both from your arousal and anxiety." Ben's deceptively soothing voice was contributing to her state of stimulation.

She was concentrating so hard on not coming that she wasn't thinking of anything else. So, he was achieving his aim of keeping her mind off her worries.

Except now, she was facing sensory meltdown.

"I love knowing I can bring you up to orgasm in just a few seconds or make you wait 'til the party is over."

The vibration increased. Selina gasped softly and shifted in her seat, sending the pulse down her back crease. She gripped the edge of the table.

"Before we got married, I asked you to submit to me."

She looked across the table to make sure no one was eavesdropping on their conversation. Christopher was chatting with Lora, her friend, who had also acted as her bridesmaid and witness at the registry. On the dance floor, the party was in full swing.

"I agreed. Didn't I?" She turned to look at him.

He nodded, but the glimmer in his eyes challenged her. "But you can only give me your full submission if you trust me and are honest with me."

She looked away, unable to meet his gaze. Cool fingers stroked the back of her neck before he gripped her nape firmly between his fingers and thumb. He turned her head toward him. When she looked up, piercing dark grey eyes held her captive. She couldn't look away or not answer his unspoken question.

"I trust you, Ben." She did. *To a degree.*

"Then you'll have no problem sharing all your worries with me. You know you can tell me anything."

"I've been waiting to dance with the bride all evening." Christopher stepped behind their seats. "I know you are newlyweds, but I'm going to have to steal her from you."

Ben didn't take his eyes off Selina, but he nodded.

"Give her a good time." The sensual way he said that made her picture Christopher running his hands over her body and Ben watching on approvingly.

She mentally shook her head, wondering where the thought had come from. She should be thankful for the reprieve from Ben's probing eyes.

Ben leaned into her. "Relax and go with the flow."

Christopher helped her up and walked her to the dance floor.

"You looked like you needed rescuing." His black eyes were filled with understanding. "Care to tell me what's going on?"

Her lips lifted in a relieved smile. She'd met Christopher first at a club, and they had hooked up on a casual basis. She hadn't been looking for anything other than the occasional booty call, and Christopher was as laid back as they come. He just went with the flow.

One day, he'd told her about his friend who was interested in her. She'd agreed to meet Ben. The rest was history, as they say.

She shook her head. "It's nothing I can't handle."

He pulled her up close. His body was firm and fit like Benjamin's, but he wasn't her husband. The sensations between her legs moved from feather-light to throbbing. Her nipples puckered hard. She rubbed herself against him.

"You smell intoxicating." His deep voice whispered against her sensitive cheeks and added to the ache between her thighs. Her heart was thumping so loudly she thought Christopher would hear it.

Selina glanced over to the high table. Lora sat in the chair she'd vacated, chatting with Ben. But his gaze was on Selina. The shadows from the dimmed lighting turned the massive grin on his face wolfish. He knew exactly how much she was suffering while dancing with his friend. He'd planned it that way.

Damn him.

"I noticed you chatting with Lora earlier. You fancy her, don't you?" She asked, wanting a distraction from the pulsing in her core. Although she hadn't thought of her friend getting together with Christopher.

"She's nice," he said, his voice noncommittal.

"Nice ... is that all?" She leaned back so she could see his face.

Chris flashed a set of white teeth in a lopsided smile. "Okay, she's more than nice." He shrugged.

Her smile widened. "You do fancy her."

He twirled and pulled her back into his arms.

"Be gentle with her," she said. "She's on the rebound from her ex."

"I'm always a gentleman." He put his right hand over his chest, his expression of feigned pain. "Moreover, I'm still getting over you ditching me for Benjamin."

"If I believe that I'll believe anything." She giggled. "I'm the one who was cheated. I asked you for a threesome and never got it. Ah—"

As another wave of electrical sensation swept through her, she arched involuntarily bringing her body closer to Chris's until the ridge of a big erection brushed between her thighs. The combination of his voice and the vibration between her legs shot her arousal to dizzying heights. All she needed was a little more friction, and she'd have a quick orgasm to take the edge off. That's all she needed. To ease the intensity. Then she'd be able to cope with whatever Ben had planned for tonight. She darted her tongue out and licked her lips.

She ran her finger on his chest in a seductive manner. "And I say you owe me. How about some pre-wedding night excitement?"

Chris laughed, a low chuckle. "Benjamin will have something to say about that, don't you think?"

Still, he didn't step away from her. So, she tried again. "He doesn't have to know, does he? Moreover, it's not as if this marriage is real, and it's not as if you and I haven't been together before."

She inhaled a deep breath. "I just need to take the edge off. Your fingers should be enough."

His expression became serious, almost stern, and he raised his eyebrow in query.

The vibrating pattern varied again. Her eyes rolled back in her head, and heat licked her skin. She let out a low moan and shut her eyes briefly.

"What are you wearing, Lina?"

"An egg." She kept her eyes closed.

"Sweet."

She didn't need to open her eyes to know that he had an amused glint in his eyes—his voice said it all. She opened her eyes anyway.

"Trust you to think it's amusing that he's got me behaving like a hormonal teenager." She pushed against his chest, breaking his embrace. "You know what. I don't need you. I've got my own hands."

She walked off, heading towards the nearest ladies' room. Inside she leaned against the closed door and took a long, ragged breath.

***

Ben watched Selina as she danced with his friend. Chris held her with one hand low on her back just above the dip of her spine and the other cupping her shoulder, close but not proprietary.

A pulling sensation in his gut made him aware he wasn't altogether overjoyed by that image.

Nonsense, considering Christopher was his best friend of many years and Selina was his wife of six hours and counting.

Minutes previously he'd been the one holding her intimately as they swayed together to the mesmerising sound of "All My Life" by K-Ci and JoJo.

He exhaled a shuddering breath, aware that his heart was pounding. Relief washed over his skin, covering him in goosebumps.

He was married to Selina.

He hadn't believed his luck when he'd watched her marching down the short aisle of the Registry Office at Chelsea Old Town Hall toward him.

She was beautiful. Stunning. Dressed in an outfit more suited for a catwalk than a wedding day—a red satin corset showing off beautiful caramel-coloured shoulders and arms. The black ruffled lace skirt with jewels sewn into it trailed in a short tail and barely covered her feet, which were wrapped in red high-heeled diamante sandals.

The sight of her had snatched his breath away. He'd struggled to maintain his calm as his body responded as if he was still a teenager and not a full-grown man who'd had his fair share of women.

His gut had tightened, and his mouth watered. How he'd wanted to taste her skin, to feel her softness against his body.

The curl of her lips as she smiled at him had been glorious. Behind the shy smile was a hint of coquetry.

Then again, there was no other woman like Selina.

From the first day, he'd met her, he'd lost himself to her—heart, body, and soul. At the time she'd been dating Chris. If you could call what they'd had dating. It had been more of a friend-with-benefits relationship.

Chris had a carefree attitude to life. His insouciant friend wasn't ready to get serious about a woman. Selina had claimed to be happy with that.

Yet, Benjamin had recognised her need for something deeper and more fulfilling. When Chris had told him of her fantasy of having more than one man at a time, Ben had known he needed to act. He'd asked Chris to arrange the meeting. The ménage a trois she'd been expecting didn't happen that night. The dominant in him couldn't allow it.

One day he'd grant her wish when he'd earned her total submission. For now, he would gain her trust and get her to share the nightmares plaguing her, night, and day.

Selina was a strong woman. A survivor. But something from her past haunted her. It lurked in the depth of her molten toffee eyes sometimes, though she tried hard to hide it from everyone.

He needed to make her realise he was no longer just anyone. He was her husband. He would protect her with his life if necessary.

His nose flared, and he gritted his teeth.

If he found whoever had hurt her in the past, there would be breaking of bones. He wasn't particularly good at forgiving and forgetting.

Across the dance floor, Selina stormed away from Christopher, her hips swaying seductively as she walked through the door out to the hallway.

Perhaps teasing her with the vibrator and letting her dance with his friend had been a push too far. He suppressed a smile. He would enjoy taking her in hand if she'd disobeyed his instructions.

He stood up and walked toward Chris. It was time to find out.

***

What was the matter with her? Why was she allowing Benjamin and Christopher to rattle her? They'd always formed a formidable duo—like brothers-in-arms. Though she'd had a casual affair with Christopher, he'd had no problem introducing Benjamin to her. He'd claimed that Benjamin had wanted to meet her. She'd fallen immediately for Benjamin's rugged charm when she'd met him, although she'd resisted him for a while. In the end, his relentless but controlled, assured way wore down her resistance.

Now she wished she had stuck to Christopher. He was a much safer bet. His laid-back attitude was a huge contrast to Benjamin's intensity.

Knocking on the door had her jumping forward.

"Selina?"

"Benjamin ... shit," she muttered low, her face heating up like a child caught with her hand in the biscuit tin.

"I'll be out soon," she said out loud.

"Open the door, Lina." The command in his voice couldn't be missed.

She fumbled with the lock and pulled the door open. Benjamin's bulk filled the doorway, his expression unreadable.

"I was just freshening up," she said, feeling compelled to explain her actions even though he hadn't said a word. She couldn't explain her sudden need to not disappoint him.

"Are you done?"

She nodded, and he moved back.

"Good. We're going to call it a night down here and head to the suite."

Her hands shook, but she wasn't sure if it was from trepidation or anticipation. She walked through the door. Ben laid his hand on her back at the dip of her spine as they walked back to the reception hall. They said goodnight to their guests and took the lift to the suite in silence.

Selina got more apprehensive when he didn't say anything. The silence lay heavy in the air. She hated it. The quiet was a more powerful tool than if he'd shouted at her. Her heart pounded with guilt.

"Nothing happened." The words tumbled from her lips, her nerves even more jittery.

"But you wanted something to happen."

"No."

"You propositioned Christopher," he said in a matter-of-fact tone and walked to the bedroom.

"Not really." She shrugged.

"Not really?" He turned then to look at her, his expression one of non-amused disbelief.

"Well, he was being Christopher, talking dirty. I just dared him to follow through."

"Even after I'd told you to wait for me. On our wedding night."

"Get off it, Ben." She couldn't control her anger anymore. Her frustration. "You and I know this marriage isn't real. Look at me. I'm hardly the blushing bride."

Ben's heat reached her before he gripped her shoulders and pulled her back. Her bare shoulders and back burned with his warmth. The ridge of his straining erection pushed against the soft curve of her plump bottom.

"Blushing or not, you are still my bride," he said, his tone calmer than she expected it. "While you remain my wife, you will keep to our agreement in and out of the bedroom."

He ran his hands down from her shoulders, in a gentle stimulating caress, leaving tingles in its wake, down her arms and stopped at her waist pinning them there.

"Ben, I—"

"You promised, Selina. You promised to accept my terms in return for my help. Have you changed your mind? If you have, say so now."

He was giving her a way out. But in truth, it wasn't an option she could entertain.

"No." She heaved a sigh.

Only a few hours into their wedding and she was messing up already. Even if it was a sham, she'd made a promise. She must keep it.

But her need to preserve herself—her heart—warred with her promise to surrender to him.

This was only temporary. She could do it.

"I'm sorry," she said.

He turned her around to face him and tilted her chin up. She stared at dark grey eyes filled with tenderness and lust. The stubble on his chin called to her soft palms. She would've rubbed her hand against his chin if he wasn't holding her arms to her side.

"I know how difficult it is for you to let go and trust anyone. But I know that deep down you crave my restraint, my dominance over you."

She made a sound in her throat, but he continued.

"It's there in the flick of your beautiful brown eyes when you stare at me when you think I can't see you."

She gasped softly.

"In the passive curve of your delicate spine, in the seductive sway of your rounded hips." He ran his hands down her spine, hips and stopped on her bottom cheeks.

Her heart pounded loudly in her chest.

"You're a beautiful woman, Lina. I desire your body, your submission, and most of all, your trust."

"I don't know what to say, Ben."

"Say nothing. For now, I want you to strip naked. When you're done, lie in the middle of the bed."

Without waiting for her response, he walked to the living room.

Strip naked. Selina stood paralysed with fear. This was the part she'd been dreading.

"Oh, and if you're not undressed in two minutes, I'll be testing out the new paddle on the bedside on your lovely arse."

No way. He wouldn't. He knew she didn't like pain. Sure enough, there was a black leather paddle, soft rope ties, and a red silk sash.

Electrified, she reached for the zipper on her skirt and pulled it down, dropping the fabric in a pool at her feet. Next, she unclipped her garter from her stockings and rolled them off along with her shoes.

She was naked except for her corset. As bare as she'd ever gotten with anybody, including her husband. She climbed onto the bed and spread herself flat on it.

Benjamin returned. He was also devoid of his clothing except for the charcoal trousers. His muscles rippled as he moved. She licked her lips, her mouth moistening at the sexy sight.

"What did I tell you to do?" He stood at the edge of the bed but didn't touch her.

"You told me to strip naked." She shifted, more anxious under his earnest gaze.

"And you know you're already in trouble for your actions earlier."

"Yes, but—"

"Still you invite more punishment by disobeying me blatantly."

She bit her lip. "I can't take it off."

"You can't, or you won't?"

"I..."

"So, you know what comes next."

"Yes," she said in a small voice, her body trembling.

"Pick up the paddle and bring it to me." He walked away into the living room.

Selina took a deep breath and rose. Though she was petrified, she picked up the paddle from the bedside cabinet. She had to be brave. Benjamin knew she didn't do pain. And he was never that harsh with his discipline. She could take it.

In the living room, she found Benjamin sitting in a straight-backed chair next to the mahogany writing desk. He withdrew the paddle and pulled her across his lap—face down, bum in the air. The vibration of the egg stopped, but he didn't remove it.

Her breathing rate increased, and she stiffened her body, using her hands on the carpet to hold herself.

"You will feel better if you relax." His hand caressed her bottom.

Before she could react, the first sharp crack landed. Pain followed. She inhaled in a quick hiss. The second came on top of the first, spreading the sting. Her eyes watered. Each smack jostled the egg as it landed on a different spot. After the sting of the third, she stopped breathing, waiting for each spank.

The pain triggered memories—ones she'd chosen to bury. They came to the surface now. And she cried silently, the tears flowing down her face.

The present merged with the past. All she knew was pain, sharp and bloody. Panicked, she fought back at the hands holding her down, kicking out. There were hands everywhere, and she was cold, trembling, praying for death.

"You're safe, Lina. I've got you," a tender voice whispered. A soothing hand massaged her neck and back. "Breathe, darling. Breathe."

She opened her eyes and realised she was sitting on Benjamin's lap, his arms wrapped around her in a cocoon, her head on his chest.

With each new breath, his spicy smoke-wood cologne acted like a safe anchor grounding her back in the present, his strong arms chasing the nightmare of her past away. Finally, she calmed, and her sobbing stopped. She inhaled deeply and exhaled in a shudder.

He leaned back and tilted her head up with one hand. On his other hand, he held a white handkerchief he must have pulled out of his trouser pocket. Cringing at what he would see on her face—streaks of tears smearing her make-up, red puffy panda eyes, her vulnerability—she attempted to hide her face in his chest.

The pressure from the pad of his thumb on her chin increased, holding her face still. The smile on his face was tinged with tenderness. "You needed that."

She sighed and nodded, lowering her gaze. "I haven't cried in years, since..."

She didn't want to go back there, to that dark place. Still, she accepted that the tension she'd carried all day was now gone. Lowering her guards and allowing Benjamin to take charge had brought her relief. Something she hadn't been able to achieve by herself. She would admit that much.

He wiped her face, gently, as if she was crystal glass.

A sense of calm invaded her mind. She tipped her head back, letting out another sigh. For the first time in what seemed like forever, she didn't mind being fragile. She felt safe in her husband's arms. Right now, she wanted to burrow in the cocoon and comfort of his muscular body.

"You don't have to be ashamed of crying. It doesn't make you any less strong or beautiful."

"I'm not beautiful. You haven't seen all of me yet."

"Is that why you hide behind the corsets? You think I won't find you attractive because of some blemish on your body. Am I that shallow to you?" He sounded hurt.

"No." She squeezed her eyes shut, regret knotting her belly.

He has a point. Benjamin was one of the most intense people she knew. He took things very seriously and never got into anything lightly. The issue wasn't him. It was her.

She had worried about people looking at her with pity in their eyes if she showed any weakness. Yet, she'd just bawled her eyes out. The look of lust in his eyes had not faded. There was no condescending disappointment in his gaze.

Perhaps he would understand when he saw what lay beneath the bones of her corset. It was one way of testing the strength of his commitment.

"I'm the shallow one. I'm afraid the desire in your eyes will die and be replaced with sympathy. I don't want your pity."

He lifted her, so she stood. His hands wrapped around her waist. Firm lips pressed against the top swell of her left breast. Warmth flared on her skin.

"This afternoon, I vowed to worship your body with mine. I keep my promises, Lina." He looked up at her, his eyes filled with sincerity. She believed him.

"Will you show me?" His tone was firm and soothing. He sat back, and she missed his touch. She wanted his hands back on her body, soothing her, pleasuring her. The only way she would get it was to succumb and strip herself of her inhibitions. The corset was a symbol of the last of her control.

The initial design for her wedding dress had the laces for the corset at the back. She'd requested a change to front-fasteners, in her bid to retain control. She didn't want to have to ask Ben to help her loosen it.

Inhaling a deep breath, she reached for the first of the fasteners with trembling hands and unhooked it. With the first one undone, it was easier to do the others. Her whole body was shaking when the final hook was undone. She gripped the edges of the corset. The hooks dug into her palms, hurting, but she ignored it. Inhaling a deep, slow breath for courage, she gradually drew the ends of the corset apart, revealing her torso to Ben.

"Who did that to you?" His voice was encased in steel.

She glanced at him sharply. His gaze was fixated on her abdomen where she was sure he could see the criss-cross of ugly dark scars.

He glanced up and met her gaze. His eyes were dark with anger. "Tell me who dared to mark your body, so I can find them and make them pay."

"I don't want to talk about it," she said in a choked voice.

Turning away, she ran into the bedroom. The sound of his frustrated growl echoed in the room. She climbed onto the bed and lay on her side, hugging her knees to her chin. Trying to blank her mind off, she squeezed her eyes shut, rocking her body from side to side. She didn't want to think about the past. Not now. Not ever again.

Firm hands massaged her back and her leg—slow, firm strokes interspaced with light, feathery ones—arousing feelings that had cooled. Gently he coaxed her until she lay on her stomach, her head on a pillow facing away from him. He pulled the egg out and tossed it aside. She gasped as her body missed the fullness.

He massaged the oil into her skin, soothing her raw bum cheeks. The calming scent of lavender and camomile transported her to a green meadow on a summer's day with stems of flowers swaying in the breeze.

The darkness of her mind slowly dissolved. Soon the tension on her shoulders and her agitation turned to serenity. Before she drifted off into a light snooze, he covered her with a bedsheet.

The sound of crockery jangling on metal woke Selina. She stretched out and opened her eyes. The bedroom was dimly lit with just the one side lamp on.

"Congratulations to you and your wife," someone said from the other room.

"Thank you." Ben's low deep voice came from the sitting room.

"You're welcome, sir. If you need anything else, just call the front desk."

She sat up. The cold air on her body revealed her nakedness. For a moment, panic swirled in her mind. She yanked the sheet up to cover her chest and swept her gaze across the room for her clothes. The paddle was back on the bedside cabinet.

She remembered, bowing to Ben's paddle, and stripping off her corset, being vulnerable and Ben taking care of her need.

She didn't hear the concierge leave. Nor did she hear Ben return to the bedroom. The skin on her arms tingled. She raised her gaze towards the door.

Ben stood there, his shirtless and tanned upper body leaning against the frame. Dark brown short hair trailed over sinewy arms, his hands shoved in his trouser pockets, hiding long fingers she'd rather have, tracing every curve on her body.

The intensity of his dark gaze snatched her breath away. Her skin flushed. Instinctively her fingers clutched the sheet tighter.

"Are you back to hiding your body away?"

It was a simple question. So why did it sound like a reprimand?

"No." Releasing the sheet, it dropped to her thighs. Her bum still ached from the paddle, and she didn't want another round.

"Good." His smile of approval filled her chest with warmth, pleasing her. He strode to the bed and sat on one end. The mattress dipped with his weight.

"I love looking at you. Get on your hands and knees."

The effect of his complimentary words surprised her. She wanted to be on display for him, needed to have his eyes worship her body, knowing that he genuinely desired her, scars, and all.

She lowered her hands and took up the position with practised grace. Well, as much dignity as she could muster when all her body was bared and under her husband's scrutiny. And desires. She clutched the sheet to hide the fact that her hands were trembling with anticipation.

With the pad of his fingers, he trailed a heated path from her shoulder to her back. She closed her eyes and sighed, tuning in to the sensations he elicited from her body.

"We don't have to talk about your past tonight." He continued his sensual caresses, over her sore bottom and tracing the crack between down to her slit. Her inside walls contracted in expectation, and she bit her lower lip.

"But I have to tell you that I want you the same as I've always wanted you."

He drew her left hand and placed it over the ridge of his erection. It felt huge, and a smile tugged her lips. She turned her head. He had a twinkle in his eyes, but it was pure desire. No pity.

"Of course, if you'd rather sleep tonight—"

"No way." She sat back on her haunches. "You've had me on edge all evening with that damned vibrator inside me. You owe me a damned good fucking."

He flipped her over before she knew what'd hit her. The quick hard smack on her bottom resounded in the room inflaming her already raw behind. She wouldn't be sitting much tomorrow.

"You'll get a damned good fucking when I say so, woman." He flipped her over again. "And I need to stuff your mouth. You're getting too lippy."

She licked her lips, and he chuckled.

"This weekend, you're not allowed to wear any clothes, except when we're out of this room, or there's someone else in here."

"What?" She frowned. Her body issues weren't just going to disappear at a flash. "Why?"

"Do I need a reason?"

The smirk on his face challenged her to dispute his words. She'd agreed to accede to him, accepting the terms of the arrangement. One of which stated that her body was his to command as he pleased.

"No," she said, gulping down her unease. If she would have clothes on in the presence of others, then she could live with putting her body on display for him for the rest of the weekend.

"Moreover, it pleases me to see you exposed to me. Just me."

Her insides clenched, skin flushing with heat. Part of her wanted to be on display for him, even if her mind rebelled against it.

He reached across and picked up the soft black rope. With it, he bound her entire body in an intricate weave. The way the rope wound around her breasts and abdomen made her feel like a precious parcel, his to keep safe and treasure, down to the pattern crossing each thigh and lower leg.

He placed a pillow beneath her head for support, and she knelt on the bed, bound hands crossed on her back, knees apart, her arse and sex exposed to him.

He stood beside her. This close, the bulge in his trousers was so close, yet so far away as she couldn't touch him.

"Beautiful," he said in a voice thick with lust.

The pads of his fingers trailed down the rope over her spinal column, past where it held her arms to her bum crease.

Tingles spread on her skin, her clit throbbed and she winced when he palmed her exposed, sore butt-cheek.

He disappeared out of her line of sight. When he returned, the red silk sash was in his right hand. Her heart thudded in her chest. She swallowed to hide her rising agitation.

"Sit up."

Holding her shoulders, he helped her raise her head and straighten her back. She knelt before him, her breasts pushed out by the cross-over rope design. Shibari. That's the name he'd called it the first time he'd bound her so intricately in his apartment. She remembered asking Ben once where he'd learnt such a beautiful skill with a rope, and he'd said the army. Somehow she hadn't thought that a Japanese art form would be taught to South African soldiers.

"Your trust is the most important gift you can give me." He brushed back strands of her hair that had fallen to cover her face. "But I realise that it will take a while for me to earn it. So, we're going to take it a step at a time."

She swallowed again, her stomach churning. She knew what he was getting at but couldn't stop her apprehension. Being blindfolded meant she couldn't anticipate what he was going to do to her and when, which terrified and thrilled her at the same time.

The first time he'd wanted to use the red sash over her eyes, she'd point blank said no. She couldn't bring herself to give up that much control to him. She'd been afraid of breaking down before him, of letting him see her so vulnerable.

Now, he'd seen her being vulnerable, physically fighting the nightmare of her past and bawling like a baby. She'd never been that unguarded before anyone else. And her world hadn't bottomed out.

Perhaps this was the time to take the next step.

"From the way you're watching me, I guess you know what's coming next. I know the last time you weren't ready, but it would please me immensely if you are ready to try this now."

He was doing that thing again with his voice. The reassuring, enticing quality back. It was the voice that could defuse an explosive situation. The one that was telling her to take another step forward in their relationship, to yield and trust him.

"Are you ready for this?"

She swallowed but still said, "Yes."

He nodded. "As always, you should let me know if you want me to stop for any reason."

He leaned in and placed the sash over her eyes, wrapping it at the back of her head. Darkness pervaded around her. He moved away. Her body lost the heat, and she missed him.

She listened out, trying to figure out where he was and knowing the pile of the carpets would muffle his bare footsteps.

Hearing nothing except the pounding of her heart, she licked her lips, her mind warring between anticipation and trepidation. Was he still in the room? How long would he leave her like this, bound intricately and on her knees? She shifted to get more comfortable on the bed, but she couldn't pull her thighs together because of the way the rope was wound around her legs.

The tinkle of crockery informed her he was back in the sitting room. Curiosity made her inhale deeply so she could figure out what meal he had ordered.

They'd eaten dinner with their guests at the reception hall. Feeling peckish, she would accept a snack.

His scent, the mix of smoky cologne and all-male spice that was pure Ben invaded her nostrils. She drew in a deep breath, her nerves calming. He was back in the bedroom.

"Open your mouth for me."

She did as he instructed, and he placed something on her tongue. She closed her mouth and allowed the taste to sink in. First, the texture was creamy. Perhaps cream, perhaps cheese. She wasn't sure. Yet as she chewed, she felt the crunch of biscuits. Then came the sweet acidic taste of the fruit.

"Do you know what you're eating?" The sound of his voice was warm and sensuous.

"Strawberry cheesecake?" She loved strawberries, and by default, any dessert made with the fruit.

"Close. On the menu, it read 'Strawberry parfait with Vin Santo, mascarpone and biscotti'."

She mewled.

His low chuckle made her chest bloom with warmth. She loved the sound of his laughter.

Cool glass touched her lips. She opened them, and he tipped the glass. She inhaled an aroma of ripe pear. The popping sounds of tiny bubbles filled the air. The liquid filled her mouth, and she tasted apples and citrus. She rolled it around her mouth before swallowing, loving the flavour.

"Champagne," she said with a smile after it had gone down her throat.

"Well done."

He continued feeding her, spooning in the dessert, she licking the spoon clean each time before he gave her a sip of champagne.

Just letting go and being fed by him relaxed her. She gave in to the sensual play drowning in the flavours and scents. He started using his forefinger. Each time she wrapped her tongue around it and licked it clean.

Some cream touched her cheek. His hot breath whispered against her cheek before his warm tongue laved the spot.

Strong fingers wrapped the hair at the nape of her hair, tugging her head back. Then he was kissing her, his lips possessing, his tongue invading. He tasted like heaven, and she moaned into his mouth. He stopped, withdrawing.

"You've been a good girl." He loosened her arms from behind and rubbed them to get her circulation flowing again. Slowly he tipped her back, and she allowed him to lay her back to the bed. He secured her hands on the spindles of the headboard.

"And I'm going to give you what I promised you."

Her core contracted, gushing wetness. He must've noticed with her thighs spread out, leaving her sex to his view. The light pressure from the pad of his fingers on her clit made her jump with the unexpected sensation before she lifted her hip to feel more of his touch.

What she'd been waiting for since he slipped that vibrator into her slit. All she needed was more friction, more of his hand, working her body like he was so good at doing. The fever of orgasm built within her, winding her body taut, so she'd be flying off the edge.

"You won't be coming until I'm buried deep inside your sweet pussy."

She groaned in frustration when the feel from his hands stopped. The metallic clank of his belt buckle and the swish of fabric sliding over indicated he was taking off his trousers. Her heart pounded in her chest. She had to stop her body from squirming visibly in excitement.

Then he was on top of her, his heat surrounding her. Flesh against flesh, he explored her body with his lips, starting from her neck, a nip here, a lick there, a suck elsewhere.

Her breasts and her belly received special attention. He worshipped her like she was a goddess, kissing every one of her scars. By the time he reached between her thighs, her body was trembling, her bud throbbing. All it took was the flick of his tongue on her swollen nub, and she was fighting to stop herself from disintegrating in the most intense orgasm ever.

Then the broad head of his erection was pushing against her wet slit. He shoved inside her, filling her, stroking her, her pleasure rising again. First, he was excruciatingly slow and steady. She pleaded, her shame at begging him dissipating.

Then he increased the tempo, pounding into her body like she'd imagined, taking her back to dizzying heights. This time she came apart, screaming his name. He wasn't far behind her, and they rode the waves together. She blanked out.

When she came to, Ben had untied her hands and removed the sash covering her eyes but left the rope around her body. She couldn't believe how intense her orgasm had been. Her body still trembled.

As he spooned her into his body, she whispered in a croaky voice. "Thank you."

"What for?" he asked as he nibbled her ear.

"For giving me the most intense climax ever and for still wanting me regardless. I feel so light like a heavy load has been lifted."

"That will never change."

She let out a soft sigh, content in his presence and promise as he nuzzled her neck.

"And actually, I lied when I said I didn't want you to wear anything all weekend. There's something I'd like you to wear." He leaned across and opened the side drawer. He withdrew a long black velvet box that spanned his palms.

Her heart raced as she wondered what jewellery it contained. Apart from her wedding ring, he hadn't given her jewellery before.

He opened the lid, revealing a platinum link charm bracelet with one charm attached.

She gasped. "It's beautiful."

"Not as beautiful as you." He smiled. "But close."

Lifting the bracelet out, he put the box away. She saw it then. The mini red corset attached to the gift. Tears welled in her eyes. She understood the significance.

"I actually thought about buying you a collar."

She frowned. She didn't want a collar.

His lips curled in a smile. "But I know you're not ready for it."

She met his intense gaze filled with determination. Then it clicked in her mind. Ben understood her a lot more than she'd given him credit for. He would never force his will on her. Her heart clenched.

"This bracelet signifies our commitment to each other and that you belong to me, temporarily at least. For as long as you wear it, you are under my protection, and I will fulfil my promises to you."

He paused, held her gaze as if reading or waiting for her to say something. But she had no objections. In her heart, she knew he would keep to his word. He wouldn't fail her. She could trust him. For that reason, she would wear his bracelet with pride.

"Do you accept to be mine, Lina?"

"Yes." She smiled up at him, her eyes filled with tears.

He took her hand, kissed her knuckles before hooking the bracelet on.

"For each layer of your shield you let go, I'm going to add a charm to the bracelet. One day, your heart, as well as your body, will belong to me."

He turned her face and kissed her. She succumbed to his power. At this rate, her heart would be his sooner rather than later. One thing was sure, married life would be fun after all.

Secrets
THE BEN & SELINA TRILOGY #2

Dedication

This story is dedicated to the 'wind beneath my wings,' my love.

Blurb

Her body is his to command, her heart his to win.

Selina bared her body to her husband and allowed him to see her and touch her like no one else has ever done. When a member of the family visits, she realizes there is still so much about her husband she doesn't know.

Ben's remorse about his family history drives his actions. Selina is his present and he'll do whatever it takes to protect her from being contaminated by his past, including revealing the shame that burns his soul.

For Selina, finding out about Ben's past means investing emotionally in a man who's only going to walk away once their temporary arrangement comes to an end. Is she ready to bare her heart to him along with the secrets of their past?

Chapter One

"Wake up, beauty." Benjamin's alert tone penetrated Selina's sleep.

She stirred slowly, her body weighed down, languid. The aroma of dark roasted coffee beans wafted around her, alerting her brain. She lifted her eyelids and blinked a few times.

Sunlight streamed in; the heavy black curtains pulled back. A light breeze coming through the open balcony door lifted the sheer white curtain beneath. Cold air kissed her shoulders and face. She dragged the bedcovers up, burrowing deeper.

At the soft hissing sound of a door opening, she rolled onto her back. Her husband strode out of the walk-in closet. Half-naked, he stood in the middle of the master bedroom, wearing a pair of charcoal chinos. His tanned torso and arms a golden beacon drawing her waking desire.

Her breath caught and held for the briefest of moments, and her pulse skipped a beat, both standard rising responses these days to seeing Ben in any state of undress.

Instead of giving in to the flare of arousal in her veins, Selina shifted, lifting her body into a sitting position, her brows knitted together in a frown. Something was wrong.

In Ben's left hand dangled a sky-blue shirt he'd just unwrapped from the laundry service, the clear branded cellophane scrunched and tossed in the aluminium wastepaper bin in the corner.

Looking over his shoulder, his gaze met hers. The corners of his compelling grey eyes crinkled, his full lips curling in a rare seductive smile she never tired of witnessing. Gifted with inherent strength and rugged features, her husband wasn't classically handsome. Striking was a better summation. To her, he was a Greek god.

Gulping down the sudden need to taste his mouth and have his weight between her legs, she quirked one eyebrow in a silent query.

"I have to go into the office this morning," Ben said with sedate calmness, effectively ruining her day in nine words.

Lowering her eyesight to where her fingers now clutched the white bed sheet almost defensively to her chest, her shoulders slumped.

"It's Saturday." *And play day*, she omitted from saying, disappointment a massive boulder in the belly.

After an initial reluctance, she'd come to look forward to their weekend ritual. She worked as a senior pharmacist in a city hospital. The pressures of her job meant that some days she was like a bottle of shaken fizzy drink waiting to explode as soon as someone opened it.

Playdays were her opportunity to unwind and de-stress. A safe environment where she didn't have to be in charge, where she could trust Ben to take care of her needs. The only times she allowed his need for ascendency over her without feeling weak and pathetic. The routine had become as much a part of her survival mechanism as sealing the memories of her past.

"I know." His massive shoulders lifted and fell in a shrug. "Moss Star provides a 24/7 service."

Letting out a soft sigh, Selina nodded.

Benjamin ran his own business. Unfortunately, it meant that he sometimes had to work at weekends or be available to his staff. And though they were married, it was still just a temporary arrangement she'd agreed to because of her brother. Her needs were secondary to Kaya's and Ben's.

Tears rose, swelled behind her eyeballs. Lowering her lashes, she fought the storm of emotions rising. As much as she tried to rationalize his reason, her stomach churned. The disappointment souring her mouth, turning to anger in her veins. After years of surviving on her own, she should've known better than to rely on anyone but herself.

In the past month, she'd come to depend on Benjamin, to need the comfort of his dominance, the mastery of his touch, the pleasure of giving herself freely to him. She'd let her guard slip, handing her scarred body into his care, trusting him to see all of her and not just her physical blemishes, to protect her.

Saturdays had become the only times they got to slow down enough to see and communicate with each other. The time they displayed not just physical affection but shared an emotional connection, too.

Who was she kidding? Maybe this was just a routine to him, a force of habit. Perhaps he didn't care one way or the other.

Relying on him had been a mistake. Starting now, she would remedy the error by finding another way to relax today. She didn't need Ben. Or anyone else.

Swinging her legs over to her side of the bed, she prepared to stand.

"Stay right there," Ben said in a firm, deep voice. Despite the calmness to his words, she didn't miss the order.

Instinctively, traitorously, her body stilled. An almost natural response to his command, masking the weeks of training it had taken to achieve. Her mind rebelled, her anger still riding her blood with each beat of her heart.

Last night she'd fallen into bed exhausted, barely able to string together two words in a sentence. Ben had seen how tired she'd been. He knew how much she needed today's play, *damn it!* A little warning would've been nice for starters.

Lifting her head, she glared at him, her obedience tottering on razor-thin wires.

"What are you doing?" he asked, the warning in his voice apparent.

In a heartbeat, his smile faded, his lips flattened, the grey of his eyes marbling, the muscles of his arms bunching. He held her defiant gaze and raised it, like in a poker game, challenging her to take it one step further into outright disobedience.

Could she dare to call his bluff?

Mentally, she calculated the distance between the bed and the adjoining bathroom. She could make a dash for it and rely on the safety of its enclosure. Since Ben had to go out, perhaps he would just ignore her. By the time he got home, her insubordination would be forgotten.

As she stared at his rock-solid body, she accepted that his current frozen state was an illusion. It was the rigid pose of a wild tiger, ready to pounce. He would intercept her before she reached the bathroom door. And then she would have to put up with the humiliation of being spanked while over his knees. Her bum prickled as if in remembrance of the last time he'd taken his bare hand to it. She'd been unable to sit comfortably for two days.

Letting out an exasperated sigh, she lowered her gaze, fixing it on the pile of zebra-print monochrome hand-woven rug at his feet.

"But I thought—"

"That's the problem. You overthink."

Bristling inwardly, she held her tongue. So, what if she overanalysed every situation? It was the one trait that had guaranteed her survival to date, and the main reason she'd come to love play days. They were the only time she didn't have to worry about thinking about anything. Simply put, it was the best stress release she knew. Better than any pill she could take. And she was a pharmacist!

Ben strode across their bedroom floor, the deep pile on the rug muffling the sound of his feet bound in Italian-made black leather shoes. His teasing smile took the edge off his stern words.

"The rules of play day still apply even though I'm going to be out. You'll follow my instructions to the letter."

He nodded toward the bedside table. She noticed the sheet of notepad on it. He'd scrawled a list of actions for her on the top.

"I'll be back as soon as I can." He shrugged his arms into his shirt covering up the chest packed solid with muscles and the smattering of short bronze hairs trailing down to his trousers.

She leaned toward the table to pick up the list.

"No. Wait until I'm gone before you read it." He disappeared into the walk-in closet.

Her frown deepened. This was a new test. Usually, when he gave instructions, he was close by to ensure that she carried them out. At first, she'd obey some and not others depending on what she'd considered her limits. But over time he'd pushed back her boundaries. But she still struggled with the side of her that didn't want to give total control to someone else.

Knowing he was always close by and would punish her had always been a strong incentive to obey his orders without hesitation. Unsettled, she rubbed her arms as she wrapped them around her midsection, Goosebumps mottling her arms. How was she going to cope when he wasn't even going to be in their apartment?

The sudden panic about Ben not being at home to make her toe the line didn't escape her. She'd learned to concede to her husband's authority and even yearned for his brand of reward and punishment. Was there shame in admitting that some penalties thrilled as well as scared her on some level?

She ignored the revealing question and focused on the source of her current unease. His presence was an anchor, grounding her in a turbulent sea ruled by her emotions and fears. In his absence, she would fail and disappoint him. Spidery cold fingers of dread crawled over her flesh.

If he asks, lie. He won't know.

Eyes closed, she rocked back onto the soft pillows behind, pulling her knees up, her mind churning over the words.

No. She couldn't. She'd never lied to him before. She wouldn't start now.

Yes, there were things from her past she hadn't shared with him. But omission was better than outright deception.

Fingers curled into her tresses. The sharp tug of her hair and her prickling scalp shocked a soft gasp out of her mouth as she lifted her eyelids. Her husband towered over her now fully clothed and standing beside the bed, his firm hand gripping her nape.

"You're thinking again," he said before crushing her lips beneath his.

Under the weight and onslaught of his mouth, she capitulated to his dominance, opening, letting him take what he wanted, and savouring this about him. Despite the harsh kiss, his soft lips and rough tongue stirred the embers of her lust. He tasted of coffee and caramel, dark and decadent, his smoke-wood and spice scent drawing her into the web of arousal he wove.

His right hand dipped down her body, rough palm skimming the soft flesh of her breast, firm fingers plucking at her nipple until it stood straight and taut. Her body jerked in response. As his hand journeyed over her contoured belly to the swell of her left hip, she stifled a whimper. Fever rose, fast and urgent, burning her flesh. Then his fingers spread her lower lips, stroked her clit, circling it once before breaching her already wet entrance.

Yes! Gasping into his mouth, she tilted her hips, giving him more access while pushing against him for more friction. Her fingers slid down to his trouser, cupping the huge, hard bulge tenting his fly. She stroked him and then moved her hand to the zipper. She couldn't wait to have him inside her.

He had other ideas.

Benjamin pulled away, ending her foray with a firm flick of her wrist and tilted her head up.

"Which play day rule have you just broken?" His grey eyes glimmered with wicked amusement.

She sighed, a mix of defeat and resignation. "The 'no touching unless you tell me to' rule."

She didn't bother hiding the frustration from her voice. She'd already earned a demerit. His next words confirmed it.

"And that sassy mouth of yours has cost you an orgasm this morning."

Like you'll be here to stop me. She made a low sound in her throat and just stopped from rolling her eyes back in her head.

By now, they should've been on the way to their second orgasm, usually in the shower. But as he was already dressed and they hadn't made love before he'd gotten out of bed, it wasn't going to happen any time soon.

He leaned back, arms crossed over his chest.

"Do you want to say something, Selina?" There was no amusement in his voice.

"No."

"No, what?"

"No, Benjamin." When he was formal, she had to use his full name.

"I didn't think so," he said, his tone still reprimanding. "Do I need to remind you of the rules for play day?"

Her cheeks flamed at his chiding tone. She wasn't a ten-year-old who needed reminders.

"I know the rules, Benjamin."

"Good. Then obey them. Unless of course, you wish to skip today's session?"

And miss out on what I've been looking forward to all week? I don't think so. Despite the change in their routine for the day, she would have to trust that he would meet his obligations. He'd promised her, and he hadn't reneged on that promise yet. She had to give him the benefit of the doubt.

"I don't want to skip. I'm sorry I was lippy. I just didn't like the idea of you going out this morning." Plus, the fact that he could command her body at his whim.

"Who is in charge of play day?" Benjamin asked in a quiet voice.

"You are," Selina said.

"Who owns your body?"

"You do."

"You keep that in mind while you carry out my instructions for the rest of the day." He tapped the end of her nose as he gave her a smile that brightened up his face and lit up her chest.

"Or there'll be hell to pay." This time he winked before heading out of the bedroom door. He stopped just outside the door.

"Be good, beauty," he said, and her heart skipped a beat, her body melting.

Whenever he used the endearment, her body and heart responded simultaneously. He made her feel beautiful though she didn't believe she was. If Benjamin thought she was, then his praise was good enough for her.

She listened to his heavy footsteps against the rug covered wood-panel flooring in the hallway. When she heard the click from the front door closing, she finally relaxed back into the pillows behind her and closed her eyes briefly, taking a deep breath in.

Benjamin's scent still floated in the air, reminding her of the notepad on the bedside. She opened her eyes and leaned over, picking up the paper.

The boldly scrawled words were of a man in control and committed to the day and the activities ahead.

In their month of marriage, she'd come to rely on one thing. Benjamin's consistency. His actions had always been measured and unfailing.

The primary reason they'd gotten married—her plans to bring her brother Kaya to move permanently to the United Kingdom—were already in motion.

Her husband gave hope that she could restore some of what had been destroyed from her past. Hope was a good thing, and she would cling to it.

Inhaling deeply to quell the tears that gathered behind her eyelids, Selina read the list.

Number one: No clothes. Do not wear any for the rest of the day. If you need to go out, I've selected your outfit for the day hanging over the recliner.

She swept her gaze to the chair. Her blue and brown layered tier dress with a sweetheart neckline hung over it, a matching blue, knitted cardigan next to it. The dress length stopped just at her knee. On a warm Spring day, the loose cotton style allowed for comfort. For the changeable British weather, the cosy wrap would come in handy.

She smiled. In that dress, she wouldn't need a bra because of the sweetheart neckline. Sure enough, number two on the list was *No underwear if you wear the clothing.*

A primary rule of play day was no clothes, for her anyway. It'd taken a few weeks to get used to the idea of walking around the apartment without clothes on.

She'd spent most of her adult life covering up and never revealing her naked body to anyone else.

Now, she stared down at the scars that lined her stomach in criss-crosses. Tentatively, she ran a finger along the jagged lines, tracing the welts. For years she'd thought them ugly and hated looking at them— always dressing quickly to cover them up.

Then on their wedding night, Benjamin had made her reveal them to him. He'd worshipped her body like he'd sworn he would, kissing each mark reverently as if she was a goddess and the scars her beautifying spots.

The same day, he'd given her the platinum and gold charm bracelet now sparkling on her left wrist. She'd worn it almost every day since, with pride and awareness.

During their short honeymoon stay at the hotel, she'd had her first taste of his play day. She'd spent the entire weekend stark naked, except when room service was delivered, fighting the continual impulse to cover up.

Somehow he'd found ways of keeping her fears at bay, so she didn't reach for the dressing gown at every opportunity.

"I love looking at your beautiful bare body." Benjamin's words had delighted as well as encouraged her.

There had been no repulsion in his eyes.

His measured actions reinforced his words. She was normal and beautiful and free. In his presence, with his praise, she was all those things for the first time in over ten years.

Now, Selina caressed her scars, running the pad of her fingers over each ridge the way Benjamin usually did. As she remembered his lips on her skin, tongue rough, wet, coaxing, and arousing, her skin tingled.

Her insides clenched. She trailed her hand down to her sex lips but stopped from parting them.

Who owns your body?

Benjamin's words rang in her mind. She'd promised to abide by his rules. Unable to touch herself, she couldn't have an orgasm without his permission.

Frustrated, she blew out a breath and picked up the note again.

Chapter Two

Buzz! Buzz!

At the second sound of the door intercom bell, Selina stepped out of the shower and reached for the white towelling robe hanging behind the bathroom door. She removed the shower cap she'd used to cover her hair and hung it on the hook by the wall radiator.

Buzz!

"Hold your damn horses," she shouted when the loud, persistent noise made her jump this time. Padding her bare feet across the cool limestone tiles, she stepped into the hallway. She nearly yanked the intercom receiver off the wall.

"Hello?" She didn't hide her irritation from her voice.

Saturday was a sacred time in the Moss household, especially this early. It wasn't even 10am yet.

"Sorry, Mrs Moss." It was one of their concierges, a usually pleasant middle-aged English man named Martin. Right now, he sounded harassed. "I thought I should warn you that you have a guest on the way upstairs."

"What guest?" Selina wasn't expecting anyone, and neither was she in the mood to entertain. The concierge had a specific instruction from Benjamin to dispose of unexpected guests on Saturday mornings. So why had he allowed one in?

"My apologies, madam." He coughed.

A tug of sympathy made her uncertain about what to say. Sighing, she leaned her back against the wall. A large painting of an African landscape hung opposite, adding a kaleidoscope of colour to an otherwise bare white wall. But she wasn't focused on the piece of art by Cameroonian artist, Angu Walters.

In her mind's eye, she pictured the concierge tugging at the black tie wrapped around the white starched shirt collar. He always dressed in uniform while on duty, and whenever he was uncomfortable, he jerked his collar.

"It's Ms Moss," he continued. "I tried to explain that you were not to be disturbed, but she insisted on going up."

Alarm bells rang in Selina's mind, and her grip on the receiver tightened. She narrowed her eyes, pulling her eyebrows down in concentration. Who the hell was Ms Moss? One of Benjamin's relatives, obviously, but which one?

This day was not turning out as she'd planned at all. First, Benjamin had abandoned her with an action list. Now, she had to deal with a family member she hadn't been warned about.

What's my husband thinking?

Closing her eyes, Selina dragged in a long breath to subdue her fraying nerves.

"Martin, who exactly is in the lift? I mean which of the Mosses?" she asked in a calm tone, lifting her eyelids, and focusing her gaze back on the painting on the wall. There was no point in taking out her irritation on the concierge who was simply doing his job. Benjamin, however, wouldn't be spared her bubbling wrath.

"Beatrice, Mr Moss's younger sister."

Just at that moment, loud, insistent knocks came from the front door. The entryway slab was constructed from solid oak wood and a core of steel. Whoever was knocking was using something more robust than their knuckles.

Instinctively, Selina pulled the wrap around her body and cinched the waist belt tightly. It was Benjamin's robe, large enough to engulf her body and trail to her feet. Yet she didn't like not having her clothes on in other people's presence.

Counting to five, she inhaled deeply to stave off the panic rising in her stomach. What was Benjamin's sister doing here? The woman was supposed to be in South Africa. And from the vibes Selina got from her husband, he wasn't close to his family.

Her husband's smoke-wood scent reached her nostrils as if he was the one cocooning her with his warm body instead of the weight of the cotton fleece on her shoulders.

She walked to the door, pressed the combination to open the lock and pulled it back. On the other side stood a beautiful woman with dark blond hair. Her skin was tanned like she'd been out in the sun, and she had a pretty, oval face. Selina noticed her grey eyes instantly; they had the same calculating quality as Benjamin's. Except these lacked his warmth.

Behind her stood the junior concierge—James, a young man in his late teens or early twenties—holding two large suitcases. The lobby was bare except for large ceramic-potted palm plants. There were no other apartments on this floor. James would've used the key lock to send the lift to this penthouse level.

She'd always wondered about the need for the double security since a key was required to reach this level but had always put it down to her Ben's work hazards.

"You must be Beatrice Moss." Selina pasted a smile on her face although the last thing she felt was cheerful. Why did her husband not mention that his sister was coming over?

"Of course, I am," Benjamin's sister said. "Are you going to let me in or just stand there all day?"

The impulse to slam the door flared. Selina didn't like the woman's bossy tone.

However, this was her husband's sibling, and her African upbringing overrode all else in this situation. She couldn't kick out a guest, mostly when it was family.

"Sorry. Come in." Selina kept her cheerful smile and moved out of the way, holding the widened door.

Beatrice walked in, or rather, waltzed in, her sweet floral perfume hanging in the air after her. The junior concierge came in behind her, carrying the luggage. She wondered how the woman had roped the boy into doing her bidding. The concierges were there for the benefit of the residents only. But from the harassed expression of his face, it seemed he was quite eager to complete the task and disappear.

"Leave it there." Selina pointed at the hallway table, which held a bouquet of fresh lilies in a white vase.

He deposited the bags next to the mahogany table and straightened up, smiling weakly.

Selina injected sympathy into her smile and voice. "Thank you, James."

"My pleasure, Mrs Moss," he muttered before exiting.

She shut the door behind him and turned.

Beatrice stood at the threshold to the living room. Dressed in a cream top and skinny black jeans with high-heeled gladiator sandals, she looked as glamorous as Charlize Theron on a casual day.

Selina had seen pictures. None did her much justice. Beatrice was physically beautiful—model skinny, straight blonde hair, and flawless porcelain skin—the epitome of modern-day beauty. Selina was the exact opposite with her hour-glass curves, curly brown hair, and scarred chocolate skin.

"So, you're the new Mrs Moss."

Was there a hint of scorn in her voice?

"Yes, I'm Selina." She contemplated extending her hand for a handshake but rejected the notion. She didn't like the way Beatrice was looking at her. As if she was something a cat dragged in off the grubby gutters.

"Did Benjamin know you were coming?" she asked instead as she walked past Beatrice, who stood taller than her in her high heels.

"Of course, he does. Where is he, anyway?"

Beatrice walked down the hallway toward the bedrooms.

"He's at the office," Selina called out and followed her; appalled the woman was walking around with the air of someone who owned the place.

"On a Saturday? That brother of mine works too hard." Beatrice pushed open the door to the guest bedroom opposite Ben's study. Fortunately, she hadn't gone to the master suite in search of her brother.

Selina exhaled in relief. She didn't have to deck the woman for disrespecting her.

"I'm going to freshen up and catch a nap," Beatrice said. "Bring my bags in here."

Gritting her teeth, Selina stomped to where the luggage was left, dragged them along the floor, and unceremoniously pushed them into the bedroom.

They both hit the dark wooden frame of the low Japanese style bed with a thud and collapsed on the floor.

"There you are, madam," she said in a rude tone.

The wide-eyed and open-mouthed shock on Beatrice's face as Selina shut the door was enough to put a smile on her face. She went into the living room and picked up the cordless land phone. The intermittent ring tone indicated there was a voice message. But she needed to speak to Ben first. So, she pressed the speed dial number one button.

He picked the call at the first ring.

"Hi, beauty." The sound of his deep voice should've soothed her. It didn't. Instead, it exacerbated her exasperation.

"Did you get my message?"

"What message? I didn't get any message," Selina replied, her voice nasally.

"Oh. I thought that was why you phoned back," Ben said. "I called to tell you my sister was on the way over to our apartment. She arrived from Johannesburg this morning."

So that was the voice message. Every Friday night, Ben set the voicemail to pick up their calls after one ring. Moreover, she'd taken a long shower this morning, using the powerful jet of the water to sluice some of her earlier tension away.

Shame. The tension was back. Her shoulder and back muscles wound so tight, her chest constricted with rage.

"Do you think it's okay to wait until the morning your sister arrives to tell me?"

He might own the luxury penthouse apartment, but this was still their home, her home, albeit for a short while. She wouldn't be disrespected. Not by him or his sister.

"If you'd listened to the message you'd know that I wasn't expecting her. She just turned up."

"Well, I was in the shower, so I didn't hear the phone." She blew out a frustrated breath. "And anyway, who does that? Who flies over thousands of miles to just turn up in somebody's house? What if there was nobody home?"

The sound of Ben's weary sigh filtered through the phone line.

"She has the code to the door lock. She usually stays over when she's in London."

This just got better.

"A family member I never met just turns up in our home unexpectedly." Her voice was loud. She didn't care if Beatrice overheard her words. "And now you tell me she's allowed to come and go as she wishes. Do I not have a say in this?"

"Of course, you do."

There was a long pause on the line in which Selina wanted to demand answers. Instead, she bit her tongue, fuming silently.

"I should've considered that you might not want her staying with us. Don't worry. I'll arrange a hotel room for her and send a car to pick her up."

His conciliatory tone and speed to remedy the problem gave her cause to pause. Did she really want to make an enemy of her sister-in-law? There were enough spare bedrooms in this penthouse to accommodate a basketball team. Moreover, when Kaya came to London, he would be living in their apartment. It was only fair to allow Ben's sister to stay.

"No. Don't book a hotel. I don't want her to go." She heaved a sigh. "I guess the unexpectedness of it all threw me. I would've liked to know in advance, that's all."

Not to mention that it was something else that was adding to screw up her routine for the day.

"Sure. I'm sorry," Ben said. After a short pause, he asked, "Where is she now?"

Selina told him, omitting to describe his sister's behaviour on arrival or Selina's reaction to her rudeness. Telling tales was never her thing.

"Are you dressed?" Benjamin's tone changed from peacemaker to seducer, deep and husky.

Heat flared on her cheeks, her pulse rate increasing. "No, I'm wearing your towelling robe," she said.

"Have you been a good girl?"

The heat spread from her cheeks down her chest and finally pooling between her legs. She shifted from one leg to the other to distract herself. Benjamin had a knack for turning her on just with the tone of his deep voice.

"If you mean as per your instructions on the list then I've tried to carry them out. But with your sister here I'm not sure what else to do."

"Did you touch yourself after I left?"

She shifted again, remembering what she'd been doing.

"I started to..." She'd sworn to always be honest with him.

"Did you climax?"

"No. I stopped before my hands reached my ... sex. I only traced the scars while remembering how you touch them."

The sound of his muffled groan made her heartbeat faster.

"I want to see you."

Her breath hitched, and her hand travelled to her neck instinctively where her pulse jumped against her collarbone.

"Are you on your way home?" she asked, her voice a tad hopeful.

"No. Go to my study."

At first, she was unsure of what he meant. Taken aback, she frowned. "What's that got to do with you wanting to see me? The door is locked."

"Stop overanalysing things and do as I say. You know the code to the door. Call me back from the phone in there when you've opened the door." He didn't give her a chance to argue and hung up.

Now she was even more curious as to what he had in mind. The study was Ben's sanctuary, and she just went in there on the rare occasions he invited her in. Her having the door code was only supposed to be for an emergency.

Since it was Playday, strictly she shouldn't ask questions. But the standard rules were out of the window with the arrival of Beatrice. Selina couldn't follow them to the letter with another person in the house. Playing their games in the presence of a third-party was a non-negotiable limit for her. Ben would have to find an inventive way to get around the restriction.

Selina walked down the hallway. Putting her head against the wood, she listened at the door of the spare bedroom. No sound came through. Beatrice must've been fast asleep. Feeling a little bit more confident that whatever Ben had planned wouldn't be interrupted, she keyed in the code to his study. The lock clicked. She twisted the handle and pushed the door open.

Butterflies fluttered in her belly, her shoulders tightening with nervous tension. It was her first time in this room alone. She paused, taking in the sight and scents, letting it soothe her.

She loved the sanctuary of his study. It smelled of wood, leather, cigars, and Benjamin. The wall behind his large solid mahogany desk was lined with wooden shelves stacked full of books—old and rare out-of-print hardbacks as well as newer ones.

The chair was covered in the softest dark brown leather that matched the two-seater sofa leaning against the opposite wall. Above the couch was another canvas painting of a family of wild lions relaxing on the Serengeti landscape. The outer wall was nothing but a double-insulated glass sliding door leading to the balcony that ran around the side of the building. The unobstructed view of the River Thames and Chelsea Bridge.

Blue sky and bright sunshine drew her to open the door. A train rumbled along the tracks in the distance, the faint sound of the travelling cars carried in the brisk wind. Though the sun was out, the wind held a slight chill.

She closed her eyes, allowing the sun rays on her face for a few brief moments. Taking one final breath of crisp air, she slid the door shut and locked it.

Her nerves more settled, she returned to the chair behind the desk, picked the phone and redialled Ben's number. He answered it at once.

"Lock the door and take the robe off," he said without preamble.

Chapter Three

To say that her heart was racing would've been an understatement. After an initial leap as if it would have exited her throat, the vital organ pounded against her chest with the force of excitement.

With knees threatening to buckle, Selina swayed to the door. She secured it, ensuring that her sister-in-law couldn't walk in on whatever Benjamin had planned for her.

She returned to the desk, the soft wool of the carpet cushioning her bare feet. At the desk, she removed her robe, folding it neatly the way she knew Benjamin preferred and leaving it on the chair. While she was happy to remove her clothes and toss them aside, Benjamin liked a tidy environment. And she'd learned to please him by adopting his style.

Even now, knowing he wasn't here, she still did it anyway because it made her feel as if she was in his presence. And he would keep her safe regardless of the physical distance between them.

She picked up the phone where she'd left it on the table.

"I've done as you instructed," she said, glad that her calm voice hid her trembling excitement.

"Good girl," he said.

Approval. She'd pleased him. A warm glow bloomed in her chest, cheery and bright, curling her lips in a happy smile.

"Now, put the phone on speaker and leave it on the desk."

When Benjamin was in this mode, his voice acquired an intense, thick quality like a baritone. The fierce and vivid cadence washed over her, mesmerizing her into compliance, the sexiest thing she'd ever heard. Her body mellowed, liquid surging within her core.

She obeyed and stood back, waiting for his next instruction. This was exactly what she loved. The freedom to just be and enjoy this lull in their otherwise hectic existence without guilt or scorn. She didn't have to think about a thing, just followed his commands, knowing that she pleased him by doing so, also knowing that he would fulfil her needs.

It was always an exchange, his command for her obedience, his pleasure for her fulfilment.

"Stand in front of the desk and present yourself."

A frown creased her forehead, and she paused, her analytical brain kicking in. Benjamin wasn't there. He couldn't see her through the phone. So how could she present her body to him when he couldn't see her?

She stared at the phone about to state the obvious but bit her lower lip instead. The rules meant she couldn't talk unless asked a question that required a response.

"Do I need to repeat myself?"

How did he know she was hesitating?

"No, Benjamin."

Unnerved, she glanced behind, half-expecting him there and stood before the desk. Back upright, shoulders squared, chest pushed out, her arms behind her back and feet shoulder-width apart, she held her body still the way he'd taught her.

"Turn around, slowly."

Strange. Still, she did as he instructed, heat sweeping over her body. In her mind's eye, she pictured his all-seeing gaze on her. Tingles spread as she came to a stop facing the desk again. Her clit pulsed, aching with arousal. She wanted to pull her legs together. Knowing it would be going against Benjamin's wishes, she didn't.

"Take the clip out of your hair."

How did he know she had a hair clip on? Her gaze swept the room, searching. She couldn't see anything that looked like a camera. Despite the intrusion, the notion of being watched by Benjamin had her womb clenching with exhilaration.

Standing naked in front of anyone else would kill her. Humiliate her. Strip away the dignity she'd fought to regain since the attack that resulted in her scars. Her husband knew it. He'd never allowed anyone else to catch a glimpse of her bare body. She pictured him sitting at his office desk, watching her via a video feed.

Was it intrusion since he owned her body? Was he sitting alone in his office playing with his massive erection while watching her naked?

"Do you want to say something, Selina?" He sounded amused.

"Can I ask a question, please?"

"I will answer any questions you have later. But for now, you are to simply obey me."

She bit her lip, her frown even more pronounced.

"If you want to stop, you know what to do," he added in a matter-of-fact tone.

If she stopped the session, then he would have to answer her questions. It would also mean giving up any thrill or release she would've gotten out of the session. She'd gotten angry with him earlier because she'd thought he was abandoning play day. If this was his way of making it up to her, she couldn't miss the opportunity.

Letting out a sigh, she unclipped her hair and allowed the thick, untamed dark tresses to cascade down her shoulders and back.

"I don't want to stop."

At this moment, he was in charge, and she trusted him to keep her safe.

"That's your second display of insubordination today. Anymore and I will suspend the rest of Playday until I've punished you appropriately. Are we clear?"

"Yes, Benjamin," she replied, her head tilted down, her gaze glued to the clawed feet of the mahogany desk. One thing was certain, she couldn't afford to screw up or get any more demerits than she'd acquired already.

"In the bottom right-hand drawer of the desk, there's a small bag. Go and retrieve it."

Without hesitation, she walked around the desk and bent to open the drawer.

"There's nothing more beautiful than your ass exposed to me like that, except your pussy. But I'll get to that in a moment."

A shocked gasp escaped her lips.

He *could* see her!

She lifted her head.

"Be still, beauty. I want to look at your lovely plump behind."

She remained bent over, her hands now propped on the desktop, shaking with both excitement and fear.

He's watching me! How?

"I love looking at it. But even better, I love touching it."

Her breath held, locked in her throat, her pulse rate increasing.

"I love the smoothness of the skin and the way it wobbles when I spank it, the way it yields to my touch, just like you yield to my command."

Her womb clenched several times as she remembered his caresses. The way he would trace the callused pad of his fingers over her bum, the firmness of his palm when it connected with her skin in a smack. She had to admit that when the spanking was for her pleasure rather than a tool of punishment, she enjoyed it.

"And your lovely tight hole ... one day I'm going to breach it."

Blood surged in her veins, pounding in her ears.

"Fill you up so you won't know where you end and I begin."

Her ass clenched tight.

"Fuck you so hard, you will pass out from the sheer pleasure of it all."

Her breathing came in short spurts. There didn't seem to be enough air in the room. Her heart was beating so hard she almost felt faint.

"Would you like that, my beautiful Selina?"

"Yes," she breathed out in a soft gasp little more than a whisper, her voice breathless, and air barely getting into her lungs.

Her head swam with all the images he'd placed in there with his words. Her mind reeled with all the possibilities. Flames of desire licked her skin. She held firm to the table, afraid she would collapse on the floor in a trembling heap of arousal.

While they'd played and she'd fantasized about it, nothing more than his tongue and finger had ever touched her back entrance before. Would he fuck her there today? She turned her head to look behind her.

"One day soon, but not today," he answered her silent question, the laughter in his voice unmistakable.

She shivered. The intuitive way he read her was uncanny.

"Now, take the bag out and empty the contents on the sofa."

She pulled out the soft cloth black bag and straightened seductively. It was amazing how much little words of admiration could affect her confidence. Now she sashayed to the couch, releasing her inner sex kitten with every deliberate step. Knowing he was watching her and that he liked her back view so much, she bent over, exposing her ass and sex again as she emptied out the bag.

"Good girl," he said. A smile played on her lips.

The items on the sofa sent her pulse racing again. There was a massive silicone dildo, a transparent glass vibrator with an anal stimulator, a pair of diamond-studded nipple clamps with magnetic chain links, and a white tube of lubricant.

One day, he'd presented the boxed items as a gift to her. They were for her use. Never having owned a sex toy, she'd soon discovered how much Ben loved using them on her.

"Anything that blows your overactive mind is a good gadget," he'd said then.

"Sit on the sofa. Spread your legs."

She did so, her body sinking into the leather, the softness stroking her back.

"As I'm not there with you, you're going to have to follow my instructions diligently. No hesitations. No coming until I say so."

"Yes, Benjamin," she whispered as anticipation and arousal fought for dominance in her veins.

"First, I want you to show me how you touch your body with your hands. Prepare yourself for me."

Sighing, she leaned back on to the sofa, tilting her head back to rest on the top. Then she lifted her right hand, stroking her neck downward, her skin soft and sensitive. Her left hand rubbed from her belly upwards, the scars there rough and hard. The contrast in textures fuelled her desire.

Carrying out his instructions meant he experienced each physical stroke and each tangible caress vicariously. She appreciated this connection they shared. It was as real as Benjamin caressing her body himself.

She palmed her breast, weighing the right one the way he did, then the other before squeezing the flesh of each with her hands. A moan escaped her lips as pleasure zinged around her body.

Rolling the nipples between her thumbs and forefingers, she tugged the tips until they hardened into points, electric vibes making her clit throb. Her core clenched with need, and she couldn't ignore it.

She slid her hand down over the smooth lips of her sex she'd shaved in the shower this morning. Benjamin had always preferred her body hairless except on her head.

"I don't want anything hiding you from me. Not your clothes and not the hair," he'd said to her once.

Afterwards, she shaved her legs and sex every other day.

"That's right. Open yourself. Let me see that tight little bundle," he said now, his voice deep, his tone controlled. But she detected a roughness in there as well. He was aroused. Knowing how much she affected her control freak of a husband, she smiled.

Using both hands, she parted the lips, revealing her erect clitoris.

"So pink and beautiful. It's crying out for my tongue, isn't it, Lina?"

"Yes!" Her voice was breathless, a shiver running down her spine.

"Flick your index finger around it. Imagine it's my tongue tracing a circle on your clit."

She did so, and a thrill coursed through her body enhanced because she pictured her husband's rough tongue teasing her.

"That's right. I'm licking it, coaxing your clit until it's erect and swollen."

She panted, fever rushing over her body.

"Dip a finger into your pussy and show me how wet you are."

Gasping with delight, she thrust her middle finger inside her soaked channel. When she withdrew it, the digit was coated in her juice up to the second knuckle, glistening in the bright daylight.

"I love that you're so responsive to me. It is me touching you, right?"

"Yes, Benjamin. Your tongue is caressing my clit, making me wet."

"Good girl. Pick up the vibrator and fill your pussy with it. Slowly. I want to see your pussy swallow it up," he said. "Don't turn it on yet. If you need lube, then use some."

Ignoring the lube, she picked up the glass sex toy. She tilted her hips up and inserted the bulbous tip, crying out softly as the cold, smooth surface penetrated her.

"That's it. Push it all the way in."

She followed his words. The object widened her insides, warming as it went in, leaving her body feeling full. When it was wholly fitted, the anal extension brushed against her back hole.

Her arousal spiked, her channels contracting around the vibrator though it wasn't on yet. If she turned it on, it wouldn't take long for her to climax, as her body was already wound so tight.

"With the other hand, roll and tug your nipple until it is stiff."

When she obeyed, her arousal spiked again, warm blood rushing to her nipples, her nerve endings sensitized.

"Pick up the clamp and attach it to your lovely, stiffened nipple."

She hesitated, staring at the clamps but not picking them up. She'd never choose to inflict pain on herself although she'd allowed Benjamin to use the clamps before.

"Do it." The depth of his tone suggested he wasn't going to allow for her to back out.

She picked the item up that looked like pincers but with flat instead of serrated edges. With shaky hands, she applied it on and hissed as pain shot from her nipple.

"Breathe, Lina."

His voice calmed her, and soon the sting dulled to a bearable level turning to delicious heat.

"Now the other one."

She inhaled several breaths before repeating the process with her other nipple, rolling it with her fingers before applying the clamp. He talked her through the pain, soothing her nerves until she relaxed again.

A month ago, she would've been unable to do or even accept for anyone to do that to her. Benjamin had proved his worth as a dominant man, quashing her fears.

This was progress in an unshakable form. One day she would trust him with the secrets buried in the vault of her mind. And that day was fast approaching.

"Good girl. Your obedience is a gift that pleases me. You will be rewarded."

She continued breathing slowly, dragging air into her lungs, the dull ache pulling her into a trance. The sound of his voice lapped at her body, a gentle ocean tide.

"As I'm not there to control you directly, the nipple clamps will act for me to keep your orgasm in check."

He knew her too well. Without the pain as a pleasurable distraction, her body was primed to explode when any stimulation hit her clit.

"Now turn on the vibrator but keep the setting low."

Chapter Four

The gentle whirring sound of the vibrator masked the devastating effect it was having on Selina's body as she let out a long keening cry after she turned it on. The setting was at the lowest. Still, her body was already aroused. The mild pulsation teased, akin to putting a drop of water on the lips of a thirsty man in the desert and expecting that to be enough. Expecting him not to want to snatch the bottle of water and gulp down the rest.

With an orgasm so close at hand, she wanted more intensity and more friction. Her overwhelming need for release fought with her need to relinquish control, to trust Benjamin's ascendancy, knowing it could only lead to the ultimate in pleasure.

"Play with your breasts. Tug the chains when you're close to coming."

That her brain could still process his instructions was a mini miracle. With an effort, she returned attention to her breasts. Using her hands to squeeze them together, turning their throbbing ache to something deliciously decadent that joined the pleasure building in the rest of her.

Her lower body was on fire, the slow rising fever that resurrected from her sex and was now spreading up her spine, belly, and chest to heat her face.

She tugged at the magnetic chain linking the nipple clamps, and the sweep of sharp pain held back the urgent rise of her orgasm. For a moment she just lay there panting, trying to refocus her mind on the tremors in her sex and not the twinge in her breasts.

Swiftly, the tenderness and pleasure balanced out, and she remembered where she was, in Benjamin's study. He was on the phone line and watching her from a secret camera hidden somewhere in this room.

He'd been silent for a while, which was unusual. He was always active, either giving instructions or participating. She tried to imagine what he was doing on the other end.

Was he naked? Somehow she knew Benjamin wouldn't take all his clothes off. It was more likely that he would unzip his trousers and release his erection into his callused hand. She chose to picture him that way.

In her mind's eye, he sat in his black leather executive chair, the sleeves of his sky-blue shirt rolled up to the elbows revealing strong, sinewy, tanned arms covered in golden brown hairs. His firm thigh muscles flexing in his charcoal trousers, the black belt and fly undone, his hefty shaft wrapped in his long fingers, the blunt head engorged, a pearl of pre-cum beading there.

She licked her lips, picturing her tongue swiping at the bulbous tip, tasting his seed while kneeling on the rough hardwearing carpet in his office. She would run her tongue along its length, licking and sucking the steel encased in satin.

Then he would wrap his hands in the strands of her hair, tugging her head back before filling her mouth with his shaft. She would suck it, swallowing him up as much as she could until its head hit the back of her throat. She would work it, his body heat as well as the scent of his musk adding to her excitement, the evidence dripping down her thighs until he swelled in her mouth and let out a loud growl, spilling his cum down her throat.

The imagery she conjured up, only worsened her fate. Passion took over, an urgent orgasm rising through her body, and she bit her lip.

Her hips bucked, her inner walls contracting around the vibrator as the butt piece continued to tease her hole. A tug of the nipple chain only increased the rate at which her orgasm peaked.

"Ben?" She pleaded, asking for permission, knowing she couldn't hold back much longer.

"Now, beauty," he said, his voice husky. "Fly for me."

The words barely registered before her climax tipped over the edge and her whole body convulsed. She screamed, releasing the pent-up stress bubbling inside her mind all week. Nothing else gave her this mindless, breathless high that surpassed all else, except submitting to Benjamin. Slumping on the sofa, her brain blanked out.

****

Benjamin's heart pounded against his chest, his blood whooshing in his ears. It took an effort to stop panting out loud, all from watching Selina's sweet submission.

Witnessing her beautiful hard-earned compliance swelled his heart with delight. It had taken weeks of training to get to this point, weeks of patiently nurturing and enforcing patterns, of rewarding and punishing as was necessary.

Yet at one point this morning he'd thought they'd had a setback. The way she'd glared at him, her eyes burning with her fury. He'd thought she would defy him and refuse to obey his instructions. Only the months of experience he'd taken to learn her character had prevented an all-out disintegration of what they'd both achieved.

With Selina, it was always about getting the right balance of carrot and stick. Too much carrot and she would get lippy. Too much stick and she would run. He'd still have to take the paddle to her lovely behind for her outburst this morning. But that could wait.

For a moment, Benjamin stared at the large television screen braced on the sidewall in his office. The image he'd previously zoomed into—of his wife sprawled on the leather sofa in his home office. Her dark tresses tumbled around her, framing her face, the rest of her body chocolate, bare, and vulnerable as it trembled.

As her body's spasms calmed, she seemed to rouse from the climax possessing her, eyes still closed.

Benjamin shifted in his buckskin seat, his discomfort more than just about the hard as granite erection in his trousers and more to do with the fact that he wasn't there with her.

During and after orgasm was the most vulnerable moments for Selina. In those moments, he liked to hold her, to encase her trembling body in his arms so that she would always know that he would protect her and bring her comfort.

By taking away her corsets, he'd taken away her safety net, which only left him to reassure and restrain her.

Then again watching her sprawled out like that, the diamond studs from the nipple clamps glittering, the glass edge of the vibrator sticking out of her glistening pussy, the welt and scars on her stomach exposed to view. It was massive progress she hadn't already rushed to cover up. A month ago, she would've been pulling the robe back on immediately.

Hell, she wouldn't have even allowed him to watch her via a video feed. She was so distrustful about cameras because she never wanted to be filmed naked.

For that reason, he hadn't told her there were several cameras located in strategic points in their apartment. They were there for security reasons and had been installed a long time before they'd been married. His line of business demanded that level of security. He'd bought the penthouse apartment more for the protection it provided than for any display of wealth.

For the last month, he'd had the video feeds disabled as he wanted Selina to get used to the environment before talking to her about the cameras.

He'd need to be at work this morning and had noticed the vehement way she'd reacted to him going out on today. Hence the decision to take their relationship a step further. A gamble which paid off with significant gains.

In the last few weeks, he'd managed to push her comfort barriers down one obstacle at a time. Gradually his wife was letting go of her inhibitions and starting to trust him totally. They still had a way to go yet. But this was progress. Warmth radiated from his chest.

"Lina, don't sleep off yet," he spoke into the phone speaker on top of his mahogany desk.

On the screen, Selina stirred, shifting her arms and legs, but she didn't get up.

"Pull out the vibrator and switch it off."

She reached between her legs, wrapped her right hand around the flat end and gently pulled out the glass phallus-shaped stimulator, her lower body arching. It glistened in the light, coated with her fluid. She would be sensitive from her orgasm.

"Now, the nipple clamps, take them off."

Her finger fiddled with the chains before the clamps came off, and she held them in her open right palm.

"Put the items on the table. Don't worry about cleaning them up. Just put the robe back on and lie back on the sofa."

She stood, her movements languorous, and did as he instructed. Picking up the robe from where she'd left it folded on the chair, she shook it out and slipped her arms into the fleece.

She looked so small covered from neck to toes, her vulnerability even more apparent.

"Take the phone."

Complying, she returned to the sofa, phone in hand, her eyes unfocused. Having a climax was such an intense experience for her.

"Lie down, Lina. Take a nap. I'll be here to watch over you, and I'll wake you when it's time."

"Okay," she said, her voice filled with emotion.

His heart squeezed tight as if in a clenched glove, his breath knocked out of him.

Her shoulders lifted in a seemingly satisfied sigh. She curled up, knees tucked in, her long dark eyelashes drooped onto her flushed cheekbones.

"Thank you, Ben." He had to strain to hear her whispered words before the phone line clicked off.

Without moving, he watched as the rise and fall of her chest became regular. She was asleep. This was a gift, watching her like this. That she'd trusted him enough to let him do it made it more precious.

Their life was moving forward, their plans in the right direction. The visa application for her brother Kaya to come and live with them in the UK was in progress. As the sponsor, he'd already sent documents showing that he could provide financially for the boy. Kaya wouldn't need public funds when he came to live with them.

A tap on his office door drew his attention. He pressed the button on the remote control, blanking the screen just as Christopher Star, his long-term best friend and joint business owner, strode in. They had a past linked from their time as mercenaries.

Though they'd shared most things, and Chris had introduced Ben to Selina, he couldn't allow his friend to see Selina in this state. It was an intimacy he wanted to share between his wife and himself. What's more, it would be a misuse of her hard-won trust.

In the past, Ben had shared women with Chris. Now seeing his friend reminded Ben of Selina's request for a threesome, something he'd yet to grant her. He didn't know if he could. Selina brought out the possessive side of him like no other. The more time he spent with his wife, the less he wanted to share her with anyone else.

Even if their arrangement was temporary.

He pushed the thought aside. For now, he had a more pressing problem.

"I came as soon as I could," Chris said when he lowered his tall frame into the seat opposite Ben. "What's going on?"

Without saying a word, Benjamin clicked the mouse of his laptop. The email screen came into view. He swivelled the device so his friend could see the page.

"Read this email."

Christopher met his gaze, concern etched on his forehead before he stared at the computer screen. Benjamin rose from his chair and withdrew a bottle of spring water from the small refrigerator in the corner of his office.

He unscrewed the plastic metal cap and lifted the glass to his lips. Chilled water travelled down his throat, cooling his insides as well as quenching his thirst.

Though he tried not to focus on them, the words in the email came to him.

I want you to come home immediately.

He pictured Uncle Leonard dictating the words to his long-suffering secretary who'd sent the message.

"What are you going to do?" Christopher's question drew his attention.

Without looking behind, Ben knew his friend's gaze was boring straight into his back. He stared out of the window of his office building located midway between Victoria Station and Vauxhall Bridge. From his window, he could see the street level. Cars were sparse on the road.

"You know how I feel about going back there," Ben said, turning around.

"Well then, just reply to him and say 'no'."

"It's not that simple. Beatrice arrived from Joburg this morning."

"Shit. You didn't tell me she was coming," Chris said, a frown creasing his face.

His friend's surprise wasn't lost on him.

"I didn't know. I only found out this morning that she was here when she called from Heathrow."

"Bea arrives the same day you get a summons from Uncle Leonard? This is just too coincidental."

Though Christopher wasn't a relative, he addressed the patriarch of the Moss family the same way Benjamin did in deference to the man who had brought him up.

"You talk as if you don't know the man. This is very calculated, and Beatrice is here to make sure that I comply with his wishes. I'm sure of it."

"I don't like this at all." Christopher stood and walked to stand next to him by the window.

"On the other hand, I could do what he's not expecting and go home with Selina in tow." A cynical smile tugged Ben's face, his chest tightening with suspicion.

"Now that would be a slap in his face." Chris barked with laughter. "Can you imagine that kind of commotion that would cause? I noticed Uncle makes no mention of Selina in the email. He does know about her, right?"

"Of course, he knows I'm married. He's showing his disdain by not inviting or referring to her. I'd definitely love the see the shock on his face when my wife shows up."

He tossed the empty water bottle into the little waste bin.

"Then again, I don't want Lina enduring my family stresses. She has enough on her plate already." Therein lay his conflict. Protecting his wife was as vital to him as showing his respect for her.

"Fair enough," Chris said. "How much does Selina know about this?"

He flicked his hand at the laptop.

"Well, she knows that my family is in South Africa, and she's just met Beatrice this morning but not much else."

"You are going to have to tell her a lot more before someone else fills in the gaps."

"I know." Ben swiped his hand through his head, ruffling the tufts of hair, letting his inner turmoil show to the one person who knew him as well as a brother could.

Discussing his family and past left him with knots of regret in his stomach. Shame made him reluctant to share them with his wife, especially as she'd been so skittish. He'd grown to care for Selina a lot more than he'd bargained for and losing her now they were on the verge of a real, permanent relationship didn't appeal to him.

"Beatrice being here complicates things. She's not exactly the most discreet person on earth."

Chris's laughter resounded in the room. "You can say that again."

Some years back, his sister had stumbled upon Chris and Ben sharing the same girl. She'd been the daughter of their cook and worked as a maid in the house. It had been on one of their breaks from active duty, and Chris usually spent it with Ben and his family except on the occasions he'd travelled back to Chechnya.

The next time Ben had returned home, he'd been fuming with rage over what he'd witnessed at the frontline of the war in Sierra Leone, only to find out the girl and her mother had been sacked.

Beatrice had reported him to their uncle who instead of putting the blame squarely where it was due—on Ben's and Chris's shoulders—had meted out punishment on the girl and her family.

When Benjamin had tried to reason with his uncle, the old man had used a very offensive racist term to refer to the girl and her family. Ben's open scorn for the man he'd previously regarded as a father begun then. He just couldn't respect a man who would treat people with such hatred and disdain.

Things changed for him forever from that moment.

Now, he was finally righting some of the wrongs from his past. There was a risk his plans could be derailed. He couldn't let that happen.

"I'll speak to Selina the first opportunity I get," Ben said and returned to his desk.

Chapter Five

An hour later, Benjamin woke Selina with a phone call and informed her he would return home soon.

Instead of feeling refreshed from the nap, irrational fears plagued her mind as she tidied up. Ben had been abrupt on the phone. Had something gone wrong? Was he trying to hide something from her? Why was his sister here out of the blue?

Discomfited, she needed a distraction. Usually, Benjamin took responsibility for the care of sex toys. However, when she was anxious, there was only one thing to do. Work. Keep busy.

Exiting Ben's study, she locked the door and returned to their bedroom. Using their ensuite bathroom sink, she cleaned out the sex toys, patted them dry with a towel, and left them to air dry on the counter. She would return them to the study later.

She dressed quickly in the clothes Ben had left out for her. The free-flowing shape of the dress flattered her curves. She loved that it wasn't clingy since the temperature had risen. Ben always said she looked pretty in it.

A smile curled her lips as she thought about her husband. She pictured his face screwed up in concentration as he read something on the screen of his laptop or when his mind was buried in thought. Did he accomplish what he set out to do today at work, or did he think about her?

A wave of dizziness passed over Selina, an ache blooming in her chest. She gripped onto the bottom bedpost, swinging round to sit on the edge of the bed.

For years she'd been drifting, never at home anywhere, or giving herself to anyone entirely. Until Benjamin. Until now. He'd found her—no, scratch that—he'd captured her. She wouldn't have volunteered to be here without his brand of persuasion. Now, she wanted to stay, yearned to belong and call this place her home.

Permanently.

Drawing in air through her nose and letting it out, the realization shocked her.

When had their relationship translated into more than a physical yearning? When did she start not just wanting him, but needing him?

No! She shook her head. She didn't want to think about this. Not now. All she needed right now was to focus on what she had to do to get through the day. Since they had a guest, Ben's earlier instructions were obsolete. She had to concentrate on taking care of the needs of their visitor. Her worries would be dealt with another time.

Having made her decision, she pulled her hair into a ponytail, holding it with a hair clip and left their room.

She found Beatrice in the kitchen dressed in red Capri trousers and a white tank top, staring into the open fridge. She must have showered. Her hair was wrapped in a white towel and her face free of make-up.

Without the glam, she appeared young, close to Selina's age.

"Did you sleep well?" Selina asked, keeping her tone light and cheerful. Despite their earlier run-in, she was willing to move on and be polite. Beatrice was Ben's sister, after all. Still, she stood at the kitchen door, her shoulders tensed, half-expecting lousy attitude.

"I did," Beatrice said but didn't turn to look at her. Her tone, however, wasn't rude. "Now I need some food."

Selina let out a sigh of relief as she stepped into the kitchen. The food she could do. Moreover, the woman looked like she needed some meat on her bones.

"I was about to make some pasta. Would you like some?" It was a little lie. But Beatrice didn't know that. Their Saturday night meals were usually takeaway ordered from their local restaurants. Sometimes Ben took her to eat out.

Since her husband wasn't home, there should be nothing wrong with her cooking instead.

"Yes. Please." Beatrice turned around, a smile making her flawless oval face even more girlish. In her left hand was a container of yoghurt she'd taken out from the built-in fridge. She shut the door and opened a drawer, removing a small spoon.

The familiar way she'd opened the white drawers and extracted the items didn't skip Selina's notice. Like Beatrice belonged here and not Selina. After all, Selina had contributed little to what was in the apartment. Okay, she'd added fuchsia-coloured scatter cushions to the sitting room sofas to break up the monotony of mink and mahogany. Apart from clothes and personal items in the bedroom, nothing in the residence reflected her personality.

Perhaps Beatrice had been here when Benjamin had moved into the apartment and suggested some of the interior design. Selina's stomach curled with unease. Inhaling deeply, she pushed back the disturbing niggle.

Concentrate on here and now.

From the vegetable rack, she took the items she needed to prepare the meal.

The sound of a phone beeping drew their attention. Her sister-in-law stretched across the counter and picked up the mobile on the black granite-topped island unit.

"Hi, Louisa," Beatrice said, phone clutched between her left ear and shoulder, yoghurt bowl in her hand as she walked out of the kitchen, her bare feet padding on the grey stone tiles. "Yes, I got in this morning."

Selina didn't hear the rest of the one-way conversation as Beatrice disappeared out of view, perhaps into her bedroom.

Glad to be alone in the kitchen, she shook out her shoulders, easing some of the tension there and focused on preparing the meal. Luckily, she'd had her groceries delivered from their local supermarket on Thursday, so she didn't have to scramble around looking for ingredients to cook with.

Still, her hands shook as she poured the fresh pasta into the pan, some falling onto the worktop. This had special significance for her. It was the first time she was cooking food for a family guest in over ten years. She wanted to take her time and prepare it well. It used to be a thing of pride for her to entertain guests. She had loved hosting family and friends. But that inherent value had been robbed from her.

Now panic ate into her mind, and she hurried with chopping the vegetables. Benjamin would be home soon, and she wanted to get this right. For Beatrice's sake.

She poured some oil into the pan and turned the heat on the hob on. She returned to crushing the garlic and chopping the peppers.

When she looked up, the oil was hot and smoking. In a panic to avoid the smoke alarm from going off, she pulled the pan off the fire in a jerky movement. It sloshed over, and some of it splashed her arm.

She yelped as her skin burned. Gripping her arm with her left hand, she rushed over to the sink. Cold water cascaded over her burnt flesh, taking away some of the stinging.

The pain ricocheted around her body, her heart pounding loudly in her ears. She gritted her teeth as she fought back the tears that misted her eyes.

"What are you doing?"

Benjamin's gravelly voice made her look up. He stood by on the threshold, his body filling the doorway, his lips pursed in a stern line. Her heart jumped in surprise and relief at his presence. She hadn't heard his return.

"Ben!" She couldn't hide her breathy voice with the realization that she'd messed up the dinner and he was there to witness it. Her earlier wish for him to come home reversed. She coughed to clear the lump in her throat and didn't meet his searching gaze.

"I'm just cooking dinner," she said in a much too cheery tone and turned off the tap. "Go and welcome your sister. I'll let you know when it's ready."

Please, let him not notice the burn.

His eyebrows pulled together in a frown as he strode across the kitchen towards her.

Feigning a calm exterior, though her heart pounded in panic, she pulled a sheet of paper towel out and dabbed it over her arm as if she was merely drying it.

Ben's long fingers wrapped around her upper right arm, his grip tight but not painful.

"Take the towel off." Something wasn't right with the calmness in his voice.

Compelled to obey, she reluctantly lifted her left hand with the wet sheet in it, nausea churning in her belly, her gaze fixated on the grey floor tiles.

"What happened?" There was thunder in his voice. She lifted her head and stared at his face. His grey eyes darkened to stormy clouds, the groove of creases on his face deepening with his frown.

"The hot oil splashed on my arm," she said in a weak voice as she fought back the tears. There was no point attempting to hide the truth anymore.

He glanced back at the cooker and saw the still burning hob. Releasing his grip on her arm, he leaned across and switched it off before turning back to her.

"Let me see that," he said in a surprisingly gentle voice. She had been expecting anger.

She lifted her right arm so he could see it better in the overhead spotlight. A patch of skin the size of a ten pence coin was already darkening.

The sound of his growl vibrated throughout the kitchen. Tingles travelled down her spine to her core. A soft gasp escaping her lips as her insides contracted. There was something about the intensity of his response that was so damned erotic she wanted to wrap her legs around his hips. At the same time, he took her fast and hard against the work surface.

"You stay right there. I'll get the first aid kit."

She watched the movement of muscles through his shirt as he opened one of the top cupboards. The fit of his dark trousers emphasized the firm buttocks and thighs inside the soft fabric. She imagined holding onto his back, running her palms along his skin. A moan built in her throat. Suppressing it, she licked her lips instead.

"Do you really think this is a good time to be staring at my behind, Lina?" His voice held reproach.

Heat flared from her neck to her face. How the hell could he have known that? She switched her gaze to the counter.

Ben placed the box containing the emergency items on it and pulled out the bottle of burn spray. Then he scooped Selina up and set her on the central island worktop. She lifted her arm as he sprayed the coolant on the spot. Eventually, the painful sting mellowed.

From another cupboard, he took out a glass tumbler and filled it with fresh water from the tap. From the emergency box, he withdrew a pack of painkillers. She stretched out her left hand as he popped two tablets out.

With the water, she swallowed the tablets and handed the glass back to him. He put the glass in the sink. Leaning against the counter, the skin of his hand turned white as his grip on the edge tightened. His shoulders rose and fell, and he exhaled a heavy sigh before turning to fix his intense stare on her.

"Why were you cooking, Selina?" he asked her in a quiet, even voice. Still, she detected disapproval, and it annoyed her. She stiffened her back.

"We have a guest, remember?" She met his gaze and held it.

He stared at her blankly for a few seconds as if he'd forgotten that his sister was here.

A couple of blinks later, he asked, "So? You could've ordered takeaway."

"Beatrice said she was hungry, so I decided to cook dinner. I didn't want to serve her food from a box. It's my first time meeting her." *Moreover, I don't want to give her more reasons to dislike me, as the brother's wife who doesn't cook.*

"Selina, we have Saturday rules for a reason. I know you think it's all a game. But it is there for your benefit as well as mine."

"Your sister is here. That changes things."

"Perhaps. We need to negotiate those changes before they can happen. You cannot act unilaterally. This is what happens when you do."

He lifted her arm to emphasize his point, his fingers biting into her skin.

"What?" She tugged her arm back. He released it. "You're implying that I'm not capable of getting through the day without one of your rules to handhold me."

He shook his head, displeasure glittering in his eyes like amber warning signals.

"I know it seems as if it's all about what I want. But this relationship is about both your needs as well as mine. The rules are there to safeguard you."

"Really? How's that?" Agitated, Selina jumped off the worktop. Though it hurt, she placed her hands against her hips, confronting him. Earlier today he'd decided unilaterally that she was ready to have him watch her through a hidden camera.

You didn't stop him. You could have at any time.

She ignored the voice of reason, reminding her she'd chosen to be watched. She'd gained immense pleasure from being spied upon and being under Ben's command.

Her insecurities held her in their grip. No matter how much she enjoyed being with Ben, it didn't change who she was. One husband had abandoned her when she'd needed him most. This one was only going to be in her life temporarily. And she was at risk of surrendering more than her body. Her heart was at stake too!

Standing barefooted, her head only came up to Ben's chest, but she stood her ground. Her vital blood-pumping organ pounded against her chest.

He paced away, turning his stiffened back, and giving her some breathing space. She exhaled in relief, grateful that he wasn't towering over her in an intimidating pose.

"I know you, how much you love your work, how hard you work," he said. "You have this thing within you that pushes you, that says it's not enough for you to give one hundred percent. You must give extra, go beyond what's required. You want to give back, perhaps because of the people who took care of you when you needed it. And this is the only way you know how."

He turned. Something in his intense gaze snatched her breath away.

"It also stops you from thinking too hard about your past. If you work yourself to exhaustion, when you come home, your brain won't engage in thought, and you can sleep 'til the next morning and start all over again."

He took a step towards her.

"Of course, what happens is that by the time you get to Friday, your brain is pretty fried and you need something to level out all that adrenaline. Otherwise, your mind and your body crash and you swing into a depression, your nightmares overwhelming you. Therefore, you've taken to play day so quickly. Because the alternative is much worse."

Tears clouded her eyes. She swiped them with her left hand. How could this man know so much about her when she had never verbalized any of it? She'd always thought his perceptive abilities were uncanny. But this was a whole new level. She didn't know whether to laugh or cry that he could see through to the murky depths of her soul.

"Have I said anything that isn't true?"

A considerable lump clogged her throat. Unable to speak, she shook her head, turning her back to him, knowing that if she met his gaze, she would crumble into a heap on the floor.

"That's why we need the rules. To keep you safe. To stop the panic attacks. To help you cope with the fear eating away at you inside."

A sob tore through her chest. She gripped the edge of the counter and bent over to gulp in air, the truth of his word corroding her resolve. She had never admitted it to herself, but she needed the safety net their routines and rules provided. It allowed her to let go without trepidation, something she'd been unable to do for so long. While she smiled at the world and worked hard at being successful, inside she was ruled by terror. The fear of the unknown, of open spaces, of big crowds, of being attacked again.

At last, she exhaled and opened her mouth to reply, but no words came out. She turned slowly letting him see the despair in her eyes. With a groan, he tugged her close and lowered his lips to meet hers, his arms circling her body in an encompassing hug.

Breaking off the kiss, he sighed and leaned his forehead against hers.

She needed his embrace, to be carried into their room so they could be locked away from the world. So, he could make right all that had gone wrong with today.

"Am I disturbing you love birds?"

Benjamin lifted his head, but he didn't release his hold on Selina. His sister stood at the kitchen door.

"Hi, Bea." He smiled warily.

Beatrice walked in. "Hello, brother."

Ben let go of Selina and engulfed his sister in a brief hug. She was tiny compared to him, but Selina could see the resemblance immediately in their colouring.

"You're looking well."

"So, do you. Marriage seems to be working for you."

Selina almost smiled. Was the woman saying nice things about her indirectly?

Ben chuckled. "I'll take that as a compliment."

"On the other hand," Beatrice looked around. "You wife promised me some pasta, but it doesn't look like it's gotten far with your arrival. I'm starving."

"Don't push your luck, Bea. Lina is a fine cook, but she's not allowed to cook on Saturdays. So, you're going to have to wait for some takeaway."

"Really? Whose rule is that?" She looked from Ben to Selina. Selina suppressed a grin. "Can't you make an exception?"

"It's my rule, and there are no exceptions. You either wait for takeaway, or you make your own dinner."

Beatrice pouted her lips. "You're going to make me cook my own food? I'm your guest."

"It's your choice."

Ben scooped Selina up and carried her down the hallway to their bedroom. Excited, she hid her smile, tucking her face in his chest. He kicked the door shut behind them, walked over to the bed, and deposited her on it.

"You stay right there," Ben said in a dangerously low voice, his expression stern. "I need to talk to Bea. When I return, you're going to be punished for disobeying Playday rules and scaring me half to death like you just did."

Her breath hitched, and her heart raced. Instead of fear, she throbbed with expectation as he strode out of the room, his scent lingering.

Chapter Six

It took all of Benjamin's resolve to walk away from Selina and shut the bedroom door behind him. That he wanted to scoop her up into his arms and hold her tight to make sure nothing ever hurt her again while making sweet love to her was one reason. It was warring with the urge to bury his dick balls deep into her dripping wet pussy after he'd spanked her bottom raw and then fuck her so hard until she begged him to stop.

In either case, walking away was difficult, the weight of the erection straining his fly telling him he wouldn't have lasted long inside her anyway. Suppose he was to administer the punishment she needed with any ounce of control. In that case, he'd have to find another way to relieve the tension in his balls before he touched her.

In the kitchen, Beatrice was leaning against a counter with the menu of their local pizzeria in her hand. A smile curled his lips. He should've known she would never cook. At least not by choice anyway. Each time she stayed in his apartment, she rarely cooked, unless you classed making a sandwich as cooking.

Back in Johannesburg, she had been spoilt by a house full of domestic servants. She'd never needed to cook.

"Luigi's is a great restaurant," he said as he started clearing up the items Selina had abandoned on the worktop.

"I know that," Beatrice said, her tone still sulky.

Ben glanced up at her and smiled. "Of course, you've ordered from them before. Just pick what you want, and I'll place the order. Either James or Martin will go and pick it up before the night concierge arrives."

She nodded.

He returned some food to the fridge, tossed the chopped ones into the bin under the sink and loaded the dishwasher with the empty pans.

When he straightened, his sister was staring at him with a frown on the face.

"What's the matter?" he asked.

"I should be asking you that question. Why are you the one cleaning up? Where's Selina?"

He laughed. "I can't believe you asked that question. Have you never seen me cleaning up before?"

"That was when you were single. Moreover, the housekeeper was here almost every day, so you didn't have to clean up the kitchen. Now you're married. You should leave the housekeeping to Selina."

He shrugged his shoulders nonchalantly. "I like tidying up. Selina is busy with something else."

"Seriously? What could be more important than her doing her wifely duties?"

"Making me happy."

"But—"

"Trust me. She is performing her wifely duties." *And more*, he omitted from saying as he smiled.

"Moreover, I didn't marry Selina for her cleaning abilities." He winked.

Bea's cheeks turned a rosy red as she blushed, her lips shaped in an O. Her expression reminded him of the time she'd walked in on him and Chris with Siba. Even after ten years, she was still as prudish. Some things never changed.

"Have you decided what you want from the restaurant?" He changed the subject.

She quickly lifted the menu, happy to refocus on something else instead of the image he was sure she'd conjured up.

"I'll have the carbonara," she said and handed the menu to him.

Ben pulled his phone out of his back trouser pocket and dialled the number for the restaurant. After placing the order that included some calamari and linguine for Selina, he returned the menu to the drawer his sister had removed it from.

Beatrice pulled a bottle of wine out of the rack.

"Would you like some?" she asked.

He nodded, reaching for two wine glasses in the shelf above his head. He put them on the table, took the bottle from his sister and opened it with a corkscrew.

"How long are you in London for this time?" he asked as he poured the Stellenbosch Roussanne, a favourite from the coastal region of South Africa.

"It depends." She lifted her shoulders in a shrug and picked up a filled glass. "I've got an audition for a play in the West End on Wednesday. If it goes well, then I could be here for a long time."

He smiled. His sister, the budding actress. While she'd performed in a few plays in their home country, she'd always dreamt of starring in a role in the London West End. Just like their mother in her heyday.

Looking at her now, she looked so much like their much-loved parent.

"I'm sure you'll get the role," he said as he lifted his glass, the delicate peachy aroma filling his nose.

"We'll see." Her upper lip trembled nervously, her smile weak. "I have to get through the audition first."

"You'll be fine. You're talented." He squeezed her tense shoulder. Realizing she was more nervous than she appeared, he pulled her into his arms and gave her a bear hug. This was his kid sister. His only sister. He'd always looked out for her, though in recent years they'd lived in separate countries.

"Don't worry about it." He pulled back and stared into her grey eyes that glittered with tears. "I know I'm going to see your name up in big lights one day."

Her lips widened, and her eyes brightened as she smiled.

"You always say that to me."

"That's because it's true."

He pulled her to the tall stool. When she hopped on, he pulled another one and sat next to her.

"You're going to be more famous than Mama was."

Their mother, Elizabeth Seagraves-Moss, had been a world-famous actress who had starred in leading roles in plays as well as movies. From the time Beatrice learnt to walk and talk, she'd always wanted to follow in their mother's footsteps.

The sound of Beatrice's weary sigh floated in the air.

"I do miss her a lot," she said.

"So do I, sis. So do I," he said in a sombre tone, his voice gruff.

"But you know, Mama. She wouldn't have wanted us to mope around. So how about we say a toast to me landing this role?"

"Of course." He lifted his wine glass. "Here's to Beatrice Moss, the new West End star."

She laughed as they clinked their wine glasses together. "Cheers!"

They sipped the wine in silence for a few seconds. It wasn't awkward, but he knew his sister was waiting for him to talk about their uncle.

There was no better time than now.

"So how is Uncle doing?"

She looked at him, her face scrunched up in a frown.

"Do you really want to know?"

"Of course, I do. I wouldn't ask otherwise."

"He misses you."

A bark of laughter exploded from his lips. Good thing he hadn't just taken a sip of his wine. Otherwise, she would've had a wine shower.

"If I believe that—"

"It's true. He doesn't show it outwardly, but I know he does."

Ben shook his head. "That man doesn't need anyone. He wouldn't know how to miss anyone."

Beatrice's jaw tightened, her eyes saddening.

"You know the two of you are so similar. So stubborn."

"I'm nothing like him." He stood up and walked away from the table. Swivelling, he faced her again. "He sent me an email—no, a summons—to return to Joburg."

She nodded.

"You know about it."

Her chest heaved as she inhaled deeply. "Yes, he told me."

"Why?"

Frown lines appeared on her otherwise smooth forehead. "Why what?"

"Why does he want me home now? He's never bothered before."

"He never bothered before because he thought you'd come home sooner. But you've moved on." She paused. "And now, you've married. He's not happy about that."

"Ha! Like I didn't know that already."

"You should have seen him. For days after you called to tell him about your wedding, he walked around like an angry bear snapping at everyone."

"Nothing's changed there then," he said.

"I'm serious. This time it's different. There's something not quite right about him. I..." She trailed off.

"What? Spill it, Bea. What's going on?"

"I think he's sick."

He pursed his lips and lifted his glass of wine. "Fine. I'll pay for him to be treated. I don't have to see him."

He turned around, ready to walk out of the kitchen door.

"He's dying, Ben. I think Uncle's got cancer." Her voice sounded choked.

He froze, his heart skipping a beat. Slowly he turned around. Beatrice watched him with a film of tears in her eyes, glistening and ready to fall.

Regardless of his feelings about Uncle, his sister loved the man like a father. Leonard treated her like his little princess, spoiling her.

"Are you certain?"

She lifted her shoulders, letting it hang in the air for a couple of heartbeats.

"I'm not absolutely sure, but he's been seeing a doctor although he says it's for nothing serious."

A tear rolled down her cheek.

"Bea, that man is as strong as an ox. It'll take more than a little illness to kill him off," he said. They'd often joked that the old man would outlive them.

She smiled weakly.

"What if it's something more serious? Promise me, Ben." She stared at him with doe eyes. "Promise me you'll go and see him and resolve this thing between both of you."

He waited for several heartbeats before responding. This obviously meant a lot to his sister. Although, he didn't think the old man was any closer to the grave than the rest of them. Finally burying the hatchet between the two of them was a good enough motive to visit his old home for the sake of his sister and new wife.

"I promise. I'll go and see him."

"Good." She jumped off the stool. "Now, they better hurry up. I need food before I can go partying."

He raised one eyebrow, half-amused. The rate at which she recovered was too rapid.

"What?" she asked, smiling at him innocently. "I'm not going to spend a Saturday night stuck indoors. I'm in London. This doesn't happen very often."

He laughed. "Oh, you are too good. So, all the dramatics about uncle was put on."

She raised her hand to her chest and feigned offence. "As if I would. He is really sick, and knowing how stubborn you can be, I had to exaggerate things a bit."

He frowned at her, feigning anger. "You know I don't like being manipulated."

"I'm sorry, but you've promised to go visit him. You can't renege on your promise."

She was right. He never went back on a promise.

"Fine. But don't ever pull that stunt again."

"I won't." She stood on tiptoes and kissed his cheek. "Thank you."

She headed for the door. "By the way, Louisa is coming over."

He stared at her blankly.

"You know, my friend that fancies you?" she smiled sweetly.

"The same one who crawled into my bed the last time?"

"Yes. She's disappointed that you're married. She's willing to crawl naked through the streets if you tell her to."

She laughed and disappeared through the doorway.

Ben shook his head. His sister's words conjured up an image of the only woman he wanted crawling around naked for him. His wife. And she was awaiting him in their room. His pulse quickened. Time for some fun.

He should really leave her alone to think about the implications of what she'd done. At least until dinner time. But he wanted to see her. And why should he deny himself? Selina was the one being disciplined, not him.

He picked up the bottle of wine and a single glass, walked to the living room. From the sideboard, he withdrew his cigar-case and took one roll out and stuck it into his shirt pocket.

On the way back to his bedroom, he knocked on Beatrice's door. She opened and stuck her head out.

"Listen out for the buzzer. The concierge will bring the food up. Get started. Selina and I will eat later."

She nodded and retreated. He walked down the hallway to the far door. His heart was already galloping at the anticipation of what would happen once he opened the door.

Twisting the knob, he pushed the door open. His heart skipped several beats, his half-awake erection roaring to life. His grip on the wine and glass tightened to stop them from slipping.

This woman will be the death of me.

Chapter Seven

A rush of fresh air from the air-conditioner in the hallway washed over Selina's bare skin like a rolling wave. A rash of Goosebumps skittered down her arms. Her shiver wasn't from the draft that had entered the room when the door opened. Instead, it was from anticipating the man who now stood blocking the light filtering in from the hallway.

She swallowed the lump in her throat as her hands, which were clutching each other at her back, trembled. Nothing else filled her with a mix of excitement and trepidation like Benjamin's imposing presence, especially when she didn't know what lay ahead.

Wool pile scratched the taut skin on her knees. She itched to adjust her posture. But she remained still, her gaze fixed to a spot on the carpet she'd chosen earlier. She knelt on the bedroom floor, her hair loose and flowing down her back like he liked it, her body stripped of her clothes, bare to the gaze of her husband whose face she couldn't see, but whose presence she felt to the core of her being.

Her heart thumped in her chest. She intended to apologize for going against his wishes, for disappointing him.

This morning when he'd announced he was going out she'd been rude and later had blatantly disregarded a Playday rule.

She could never offer herself to any other man the way she presented her body to Benjamin. She knew that now. In that sense, *he* was the Master of her body.

She sucked in her breath and blinked several times as her eyes stung with the realization. Her stomach tightened.

Her heart wasn't far behind. She would offer it to him if only she could trust that he felt the same thing for her.

He cared about her. That much she knew. The way he'd stood up for her with his sister had warmed her heart. Now she wanted to reward him the way she could with her whole-hearted submission.

She should've trusted that he would fulfil his pledge to her always. She needed to learn to give her total trust to him.

She wanted to tell him all this—to share what was in her heart. But words always failed her.

So instead here she was, bare and on her knees, in a pose, she hoped conveyed her remorse and capitulation more than any words she could conjure. Between her lips was the black leather paddle. She took shallow breaths through her nose, silently counting to stay calm. Yet every fibre, pore, nerve-ending was tuned into the man who still stood by the doorway.

He didn't say anything.

Was he angry at her? Pleased? What? She wanted to look up and see his expression. But that would negate the purpose of her actions.

She was presenting herself to him, ready for his authority, whichever form it took be it chastisement or enjoyment.

After what seemed like an eternity but was only a few seconds, Benjamin strode across the room. The door clicked shut. His dark trousers and polished shoes came into view and disappeared behind her. He remained silent, though his spice surrounded her.

She inhaled deeply, comforted by his familiar scent.

Soft hissing, a flow of warm air, and the chug of a train in the distance informed her that the balcony door was opened.

Fabric rustled.

Foam sighed.

Wood creaked.

She pictured him sitting in his favourite chair, an antique red upholstered Victorian armchair he sat on to smoke his cigar on the balcony.

Glass tinkled and thumped on a dulled surface. The scratch and sizzle of a match and a sucking sound told her he'd lit a cigar.

"Come here." The quietly spoken words were at a baritone level that had her core vibrating.

Selina lifted her head and looked in the direction of his voice. As she'd imagined, Benjamin sat in his chair on the balcony puffing on a cigar. Beside him on the low mahogany table was a bottle of wine and a glass half full.

The sun descended behind the roof of houses, the horizon an orange-purple mix. The rays reflected on the Thames.

She hesitated as she grabbed the foot of the bed so she could stand. Though they had no neighbours on this floor or above to spy on them, if someone had a pair of binoculars, they could watch from the bridge or one of the houses across the river.

"Crawl to me," he said, the gentle depth of his voice irresistible, his gaze connecting with hers and never wavering.

She sucked in a sharp breath. He really meant it. Somehow the way he stared at her encouraged her. She placed her palms on the carpet and started crawling. She pictured the grace of a cat as it padded across the floor and mimicked its movements.

Having Benjamin's mesmerizing gaze on her naked body boosted her confidence. Her movement improved, becoming fluid. She felt sexy. Hands first, she stepped into the balcony and stopped in front of Benjamin, still on her hands and knees, awaiting his next command. The slab of stone that made up the balcony floor was hard and cold. She ignored the discomfort and focused on the man in front of her, for whom she would do anything. The thought sent warmth spreading over her body and her heart clenching.

For Benjamin, she would endure most things.

Chair creaking under his weight, he pushed to his feet and walked back into the bedroom. Selina kept her gaze riveted to the spot he'd just moved from. She didn't want to look around her. If she did, then the panic simmering in her veins would boil over, and she would run. For once, she wanted to do this right without panicking.

Keeping her gaze fixated on the chair kept her focus on Benjamin. She could imagine he was the only one who had eyes for her, the only one watching her.

He returned, tossing a brown, velvet cushion on the floor beside her. He sat back in the chair.

"Kneel on the cushion."

She adjusted herself on it, glad for his consideration. Her breasts jutted out as she folded her arms at her back, her thighs spread open, the way he liked her to present her body to him. Whether it was from the breeze or Benjamin's accessing gaze, her nipples tightened into points, cream running down her thigh, her skin flushing with heat.

How she wished he would touch her! A gentle pat on the head, a brush of his sensuous lips against hers or a thrust of his fingers into her sex. Not fussed, she needed a physical connection to enhance this emotional connection she currently shared with him.

Placing the cigar on the marble ashtray with one hand, he leaned forward, the other arm outstretched, palm open and upward. Opening her mouth, she allowed the paddle to drop into his hand.

"What's the paddle for, Selina?" he asked, his tone amused.

"You said I was going to be punished."

"I said? And why should you be punished?"

"I've been bad, Benjamin. I disobeyed our rules and ended up burning my arm. I have no rights to mark my body without your permission."

"Yes, your body is mine. And you've earned this punishment. But you don't get to decide how I punish you, Selina. Do you understand why?"

"Yes, Benjamin."

"Tell me."

"On playdays, I have no decision-making powers, except the choice to participate or not. If I choose to participate, I'm simply to let go and obey, trusting that you know the best for me."

"Good girl."

He put the paddle on the table beside him and picked up the cigar again. He took several puffs, the smoke curling upward, marking the air with his presence. She knelt there content and happy to finally be with him after they'd spent the whole day apart.

Something was calming about watching him smoke, although she didn't like the fact that he did. She was a pharmacist who worked in a busy London hospital. She'd seen the effect of smoking on patients. But she accepted it as a quirk of his. And prayed that there was no damaging effect on his body. There were cases of smokers who didn't contract lung cancer. She hoped her husband would fall into that category.

They stayed like that for several minutes. She forgot about the world around them, only reminded occasionally by the odd hoot of a car horn or rumbling of a train on the tracks. The shadows deepened. The smouldering ash at the tip of his cigar glowed. Light filtered through the curtains from a dimmed lamp in the bedroom. Benjamin must have turned it on when he'd gone into the bedroom to collect the cushion.

Returning the cigar to the ashtray, he shifted in his chair.

"Unbuckle my belt," he said.

Glad for an opportunity to touch him, she rushed to do his bidding. Her hands trembled as she grabbed the metal buckle and unclipped the leather belt from it. She held each end in her hands.

"Now the fly, unzip it."

She stared at his fly. The bulge beneath appeared huge, and her eyes rounded.

She'd had some relief today.

However, Benjamin had an iron-clad control and only ever climaxed when he wanted, which was usually while he was inside her.

She placed her hands on his thighs, the muscles beneath toned and hard.

"No hands, Lina. Use your mouth."

No hands? She raised her gaze and saw his eyes glittering with quiet amusement. He nodded. Leaning in, she used her lips to move the flap of fabric covering the zipper. The metal was hard between her teeth as she tugged it.

Perspiration coated her back. She sucked in shallow rapid breaths. The woody tobacco scent of him filled her nostrils, increasing her arousal. The gritty sound of the zipper coming undone increased her anticipation.

Eventually, she got it lowered. Beneath his black boxer briefs were stretched.

She looked up again and licked her lips. He'd said no hands, so it would be difficult to get to his erection without his help. However, he hadn't told her to do anything else. So, she waited.

He lifted his right hand from the arm of the chair and slid it inside his trousers. When his hand came out, it was wrapped around his shaft. She was so eager to get it in her mouth; she looked up at him again.

With a nod of approval from him, she leaned in, flicking her tongue out around the smooth tip.

The sharp hiss of his indrawn breath coaxed her. With his hand on the base of his length, she continued her exploration with her mouth, licking, kissing, and caressing it with all the attention she could give. The bundle of muscle and nerves felt like velvet steel on her tongue and smelled of musky sex.

She continued her attention, worshipping his dick as much as she could without her hands. His light grunts increased in pace.

"Enough teasing, Lina. Open up."

She smiled, knowing she had affected him. One of the perks of being on her knees was the sounds of pleasure her husband made. Fulfilling his need delighted her.

She opened her mouth. Benjamin wrapped his fingers into her hair, gripping the strands and guiding her lips over his length. He bobbed her head up and down as her mouth slid up and down over him. When she'd mastered the rhythm, his hold on her hair loosened a little, and she worked her mouth over him.

He slid in and out, a smacking sound filling the air as the tip hit her throat. She sucked her cheeks in and puffed, mimicking the way he puffed on a cigar.

"Oh, Lina."

She glanced up, and Ben had tilted his head back to the top of the chair, his left hand gripping the arm of the chair. The whites of the knuckles showed through as she knew he fought for control. But in this battle, she intended to win.

Break his control, just once, a devil on her shoulder whispered.

Her husband was the king of control.

As he used his hand on her hair to control her movements, slowing her down when she got too fast, she added another dimension to wrest that from him.

Her body buzzed with her arousal. She pulled her thighs together, squeezing them for some relief but didn't get much. She started humming in her throat, using the extra vibrations around Ben's erection to push him closer to the edge.

A loud groan erupted from Ben. He yanked her head off his length just as an arc of semen shot over her face and chest, marking her body in white cream. A sense of satisfaction rolled over her body, but she stopped from smiling until she could see his expression.

He lifted his head. Relief washed over her.

His lips curved in a smile. "You're a troublesome girl, Lina."

The harsh edge to his words was softened by the twinkle in his eyes.

She licked the bit of cum around her lips but left the rest on her body. She loved wearing his mark. It made her belong and emphasized his possession.

Taking a handkerchief out of his trouser pocket, he cleaned himself and tucked his length away.

"It seems you're determined to be paddled. I'm going to enjoy tenderizing your beautiful ass."

She tilted her head down, hiding her smile behind the dark tresses of her hair. She knew that pushing him and trying to take charge of blowing him would earn her a chastisement. And somehow she looked forward to it.

"Stand up and hold onto the railing."

She stared at him wide-eyed, fear seeping into her body for the first time this evening. Was he really going to do this now? Outside? In public view? It was one thing to kneel naked and give him a blow job. Her body was obscured. The only way to see her was from above, which was impossible without a helicopter or from the roof.

But if she stood then people could see her from the street!

"You're going to be a good girl and take your punishment like you deserve. And you are my good girl. Aren't you, Lina?"

"Yes, Benjamin." Her voice was breathless as her throat suddenly constricted, and her skin flushed.

When he spoke to her like that, she couldn't resist him, despite her own fears. Pushing off the floor, she stood, holding onto the railing, and shut her eyes.

The chair creaked again, and she felt his warmth on her back although he wasn't touching her.

"Open your eyes and look at the world at your feet, Lina."

His warm breath whispered on the skin of her neck, making it prickle. A tremble travelled down her spine. Compelled, she lifted her eyelids. The Chelsea Bridge was lit up with bright amber and white lights in the distance, cars rolling along in either direction. Across the river, the trees on the embankment obscured her view. She surmised that if she couldn't see the people walking along the pavement, then perhaps they couldn't see her either.

"You know I would give you the world if only you would trust me." He continued, his low voice turning her insides into mush. Her breaths came in short pants as she fought to control her feelings.

"You're getting twenty. Ten for this morning and ten for this evening," Ben whispered before biting the soft lobe of her right ear.

She let out a soft gasp, more fluid dripping down her thigh.

"Count them out."

Thwack. Leather connected with the soft flesh of her right bum. An ache bloomed. She bit back the yelp, using her breathing to ease out the sting until it settled low in her belly.

"One," she whispered in a hoarse voice.

Chapter Eight

Two things surprised Selina as she sat naked on Benjamin's lap on the balcony, his large frame encasing hers, a cocoon of warmth and male spice. His hand caressed her back from nape to spine tail, his voice whispering soothing words in her ears, her behind raw and enflamed.

First, she'd stood at that railing as instructed by her husband. Her gaze riveted at the river below watching the ebbing and flowing of the murky water. She hadn't panicked for one moment.

Her brain had finally figured that even if someone could see them up here, all they would see was the silhouette of a couple standing on the balcony. They wouldn't be able to see exactly who it was or any details.

Secondly, she hadn't broken down into a pile of sobs and cried like a baby. She'd stood there counting out every thwack, every thud, her body jolting from the impact, her face flinching at each contact and yelps escaping her lips. But she hadn't cried.

And she wasn't sure why? Perhaps it was because he hadn't held her across his lap this time. Whatever the reason, a new level of satisfaction bloomed in her chest. A massive step for her and their relationship. She was happy, even with a tender bum.

Using a soothing salve, he'd gently massaged it into her sore backside taking the paddle sting away. It would still ache for a day or so.

Lifting her up, he carried her into the bedroom and placed her on the bed. The bulge in his trousers looked painfully huge. He must've seen her staring as he chuckled lightly.

"As much as I'd like to make love to you right now, you need to eat. And so do I."

He walked to the bathroom and came back with the towelling robe. He opened and held it up.

"Oh." She frowned and hesitated. "I need you, Benjamin."

"I know. Food first. I also need to talk to you. Something came up."

The tone of his voice indicated it was something serious. She stood from the bed and walked to him, her earlier unease returning.

"What is it?" she asked as she slipped her arms into the sleeves of the robes.

"We'll talk at the table," Ben said, his breath warm and tickling her neck as he wrapped the robe around her front and tied the sash for her.

His arms squeezed her body in a hug that was both comforting and tender. When he released her, he took her hand.

"Come on." He tugged her, and she followed him out.

She went into the dining room to set the table while he went to the kitchen.

He returned with the boxes of food still in the warmer and placed them on the table.

She transferred the food into the dishes.

He sat at the end of the table, and she sat in the first chair on the right side. Silently they ate for a while. She enjoyed this part of their Saturday ritual as much as she enjoyed the rest. This quiet companionship, observing each other, listening to the sound of their heartbeats and crockery, it was soothing. He'd said he wanted to talk to her, so she waited until he was ready to say what was on his mind.

"I got an email today."

"An email?" She snorted. "Welcome to the twenty-first century, caveman."

His warm laughter echoed in the room. "Hey, trouble. Be quiet before I go all caveman on you."

She covered her mouth, stifling her giggles. "Okay. Sorry. Who was the email from, and what was it about?"

He eyed her for a minute and continued. "Uncle Leonard sent me an email. Well, his secretary did. I'm being summoned to Johannesburg."

"Summoned?" She resisted the urge to laugh. "Does anybody in your family know how to ask anything nicely?"

He raised one curved brow in a mix of surprise and warning.

"Anyway, that aside," she continued. "Why is he *summoning* you?"

"The email didn't say much, but Beatrice seems to think he is unwell."

"Oh ... then you have to go and see him."

He stayed silent, just watching her.

"What is it about your uncle that sets your teeth on edge, Ben? Talk to me."

"He is a mean and vile man. Sometimes I wish he wasn't my uncle."

He took a sip from his tall glass of water before continuing.

"My father died when I was a little child, and Beatrice was no more than a baby. As a boy, I looked up to Uncle Leonard as a father figure until I saw him for who he truly was—a bully who preyed on the weak. You don't want to cross him. He crushed those who opposed him with his army of mercenaries. When we weren't busy fighting for those he wanted in power, we were fighting his personal wars. Walking away from him and my family legacy was one of the hardest things I did."

His voice roughened with emotions.

Selina had never heard Benjamin this agitated before. Reaching across, she covered his right hand with the left one, offering comfort.

"I told you my uncle, and I haven't been getting along for a few years."

"Yes, but you didn't say why."

His Adam's apple bopped as he swallowed.

"Years ago, when I lived in South Africa, I had a thing for this girl whose mum used to work for us."

Her disquiet rose. She withdrew her hand from Ben's.

"Was it serious?" She feigned nonchalance, but her chest constricted at the idea that Ben had loved someone else.

"I was a young man, and Siba was a really nice girl. In those days, I had these wicked urges, and she was the only one who could handle them, who understood them."

Selina gripped the seat of her chair tightly. It was one thing to find out that Benjamin liked another girl but quite another to know that they'd had the kind of relationship she now shared with him.

Jealousy roiled in her belly, rising to her throat, and leaving a bitter taste on her tongue.

"So, what's it got to do with your uncle?" she asked, wanting to move the story along. She'd rather not hear about his great relationship with the girl.

"Bea saw me with Siba and Chris once and told my uncle, who sacked the girl's mother and sent them away."

She had stopped listening after she heard Chris.

"You mean you and Chris slept with the girl?"

"In those days, we went as a double act." She should've read meaning into the curious stare he gave her. Yet all she could picture in her mind was Ben and Chris with this girl, inflaming her jealous rage.

"Anyway, that's hardly the point."

"What is?"

"I confronted my uncle about sending her away, and some things he said about her were very unpalatable. And I know he disapproves of my marriage to you."

"He hasn't even met me."

"That doesn't matter to him. He is a dinosaur who believes in preserving the purity of the white race. He thinks I married you as revenge for Siba."

"What? You mean your uncle is a racist."

"That's why we fell out."

"And now you've married me to get back at him."

She pushed back her chair.

"Selina, wait. I—"

"No. I won't. I don't want to hear any more."

She pushed open the door and stormed out. It took all her willpower not to bang the door shut.

How could Benjamin not tell her something this crucial before he married her? Of course, she wouldn't have married him if she'd known her in-laws would turn out to be card-carrying members of the Aryan nation.

She walked to their bedroom and locked the door when she got inside. She needed some space to think. Words, images swirled in her mind, threatening to blow the lid off the tightly sealed cauldron of her past.

In the bathroom, she turned on the shower and stepped under it. It was a quick wash before she got out and dressed in a pair of black jeans and a white t-shirt. She wasn't going to wear what he wanted her to wear today. She'd effectively called an end to play day. She was brushing out her hair when there was a knock in the door.

"Ben, I don't want to talk to you right now," she said.

"It's not Ben. It's Beatrice." The reply came.

"Oh, hang on."

She unlocked the door.

Ben's sister stood in the hallway.

Selina peeked out but didn't see Ben.

"Can I talk to you for a minute?" Beatrice asked.

"Sure. Come in."

She moved aside so Beatrice could walk in. Her sister-in-law strode to the bed and sat on it.

Selina shut the door again.

"I'm sorry, but I heard the two of you arguing, and now Ben is sitting in the living room, looking like a storm is about to hit him. I hope I wasn't the reason you were fighting."

"What do you care anyway?" She really wasn't in the mood to suck it up anymore.

"Look, I know we didn't exactly start off on the right foot. But Ben is my brother, and I love him. And it seems you make him happy."

Beatrice's words earned her a reprieve and Selina bit back from laying into her. She sighed.

"The argument wasn't about you if you must know."

"Then it must be about Uncle Leonard. Don't let him come between the two of you. I know Uncle Leonard isn't exactly everyone's cup of tea. But he just needs to adjust to the fact that Ben has changed and is married to you."

"Hang on a minute. What do you mean by Ben has changed? Changed from what?"

"You should know this already since you're from Sierra Leone. Isn't that where you two met years ago?"

"No. I only met him last year." Selina frowned; the earlier niggle returning to prick her mind. There were still missing pieces to the Benjamin jigsaw puzzle. "I mean, I know he's mentioned he's been to Sierra Leone, but we didn't meet there."

"Okay. When he worked for my uncle, he was sent to Sierra Leone as a mercenary. Uncle Leonard is one of the biggest arms dealers in Africa. Anywhere there's a war in Africa, you can be sure Moss PLC has supplied half of the weapons. And he has his own army, which Benjamin used to be a part of. Anybody could basically pay them to fight their war for them. But when he came back, he was a changed man. It was after that he had a huge fight with our uncle and moved to London. Luckily, he was born in the UK, so he had a British passport, and the transition was easy for him."

Ben had supplied weapons for the Sierra Leonean war? The same catastrophe that had destroyed her life as she knew it? The churning in Selina's stomach increased, and she fought not to throw up her dinner.

"Are you okay?" Beatrice asked, concern lacing her voice.

"I need to get out of here," Selina said.

Still stunned by the information she'd just received, she staggered to the closet and snatched her handbag and shoes. Then she walked out of the room.

"Where are you going?"

She ignored the question and headed down the hallway toward the door. As she walked past the entrance to the living room, she caught a glimpse of Ben with another dark-haired woman she didn't recognize.

The ball of emotions inside her chest swelled, taking on gargantuan proportions. Jealousy, anger, and revulsion rolled over in one avalanche.

She punched the code to open the door. Her hands shook so hard, and her eyes misted. The door didn't open.

"What's going on?" It was Ben's deep voice behind her.

"I don't know," Beatrice said, concern lacing her voice. "I was just talking to her about Sierra Leone, and she suddenly picked up her bag and walked out."

"Sierra Leone. Why the hell did you have to bring that up?" he snapped at his sister.

"I was only trying to help." She sounded offended.

A hand settled on Selina's right shoulder. Her body recognized the weight and warmth of Ben's touch and quickened. She hated herself for responding to him even when she shouldn't.

"Don't—" She flinched. "—touch me."

She swivelled to face him, fiddling with the link on the bracelet on her wrist, but she couldn't undo it. *Damn, shaky hands!*

"You know what, take this off." She lifted her arm.

He stared at her, his gaze like lightning.

"You don't mean that." His voice was too quiet, like the calm before the storm.

"Yes, I do." She knew exactly what it meant to wear this bracelet, and right now, she could not bear to look at it. "I can't wear it because I don't trust you." The illusion created in her mind was false. This was no haven for her. "And if I didn't have to wait 'til the final decision from the Home Office about Kaya, I'd be chucking the wedding band at you right now, too."

His body was so still apart from the tick of muscles in his jaw.

"Take it." She flicked her wrist at him again.

Quietly, he reached out and unclipped the bracelet. It dangled from his fingers.

"You can give it to her." She nodded in the direction of the dark-haired woman. "She looks like she wants it a lot more than I do."

Selina turned around to try the door again, but a tight band of fingers gripped her upper arm.

"This is what you do best, isn't it?" Ben bit out through clenched jaws. "Running instead of facing your fears. But the truth is that you can never outrun them. They live inside you growing every day into giant monsters when you can choose to reduce them to the size of ants and crush them. But no, we can't hurt sensitive Selina."

"I'll have you know, you're not the only one hurting, Selina. But do you care? No. You've just shown me that you don't."

Mouth agape, she stood there staring at her husband livid with anger for the first time since they'd been married. He reached behind her and punched in the keycode furiously. She heard the door click open.

"Go on then, run, Selina. Run, if it makes you feel better."

Chapter Nine

"Everything is going to be all right, you know," Lora said.

Selina sat on the chocolate print sofa in her old house in Finchley, a north London suburb. Her head on her best friend's shoulders as she fought not to break into another bout of sobbing. Lora's magic fingers worked magic on her tense shoulders.

On arrival, Selina had already been physically sick. Her emotions raged, a stormy sea, choppy and dangerous. She raised her head.

"How's that?" she asked, her voice choked with the sentiment. "First, I find out I'm not as special as I thought I was to Ben. Then he tells me his uncle is a white supremacist. Come on!"

"And if all that isn't bad enough. While my family and friends were killed, Benjamin and his family made money from all the weapons killing them. How do I reconcile those two things?"

"It really is a hard pill to swallow, Lina."

"To think that all this while I've been living in his apartment, bought with blood money. I can't live there anymore."

Shuddering, she covered her face with both hands.

"It's a good thing you kept your room here. You can always move back in."

Selina lifted her hands and nodded.

Lora scrunched her face up. "But what are you going to do about Kaya's visa application? You're supposed to be living with Ben. What if someone from immigration pays you a visit?"

Selina stood and paced the room. The familiar scent of cherry blossoms from the air freshener surrounded her.

"I really don't know what I'm going to do," Lina said.

Resigned, she sat down again and picked up one of the violet velvet scatter cushions, hugging it to her midriff.

"Why did I let another man con me? Stupid me. You would've thought that after everything I went through the first time around I wouldn't let myself be deceived by another man."

"In this case, you weren't the only one who was deceived. I genuinely thought Ben loved you. The adoring way he looked at you on your wedding day, I would've given anything to have a man look at me that way."

Selina snorted. "Ben doesn't love me. He is incredibly good at putting on an act."

"I don't know, Lina. What I saw looked genuine enough. Are you sure he hasn't moved on from his past? Perhaps that's why he fell out with his uncle."

"Even if he has moved on, it doesn't mean that he doesn't have blood on his hands."

"I know—"

A phone buzzing interrupted her. Selina reached in her bag and pulled out the offending object.

Benjamin.

She dropped the phone on the sofa. "I don't want to talk to him."

Lora grabbed it. "Do you mind if I talk to him?"

She shrugged. "Be my guest."

Her friend answered the call and put it on speaker.

"Hi, Ben. It's Lora."

"Hi, Lora. I take it that Selina is with you."

"Yes, she's here. But she doesn't want to talk to you."

"That's okay. I was expecting that. I just wanted to make sure she was okay. She left the apartment without saying where she was going. Since it's almost midnight, I needed to make sure she was safe."

"She's fine. Well, as fine as she can be considering."

"No problem. When she wants to talk, I'll be here. There are things I need to say to her, but I'd prefer to talk one-to-one. Anyway, whatever she decides, I will still fulfil my obligations to her."

Selina gasped, taken by surprise by his candid words.

"Selina?"

"Hold on," Lora said and put the phone on mute.

"Talk to him please, Selina."

She shook her head.

Lora sighed and un-muted the phone. "I'm sorry, Ben. She refuses to talk."

"I'm sorry, too," he replied. "Good night, Lora."

The phone line went dead.

"You know you're going to have to talk to him soon. If he didn't care as you said, he wouldn't be calling to make sure you're okay."

"It will have to be later because I don't want to speak to him right now. I'm going to bed."

However, sleep proved elusive. She got up in the middle of the night, watching movies and eating ice cream. She couldn't keep Ben out of her mind, rolling playback on their time together.

There'd been nothing erratic about him, so perhaps it was unfair comparing him to her ex who'd been a scheming coward.

While Ben was determined, he was never manipulative. Even now curled up in bed, she missed his warmth, his soothing words, and his safety.

That's it! She'd always felt safe with him. The Ben she knew could never knowingly cause harm to innocents, could he?

She needed to talk to him.

Only managing an hour's sleep, she called a taxi when she woke up just after dawn. It would be an expensive ride back to Chelsea. But, she needed to see Ben.

She showered and dressed in the same clothes she'd worn the previous evening. After a weepy goodbye to her friend, she headed back to the apartment in the taxi.

"Good morning, Mrs Moss." Martin greeted her.

"Morning, Martin." She smiled at the man before entering the lift. In the foyer outside their front door, she hesitated before keying in the lock code, apprehension knotting her belly.

Taking a few deep breaths, she pushed the door open. Silence greeted her. Slipping her shoes off, so she didn't wake anyone, she padded quietly past the empty living room, toward the master suite. Ben wasn't in there, and the bed was still made like he hadn't slept in it. She wondered where he was.

Ready to go searching for him, she noticed a packed travel bag next to the bed. Panicked, she rushed back out toward the study the only other place she thought Ben might be in. Knocking yielded no response. She keyed in the code and opened it.

Her heart stopped. Classical music poured through the speakers hung on the wall.

Ben sat in the leather chair facing the wall-to-ceiling window. He didn't even bother to look at her when she entered. Though she was sure, he knew it was her. With cautious steps, she approached him so she could see his face.

"Ben?"

His eyes were bloodshot, his hair dishevelled where he'd been running his hand through them all night. He was in the same clothes he'd been wearing from yesterday, the sky-blue shirt and charcoal trousers looked rumpled.

He glanced up at her and swivelled around.

"I guess you came to pick your things. There's no need to. I'm travelling to South Africa. So, you can stay here. When I come back, we'll work out an arrangement that won't derail your brother's visa application."

"Ben, I..."

"Selina, for what it's worth I'm sorry. If I'm honest, I feared the day you'd find out about my family because I knew it would be the beginning of the end for us. Even I find it difficult forgiving my uncle, and I chose to distance myself from him. I don't see any reason why you should forgive me."

"There are plenty of reasons. You are nothing like your uncle."

He wasn't, and she hated Ben comparing himself to such a bigoted man.

"In your defence, the things you did then can be dismissed as youthful folly. And when you realized what was going on, you chose to do the right thing and walk away. A courageous move, in my opinion."

He fixed his inscrutable gaze on her and didn't speak as if expecting her to say more.

"I need to explain to you why I freaked out yesterday. Can I sit down?"

"Please." He waved to the sofa.

She sat on one end, making space for him to sit, hoping he would take her hint. She didn't want him towering over her, unnerving her. Instead, he remained in his chair.

"Ten years ago, I was an eighteen-year-old girl excited and getting ready to marry the man I loved. It was a huge traditional wedding ceremony with members of both families there."

She closed her eyes reliving that day.

"Halfway through the ceremony, gunmen arrived causing chaos. There was shooting and screaming, people running, falling, wounded, and dead."

"At first I was holding on tight to Tony. He was my new husband, and he would protect me. What he didn't have in looks he made up in youthfulness and ambition. One of the militiamen gave him a choice, give up your new bride or both of us would be killed."

Tears misted her eyes.

"He turned to me and said what would be the use of both of us dying. He said I should go with them, that they wouldn't hurt me. After all, I was a girl. I begged him not to, but he told them to take me. They dragged me away. From that moment I never saw my parents or brother again. I was a captive and taken to their enclave in the bush where I was kept with some other girls. I fought the men who wanted to rape me. That's how I got the marks on my body. They said if I didn't cooperate, they would mutilate me and leave me for dead. No other man would ever want me."

Her tears had now been falling so steadily that she didn't see Ben get up and walk over until she felt the gentle dip of the sofa and his arms lifting her onto his lap.

She sighed and sank into his warmth and safety, giving her the strength to carry on.

"The cuts hurt badly and without proper attention got infected. I caught a fever. Next time I woke up, I was in a hospital in the city. Apparently, we'd been rescued by some soldiers. An aid worker arranged for me to come to the UK as an asylum seeker due to the extent of my trauma."

He went very still for a moment before taking a handkerchief and wiping her face. He pulled her in tightly, his chin against her head.

"The pain from the physical wounds I can live with, but what still hurts me the most is the thought that someone who professed to care about me could abandon me so easily without a fight. He was supposed to protect me, but he sold me so cheaply."

"Your ex was a coward. He didn't deserve you."

She shrugged. "I never trusted anyone after him … until I met you. With you, it's been a struggle to keep my guard up. And to find out so much about you and your family's role in Sierra Leone just took me back to that bad time. I kept thinking you will do the same thing Tony did to me."

"You do know that I would rather give up my life than allow any harm to come to you," he whispered into her hair. "I love you. I think I've loved you from the moment I first saw you."

Holding her breath, she let his unexpected words sink in, her insecurities coming to the fore for a moment. She lifted her head and met his gaze. The intensity and warmth of his grey eyes were seas of sincerity she could drown in. Why had she doubted him?

"Before I met you, I didn't believe I could let go and trust someone else again. You've proven to me that there is still someone worthy of my trust with your honour and integrity. I'm so happy I met you. There's nothing I'd like more than to stay in this apartment, but it is tainted with blood money, and I can't live here knowing what I know."

"Tainted with blood money? What do you mean?" His forehead creased in a frown.

"Your family makes money from the death and suffering of innocents, including my family. You must have used the money you earned to set up your business and buy this apartment. I can't stay here."

He shook his head.

"No, Selina. When I left Joburg, I left with nothing. The money I earned from my days as a mercenary, I gave to Siba and her family as reparation for the distress my uncle caused them."

"Oh? I don't understand." She waved her hand to encompass everything, including the apartment.

"When my mother died, she'd left an inheritance for Bea and me in a trust fund. She was an old-money English heiress. She owned a small fortune in property estates. That was where I got the money to start up the security firm with Christopher. There's no blood money here."

"Oh, that's such a relief to hear." She hugged him tightly.

"Does that mean you'll stay?"

She leaned back. "Yes and no."

"I'll stay, but first, I'm going with you to South Africa if you can wait a week so I can arrange to take time off."

He lifted her and put her back on the sofa before standing up.

"Did you not listen to a thing I said about my uncle?"

"I did. But as you said yesterday, I've got to stop running and face my fears. Since you're going to face your fears, I need to stand by you. And how else am I going to show you that I trust you completely?"

"You don't have to do that."

"I do ... or don't you want me anymore?" she asked hesitantly.

"Oh, I want you like I've never wanted anything else before. More to the point, I need you as much as I need the air around me. In our relationship so far, the emphasis has been on me owning your body. The truth is you own my heart, my very soul. Last night you shattered it when you returned my bracelet. For the first time in my life, I knew what it was to be broken-hearted."

She followed his gaze to where the bracelet lay discarded on the table.

"I'm so sorry, Ben. I wasn't thinking straight."

She slid off the sofa onto the floor and knelt before him. She fixed her gaze at his feet.

"Please put the bracelet back on me."

"No. Not yet."

Anxiety tightened her chest, making her woozy. *What have I done?* She'd allowed her fears to take over. This was the result.

"Stand up, Selina."

She lifted her gaze, tears clouding her eyes. He scrubbed his hand over his head, messing up the unruly hair even more. With a heavy heart, she sat back on the sofa.

"The next time you wear this bracelet, I want there to be no doubt in your mind that you belong to me, all of you—your body, your heart, your very soul."

She sucked in a breath and closed her eyes.

"And you can't make that decision until you've been to Johannesburg and seen where I've come from. Once you know everything about me and you're certain in your heart, I will offer you the bracelet again."

Disappointed, she bit her lower lip. Without the jewellery, she felt lonely and insecure. Still, she accepted he had a point.

"Okay ... but do I still have conjugal rights?" she asked glad that all wasn't lost.

A smile brightened his face.

"If you want them."

"I do."

Chapter Ten

"And there I thought I would have to tie you to our bed and tease you until you begged me to fuck you."

"You can still do that."

"Nah." He shook his head as he strode to her. "I don't have the patience for that."

He lifted her onto the table, pushed aside the contents, and kissed her. Sensation spiked through her body. His hands roamed over her, caressing every inch of her torso.

He stood between her legs, his thighs stiff, and his erection pushing against her belly.

Then he took her clothes off, starting with her t-shirt, then her jeans until she was standing naked before him.

"Beautiful," he murmured, his low voice making her stomach do flip flops.

She shifted from one leg to the other.

"Don't move. I want to look at you."

Stepping back, his heated gaze swept from her face to her painted toenails. A trail of tingles swept over her skin.

He observed every inch, tracing the oval shape of her face with the pad of his index finger.

From her pouted lips, down to the delicate neck column, her tautened nipples, the swell of her breasts, the rough stomach scars, her curved hips, the smoothness of her legs and the hairless mound of her sex.

"Your body was created to be worshipped. Turn around."

She rotated, slowly, trying hard to quell the trembling that had erupted from her core and was now spreading through her body.

"I want to love you, cherish you, and protect you for as long as we both live."

Then he knelt before her, drawing in a deep breath as he parted her hooded flesh.

"Do you know what seeing you so wet for me does to me? Your scent is enthralling, and I can't wait to taste you."

Gasping, her breath caught in her throat.

He leaned forward, his mouth connecting with her core.

The ground shifted. Her knees buckled.

His grip on her hip tightened, keeping her upright as he delved deeper with his tongue.

A tremor ran through her body, pleasure rising like a fever. She clutched his shoulders, steadying herself. Nothing else compared to the sensations he elicited from her when he was touching her like this. Not the orgasm she'd had yesterday with the aid of the sex toys under his command nor even her own fingers could give her this much exhilaration.

He teased her, his tongue circled her clit, and then his teeth nipped at it. Her breath rasped in her throat when she suddenly couldn't breathe easily. Tightening her grip on his shoulders, her fingernails scraped his skin.

Gosh, she wanted him inside her.

His mouth continued exploring, teasing, tongue circling, probing, wriggling, teeth scraping, nipping, and lips sucking and blowing.

She was mindless, and her body was canting out of control.

"I ... need you." She couldn't even string together a sentence. "Inside me ... please."

"Not yet."

Warm air feathered her already sensitive flesh, adding to push her closer to the edge. He thrust his fingers inside her. She didn't know how many. Wet sounds combined with the rasping sound of her breathing. All she knew was that they filled her up. His mouth against her mound and his hand's friction inside her drove to hover uncontrollably over the abyss. She held back just about.

Something primal within her still wanted his control, his permission despite everything.

"Ben?"

"Come for me, Lina."

And she tumbled, headlong, into pleasure, powerful and mind-blowing. He was there to catch her and hold her as her body jerked from the shock. When she came to, she tried to stand, but her body was limp.

As always he was there, thinking ahead. He stood up, scooped her into his arms and set her on the table.

Samuel Barber's Adagio was playing, the sensual music heightening her mood.

"Later I'm going to take you back to the bedroom, tie you to it, and love you until you're sated. Then I'm going to blindfold you and feed you breakfast so that all you have to do is focus on enjoying the here and now."

"I'd like that."

He started undoing his shirt buttons and ripped it off. Buttons flew, and he tossed the shirt on the sofa. This was the first time she'd seen him throw his clothes like that. He was usually more methodical. He undid his fly, pushed his trousers down, and stepped out of them.

She'd seen her husband naked before. But each time was a little like the first time. He was glorious. Powerful. Masculine. The strength of broad shoulders, the slim hips, the protective arms, the hard thighs, and the rigid, glistening erection.

"But for now, I'm going to bury my dick deep into your pussy and just feel you, Lina." His voice was gruff and packed with heat, just like his gaze.

"I'm not going to be slow or gentle."

"I don't want you to be."

He nodded. "Lean back on the table, anchor your body with your hands, so that it's curved up, your breasts in offering to me." His voice was so low, just above a whisper.

A part of her melted in response to his command. She needed this man. He didn't need to shout at her for her to do his bidding. His gentle whispers were enough to get her carrying out his instructions.

"Now, spread your legs. I want to make sure you're ready for me."

She moved her legs apart, eager to have him between them.

"Oh, you are such a good girl. I love the way you get so wet so quickly."

He pressed his thumb on her swollen clit. She nearly jumped off the table but tightened her grip, anchored down by the thought that he wanted her there.

Gripping her hips, he positioned his hips between her legs, the broad head of his cock nudging her entrance. She held her breath in anticipation.

With one shove, he pushed in, her insides welcoming his hardness, clenching. She moved her hips to accommodate him in her tight channel, rising to meet him. He withdrew and plunged deeper, harder.

She cried out, letting go, letting her body relax and accept his supremacy for these moments.

"Oh, Lina. You are so hot, so slick."

With one hand he gripped the back of her head in a handful of hair and tugged her forward. And then he was kissing her, his tongue thrusting back and forth, marauding, just as he started moving his hips in a similar motion.

He raised his head, locking gazes with her.

"If you let me, I will love you 'til the day I die." His voice was gravelly with emotion.

Her heart clenched in response. She believed him. He would never hand her over to be harmed. She was back in that mindless zone again, all sensation and no thoughts. His motions drove her closer to the edge. His thrusts were fast, hard, deep, plunging, withdrawing, taking, and giving. Driving her insane with overflowing need.

She cried out, forgetting even how to breathe, letting his body's impact on hers control her intake of air. She lifted her legs, crossing her feet over his taut butt cheek, using them to feel his body since she couldn't touch him.

Soon the wave was rising, cresting taking her to the zone where she could only think with her heart.

"I love you, Ben," she said just as she surfed the tip of the wave.

"And I love you, too, Lina. Fly for me."

How could she not? She let go and flew, knowing he would always be beside her, guarding her body and heart.

With a loud grunt, he pumped his seed into her clenching channel that milked him until he collapsed on top of her. He took most of his weight on his arms instead of crushing her body.

She didn't know how long they stayed there, their harsh breathing mixing with the classical music.

He put his hands under her and carried her to the door.

"Ben, we don't have any clothes on. What if Beatrice comes out?"

He chuckled. "One thing you need to know about my sister, she doesn't get out of bed before 9A.M. at the weekend, especially after she's been partying all night."

She smiled. "I think we might want to take a cue from her and get some sleep, too. I didn't sleep much last night, and it looks like you didn't either."

He took her back to their bedroom, laid her gently on the bed, and joined her in it, pulling the sheet over them as he spooned her body.

"Why did you tell me to give the bracelet to Louisa?" he asked. Soft lips brushed against her right shoulder, a warm shiver slithering down her spine, warring with the shame tightening her belly.

Burrowing into the pillows, she hid her face.

"I'm sorry," she said in a muffled voice.

Warm lips continued their journey on her back downwards, soon joined by questing fingers, creating soft brush strokes on canvass. Awareness flared again, overshadowing her remorse.

A mewl escaped her lips, and she melted into the sheets.

"Have I ever given you a reason to think there was someone else?"

Mind lost in the sensations taking over her body, it took her a few seconds to process his question and the censure in his tone.

"No. Never." Her face heated with guilt again, and she shut her eyes.

Firm fingers clasped around her lower arm as another hand tugged her until she was lying on her stomach.

"And yet you questioned my integrity in the presence of my sister and her friend."

A clicking sound. Metal bit into her wrist. Alarmed, she yanked her head up from the pillow. Sure enough, chrome cuffs linked her right hand to the bedpost. Punishment cuffs! He only ever put them on her when she was about to be reprimanded for her demerits. She pulled, and the rings clanged and stayed, the metal biting into her skin. Her bum cheeks were still sore from yesterday's paddling.

She swallowed down the panic and turned to meet his gaze. Grey eyes filled with quiet reassurance. There was no anger. No disappointment. Was there a glint of amusement?

He stretched out his hand, palm open, waiting.

The significance of his gesture wasn't lost on her. She read his actions. Consistent. Reliable. Self-controlled actions.

"Your submission is a gift. It is for you to offer it freely, not something to be forced out of you or taken by force," he had told her once.

And he had never taken it. If that didn't make him trustworthy, what did?

So why do I continually fail him?

Lifting her hand, she placed it into his.

"I just didn't like the way she was looking at you." Despite her shame in admitting the truth, she felt better saying it out loud to him. "I was jealous. I'm sorry. I should've trusted you."

"You should've," he said. "I have no interest in Louisa, not now. Not ever."

He leaned down and brushed warm lips against her knuckles, straddling her. His hot, bulging erection pressed between her ass cheeks.

"The only woman I want kneeling at my feet, the only one I want to fuck and make love to is lying beneath me right now."

Arousal flared again, dripping down her thigh.

He secured her left hand to the other post. She tested the binding again, and it rattled.

Thoroughly secured, she swallowed again, the sound loud in her ears. Panic and desire fought for dominance in her veins.

He disappeared. She heard a drawer opening.

"So, do you trust me now?" His deep voice resonated within her belly, a hint of uncertainty, adding gravels to the sound.

Her stomach tightened, and momentarily she hated herself for putting that uncertainty into him.

"I do, Benjamin." Tears clogged her eyes and dropped onto the pillow. "I'm sorry, I haven't been good enough for you." Her voice was choked.

A hand brushed her hair away from her face. Warm air whispered on her cheek before his lips pressed against her skin, kissing her tears.

"Shhh. No crying, beauty." His voice was low and velvety. "You're perfect for me."

She opened her eyes and stared at him, unbelieving his words.

"Yes, you have always been perfect for me."

"Even when I was stubborn and disobedient?"

"Even then. I expected it." He smiled, the luscious uplift of the corners of his lips that always got her heart racing.

"A strong, beautiful woman like you who hadn't trusted any man in the past ten years wasn't just going to fall to her knees for me without my working for it."

She quirked her eyebrow, allowing a smile to touch her lips.

"I'm good. But I'm also realistic. It would've been arrogant of me to expect any different from you. Our relationship is about the journey as much as it's about the outcome. Do you understand, Lina?"

A hard tap against her bare bum made her flinch. The links jingled. A dull sting spread warmth out from her right tender cheek.

"Yes, I do, Benjamin."

"Moreover, a well-behaved Lina means I won't get to do this—" he tapped the other bum cheek. Harder. She winced. "—often. It makes you vulnerable, and I'm the one who gets takes care of you afterwards."

"Why?" The word just slipped out.

His hand paused on her skin. "Don't you know by now, Lina?"

In that instant, it all came flooding into her mind, suffusing her soul.

"Your reprimands are a way you show your love through your patience and self-control. Without it, I don't think I would've made progress with relinquishing my fears and trusting again."

She heard him sigh. Was that relief?

"It's always my pleasure to love you in all the ways I can," he said and reached for her left hand. He released the cuff and massaged her wrist.

"You've earned yourself a reprieve. For the first time since you signed the agreement, I think you finally understand the purpose."

Relief washed over her body like a sea breeze. He also released her right hand. When he shifted his weight from her body, she sat up. She hooked her arms around his neck before kissing him, injecting her gratitude into the passionate exchange.

He looked amused when she came up for air.

"What was that for?" he asked as he laid back on the bed.

"Thank you for being so understanding," she said, settling next to him, her hand on his chest and her leg over his.

His lips brushed her forehead.

"So, you didn't sleep, huh?"

"Yes, one thing I found out. I don't sleep well without you, Ben. I will happily share your bed for the rest of my life."

"And I will happily share the rest of my life with you."

Scores
THE BEN & SELINA TRILOGY #3

Dedication

This book is dedicated to everyone who has kept faith with Benjamin and Selina's journey. From my fellow writers, Michaela, Doris and Jennifer who cheered me on when I wrote the first book of the Passion Shields series, Scars, to the wonderful readers who have read each of the books and loved it.

I also want to give a special mention to two beautiful ladies who have been so passionate about this series that my eyes water even now as I think of their praises. Sharonda and Felicia, this book is for you both. You rock!

Blurb

His love possesses her. Will it protect her too?

Benjamin has proven how much he cares about his wife, Selina. She pushed him to shred his iron control and bare his soul to her. In return he's earned her much guarded heart as well as her body.

But her past has finally caught up with her and scores will have to be settled before they can have a happy ending. Can Benjamin's love protect her from those who seek to destroy both of them? Or will she finally lose the man who's possessed her body as well as her heart?

Chapter One

"We found him." Kenny Cruz's words boomed as soon as Benjamin Moss strode into his office. "We found Tony Kana."

Christopher Star, his best friend and business partner, shut the door they'd just walked through. Ben strode across the hardwearing black carpet covering the floor and settled in one of the dark leather armchairs in front of the large black lacquered table that Kenny sat behind. Almost every white wall was covered by flat-screen TVs displaying different angles of Bar Atlantic, Kenny's night club. Kenny was big on surveillance and control.

Control was something Benjamin fought to maintain after receiving the expected bad news. Expected, since he'd ordered the investigation to find the man right after his wife, Selina, had revealed the atrocious things that happened to her before their marriage. Bad, because Tony Kana being alive provided a threat to the woman who meant more to Ben than all else.

"Where did you find him?" The quiet tone of Ben's voice belied the knot that had suddenly formed in his stomach and the rising fizz of rage in his veins.

"In Sierra Leone," Kenny said, a slight West African lilt in his voice as he relaxed back into his armchair. The leather seat seemed to squeak in protest under the sturdy weight of the dark-skinned man built like a bull. As ex-military, he was one of Moss Star Security's finest and one of Benjamin's closest friends. "The man was not difficult to find, seeing as he is a celebrity of sorts out there."

"Celebrity?" Chris asked as he lowered his tall frame into a chair. The quiet hiss of foam filled the silence following his question.

"He is a well-known businessman. One of the few who have benefited from the different projects of rebuilding Sierra Leone since the war. He has a huge house in an exclusive estate in Freetown with his own personal army of bodyguards. He's living it large out there."

Damn! Benjamin clenched and unclenched his hands, the only outward sign of the news' effect on him. This complicated matters. Was the man just protecting himself from the impact of a country still coming to terms with the aftermath of a bloody civil war? Or was there a more sinister reason for all excessive security?

"Underneath it all, the man is a crook. He's got a finger in every crime pie. Be it drug smuggling, human trafficking or gun-running, he dabbles in it. "

The unholy trinity of organized crime. The scourges of any civilized society and for a nation still on its knees after a recent civil war, these crimes were another means of ruining already devastated lives.

"Fuck. Are you sure about this?" Ben rolled his shoulders violently. If Kana was such a powerhouse, it would complicate the hell out of their trip to South Africa.

"My sources have never failed me before." Kenny reached in a drawer and pulled out a small memory device the size of a button. "Everything he could get hold of is in there. Surveillance photos, company records, bank statements and audio recordings."

Ben took the gadget from him and slid it into his inside jacket pocket. He would have to go through the file when he got home.

"I want him under surveillance for the next few weeks," he said. "At least until Selina and I are back in London after our trip."

"Sure." Kenny nodded. "I'll let them know to maintain the status quo."

"Does she know you are investigating this man?" Chris asked.

Ben turned his head sideways and stared at his friend for one long moment, not really seeing him as he turned the question over in his mind. Selina had always struggled to come to terms with her past. Apart from the one occasion when she revealed the traumatic series of incidents that led to the scars on her body, she had refused to discuss it.

To be honest, he didn't want to drag her back to that dark place. Watching her as she broke down and relived those scenes broke his heart. He couldn't put her through it again. He wouldn't.

"No. She mustn't find out," he said to his friends in a determined voice, his brows furrowed, his muscles tight. "This will set her back, and I'm not going to let that happen."

"She's going to Sierra Leone. There's a possibility she's going to see him."

"Not if I can help it. Left to me, she wouldn't be going. But she insists she wants to travel back with her brother. His visa is ready. And since we're going to

South Africa, it made sense to come back via Freetown."

"Makes sense," Chris replied contemplatively.

Cold beads of sweat broke on Ben's forehead despite the freezing temperature of the office. The whole trip to Africa filled him with unease, with a sense of disaster coming his way. There was a chance he would lose the woman he loved permanently.

She'd already run from him once after finding out some of his past. She'd returned his bracelet—the charmed one he'd given her on their wedding night, the one evidence that she belonged to him. That she'd willingly given herself to him.

He pulled the bracelet out of his pocket, fiddled with the ruby corset charm, regret making his chest heavy. He carried it with him everywhere, a constant reminder of what he'd nearly lost, could lose.

"Isn't that Selina's bracelet?"

Ben raised his head, drawn from his reverie by Christopher's question. The knotted frown on his friend's face showed he understood the significance of the bracelet although they'd never discussed it.

"Yes." A lump in his throat made his voice hoarse, and he swallowed to get rid of it. "She told me to take it off the night she found out about my past, about what we did in Sierra Leone."

"You told her everything?" The shock in Kenny's voice was unmistakable. He reached behind him and transferred the bottle of Cognac and three short ball glasses onto the table.

Ben, Chris, and Kenny had been in Sierra Leone at the same time for different reasons. A shared past that linked them both viscerally and physically. The horrors of the war had changed all three of them.

Ben sighed, remorse slumping his shoulders. "A part of me wishes I had. But she walked out before I could reveal everything. And when she returned..." He'd been more focused on relief, the easing of the tight knot in his chest, than in continuing a difficult conversation.

"This is messed up," Kenny said as he passed a drink to each man.

"You can say that again." Ben cupped the glass in his right hand, the long stem between his third and fourth fingers as he rotated the dark red-amber liquid slowly. He sniffed and allowed the blend of vanilla and nuttiness in the aroma to pull him from his funk.

His friends had all relaxed into their seats. Unlike brandy or whisky, cognac was not a drink to be rushed. Best savoured leisurely. As mates, they enjoyed this little ritual occasionally, especially when they needed to take a step back and work through some challenging issues, like the one at hand.

Ben tilted the glass again and brought it closer to his nose. This time he scented a hint of caramel in the aroma. Lifting the glass to his lips, he tipped cognac in, allowing enough to coat his tongue from the tip to the back of his mouth. The flavours of fruit and spice smacked his palate. He swallowed the smooth drink. A hint of bite remained.

"I know Selina can be stubborn," Chris said after moments of silence while the men drank. "But is she refusing to take the bracelet back?"

"No. She wants it. But I can't give it back to her until she knows everything about my past. I can't trust that she won't throw it at me when she finds out what my life was really like." Ben sighed, giving in briefly to the fear of what it would do to his heart if she spurned him again.

"I don't blame you," Kenny said, sympathy lacing his words.

"Shit," Chris muttered under his breath.

His friends understood his predicament. They were dominant men. Although Chris wasn't in a committed relationship, he had dated Selina before Benjamin met her. Kenny, on the other hand, had been married once. Still, they both understood his need for Selina, his overwhelming desire to have her submission.

She was a beam of light shining on the darkness that had lived in his soul since he was a teenager. He loved her. Wanted to possess her like no one ever did.

As a man who made a living from protecting others, no one drew out his protective instincts like Selina did. And he would make sure she was protected no matter the cost to him. If it meant taking down Tony Kana, he would do it in a heartbeat.

"I want to know everything Tony Kana does from now on. If he as much as sneezes, I want to hear about it." Ben tossed the rest of his drink down his throat as the need to be with his wife overwhelmed him. He stood and headed toward the door.

"You've got it." Kenny nodded as he stood too.

"Thank you," Ben said before punching the button to call the elevator. Chris stepped inside with him when the door opened.

"Why are you so bent on tracking this guy?" his best friend asked. "Is there something I should know?"

Ben had asked Kenny, who had contacts in West Africa, to help him find Tony Kana but he'd never really explained to his friends why.

"Kana is Selina's ex-husband," he said in a matter of fact tone.

"And?" His friend understood him too well.

"He's the reason she has body issues."

"Body issues?" Chris's face puckered in a frown.

"When you dated her, did you ever get to see her fully unclothed?"

His friend's dark brows drew together. "No. She always insisted on having those corsets on. They were damn sexy, so I never minded. Although once I walked into the bathroom while she was in the shower and she nearly screamed the place down because she wanted me to get out."

Benjamin closed his eyes and sucked in a breath to stave off his rising anger. "Her abdomen is covered in scars. Someone cut her up pretty badly."

"Kana?" Chris growled the question.

"No." Ben opened his eyes and stared at his friend. He could see his anger reflected in his friend's eyes. "But he might as well have wielded the knife himself. He handed Selina over to the militia who wanted to use her as a sex slave. She fought back, and they mutilated her for disobedience."

"And all you want to do is watch this guy? I want to put a bullet right between his eyes."

"Selina doesn't want any more bloodshed. I must respect her wishes. Doesn't mean I can't take the guy down another way."

"Right." Chris nodded. "He has to pay."

"Oh, he's going to pay. No doubt about that."

They entered the bar, and loud music erased the need for further conversation.

***

"I wish I was the one going to South Africa," Lora's voice was loud as she lifted her glass of rum and coke. "You're going to have such a great time out there."

Selina nodded her head. Her best friend was right, yet she couldn't avoid the anxiety knotting tight in her belly.

Fingers twisting the seam of her skirt, her gaze swept across the dimly lit space. Music thumped out of hidden loudspeakers. In the far corner, multi-coloured strobe lighting bounced off bodies swaying rhythmically to the house beats on the dance floor.

Revellers dressed in finery meant to seduce chatted and drank—only the crème de la crème were allowed in this members-and-their-guests-only club. On rare occasions, they permitted non-members in, the gate fees alone guaranteed the class of people walking through the ornate archway.

"Tell me about it," Noni chimed in. "I'm so jealous."

Selina glanced over to the woman. Noni's sweet smile had no malice in it.

"Says the woman who spends every summer in Marbella," Selina replied. "Moreover, your in-laws are the nicest people ever."

Noni giggled. "I must be the luckiest woman ever. Juan's mother is just the best. She pampers me every time we go over to Spain. Even my own mother doesn't fuss over me that much."

Searching the crowd, Selina found the person she was looking for as a sad pang washed over her.

By the dark wood bar running the length of a corner, Benjamin stood with a group of men who included Juan Roberto, Noni's husband and Christopher Star, Ben's business partner. The men all worked at the same firm, Moss Star Security, owned by both Ben and Chris.

Every quarter, Noni, as the office manager organized one of these events. It was an opportunity for the men and their partners to relax and socialize away from work.

"Shame, not all in-laws are like yours, Noni," Selina said ruefully before taking a quick sip of her Mojito. The sweet kick of rum and zest of minty lime exploded on her tongue.

Noni leaned closer and lowered her voice so that only Selina and Lora could hear her. "Is Beatrice—" she flicked her stare over her shoulders in the direction where Ben's sister sat with her friend, "—giving you a hard time?"

Selina dismissed her concern with a wave of a hand. "I can give as good as I get with her."

"What's the problem? You don't seem too excited about going to SA."

"Finding out your in-laws are white supremacists can do that to a girl," Lora interjected.

Selina rolled her eyes heavenward. "Lora!" she chided her friend.

"What? I'm only telling the truth." Her friend crossed her legs and leaned back into the ox-blood leather sofa.

"Beatrice is just behind us. She can hear you," Selina ground out through clenched teeth.

"Are you guys serious?" Noni's mouth was agape, her brown eyes widened. It must've been a shock for her to hear such news about her boss.

Selina did a quick look at where Beatrice sat with her friend Louisa. The two girls seemed deep in conversation, laughing and drinking.

She puffed out a slow breath and turned back to her two friends.

"It's just Ben's uncle who's involved with all that nonsense. He doesn't believe races should mix, get married, or have children. Certainly not black and white anyway. He raised Benjamin to believe that."

"What? You've got to be wrong." Disbelief marred Noni's expression, her voice taut. "Benjamin doesn't behave like that at all. I mean, he gave me a job right after I left University when it was tough finding a job in London. But he gave me a chance. In the time I've worked for him, he has never made me feel inferior."

Noni glanced over to where the men stood oblivious to what the women talked about.

"I mean, I have a great time working at Moss Star. I met Juan there, for goodness sake. He loves me, and I know Benjamin worships the ground you walk on, Selina. So, it's a bit difficult to believe he was brought up in a KKK environment."

"Of course, it's not Benjamin. He's not like that at all," Selina reassured her friends. "He walked away from all that years ago, and he hasn't been back since. This will be the first trip back for him."

"Oh." Noni placed a warm hand on Selina's lower arm. "Now, I understand your apprehension."

"But you shouldn't worry," Lora added. "Benjamin has your back. He'll never let anyone disrespect you."

Selina stole a glance at her husband as a frown creased her face. She believed Benjamin would protect her as much as he could. He'd defended her with Beatrice, his sister, hadn't he?

Still, the dark pressure at the back of her mind didn't go away. Something was off with him, and she knew it had to do with their upcoming trip to South Africa.

"You know what they say about blood being thicker than water." Selina blurted out the words before she could stop herself. She'd been thinking about this for weeks since Beatrice had turned up in their London apartment with a message that Ben's uncle wanted him to return to South Africa.

"What if he can't say no to whatever the man is going to ask of him?"

"He walked away from his uncle before. He can do it again," Lora replied, placed her hand on Selina's knee and squeezed reassuringly. After a moment, her best friend's face puckered in a frown, and she asked. "Or is there something else?"

"What if the man is dying? Ben can hardly refuse a dying man's wishes. I know what I felt like when my parents died. I would've done anything for them." Her throat clogged up as emotions churned in her mind.

"I agree with Lora. You need to stop worrying, Lina. Ben loves you."

Selina tipped back her head and swallowed the rest of her drink.

"Here, let me get you another one," Lora said. "And then we're getting on the dance floor. I'm not having you mope around for the rest of the night. We're meant to be having fun, not behaving like old women."

Noni giggled. "I don't know about the two of you, but I'm far from being old."

"Yeah and that's why you've been on diet coke all night long." Lora snickered.

"If I tell you something, promise to keep it a secret."

"Come on, then."

Selina and Lora leaned towards Noni.

"I think I'm pregnant."

"You think?"

"I'm doing the test tonight. I was waiting for Juan to get home before I did it. I didn't want to find out alone."

"Wow, that's exciting!"

"And romantic!"

"I know."

They all clutched hands in excitement.

"You have to tell us as soon as you find out."

"Ehm." Noni cleared her throat. "I think Juan and I will be celebrating if it's good news. So how about I call Lina tomorrow and she can tell you, Lora."

"Of course." Lora laughed and stood to head to the bar. "A Mojito for Lina and diet coke for you, Noni."

"Yes," Selina replied.

The back of her neck prickled, and she flicked her gaze to the men. Benjamin's stormy grey eyes held her in their thrall. Even with the distance between them and revelry going on around them, his censure whipped her mind. Of course, he couldn't have heard what she'd ordered. Still, guilt pelted her body with heat.

"Know your limits, Selina," he'd told her once after she'd had too much wine following a tough day at work. "Getting drunk never solves anything."

Although she'd been pissed at first that he would try to restrict her, she'd seen his point when she'd woken with a nasty hangover the next morning.

Two Mojitos were her limit considering she'd also had a glass of wine before they left home. She already had a gentle alcoholic buzz surrounding her.

"Lora, just get me a small bottle of water." She raised her voice so Lora could hear above the music and chatter. And, for Ben's benefit. "I'll need it if we're dancing."

With an almost imperceptible nod of his head, Benjamin's eyes gleamed his approval. All was right with the world again.

Since their big bust-up, the night Beatrice arrived and the subsequent make-up the next day, Selina had tried her hardest to be the best submissive to Benjamin.

Gently she rubbed her right wrist, her heart clenching sadly at the loss of the platinum link charm bracelet with the red corset charm. She missed the bracelet and regretted her rash decision of making Ben take back the bracelet the night they'd argued.

She hadn't realized how much she'd hurt him by her actions until she'd returned the next morning to find him at his desk in the office. He hadn't slept all night.

Though she'd begged for the bracelet back, Ben had refused, promising to offer it to her after their upcoming trip to his hometown.

Its absence on her wrist left her feeling unanchored and lost. She associated the bracelet with Benjamin's dominance and protection, his love and safety. Without it, she felt like she was floating in a turbulent sea lacking direction and would be swept away by a storm.

For this reason, she'd been on her best behaviour since. She would earn the bracelet back, or she would die trying.

***

Benjamin punched the code into the keypad to the penthouse with his right hand while propping Beatrice on his hip with his left hand.

"Did you know she was drinking so much?" he asked and turned his head to the right to give Selina a quick glare.

Spine stiffening, Selina frowned as she held on to her sister-in-law's clutch purse. She didn't like Ben's expression. "Of course, I didn't. She sat with her friend, and they disappeared a few times. Was I supposed to be minding her?"

"Hey, the two of you need to lower your voices," Bea said in a slurred tone as Benjamin carried her across the threshold.

Lina stepped in and let the door shut behind her. She leaned on the table in the hallway and reached down to remove her shoes as was her habit whenever she arrived home. She loved to walk around barefooted on the polished wooden floor.

"Keep them on," Benjamin said as he carried his sister unceremoniously down the hall to her bedroom. He didn't look at Selina, but the skip of her heart told her the instruction was for her.

Obeying, she followed. He deposited Bea on the bed, and she flopped over like a rag doll. Selina knelt and started removing Bea's strappy blue suede stilettos.

"You need to stop drinking so much," Ben said in a stern voice and ran his fingers through his hair in a gesture Lina knew as frustration.

"Now you sound like Uncle Leonard." Bea's words were annoyed, her eyes closed.

Benjamin's jaw tightened, and he crossed his arms. "Perhaps you need to go back to South Africa. In fact, I'm booking you on the same flight as Lina and I."

Bea's eyes flew open, lips pouting.

"You can't make me." His sister sounded like a petulant child. "You're not my father."

Bea rolled over and started crying quietly, her body racked with her sobs.

Selina placed her hand on Ben's upper arm, bunched across his chest.

"Please, let her be for tonight," she said. "I'll talk to her."

After a moment glaring at his sister, Benjamin blew out warm air and redirected his gaze to Selina. Lines around his grey eyes softened.

"Okay." He turned around and strode out.

Beatrice jumped out of bed and ran into the adjoining bathroom. The sound of retching filled the room. Selina was thankful she hadn't had that third Mojito and wasn't on the receiving end of Ben's wrath. Being drunk enough to be sick was not a good look on any person.

When the retching stopped, Selina walked into the bathroom to find Beatrice laying on the cold tiles. Lina flushed the toilet and manoeuvred Beatrice into a sitting position. She turned the sink tap on and wet her face towel, then used it to wipe Beatrice's face and neck.

"Why are you helping me?"

Selina shrugged. "You're my sister-in-law."

"I haven't always been nice to you," Bea said, her tone rueful. "I call you a witch behind your back."

"Oh, don't worry about that," Lina replied. "I call you a bitch when you're not looking."

They both stared at each other for one long moment. When Beatrice cracked a smile, Selina started laughing, and Beatrice joined her.

"You really are the best woman for my brother," Bea said when she stopped laughing.

"Aww, you really think so?"

"Yes, I do. You will do simply fine when you get to South Africa."

Selina's stomach knotted even tighter. She didn't want to discuss the upcoming trip or her insecurities about her sister-in-law. So, she changed the subject.

"You have to stand up," she said. "I really can't carry your skinny ass all the way to the bedroom."

"You think my ass is skinny?" Bea said as she leaned on the bathtub to push herself up.

Selina hooked her arm to help. "Yes, it is."

"Aww. That's such a lovely compliment."

Beatrice straightened and stood in front of the sink. She picked up her toothbrush, applied paste and started brushing her teeth.

Selina laughed. "It isn't meant as a compliment. Real men like the soft cushion of a fat ass when they're pounding into you." She patted her bottom. "And according to your brother, he likes the way mine wobbles when he spanks me."

Beatrice's face turned beetroot red, and her eyes widened in the mirror. She bent over and spat out the paste.

"Benjamin spanks you?" There was disbelief in her voice.

"Yes, deliciously so."

"Oh. My—" She lifted her hand and covered her mouth. After a few seconds of watching their reflection in the mirror, she wiped her mouth and turned to face Lina. "You like it?"

"Of course, I do. It is the sexiest thing when it's not a reprimand."

Bea went red again.

"Surely you know your brother is kinky in the bedroom. He said you walked in on him and Chris once with a girl."

"He told you about that?" Beatrice averted her eyes and walked past Selina into the bedroom.

"Come on, Bea. Are you really that naive?"

Bea shrugged and turned to stare at Lina, worry lines on her forehead, and her lips turned down in a sad curl.

"My mother was a successful actress, beautiful and sexy and glamorous. A lot of people expect me to be like her because I look like her."

She pulled down the zip of her blue silk dress and shimmied out of it, revealing her strapless matching baby blue lace bra and panties on her golden tanned skin.

"But look at me." She withdrew a long nightshirt from a drawer. "I'm neither sexy nor successful. My ex actually called me frigid."

There were tears in her eyes, and a drop rolled down her cheek. She covered her face with both hands and slumped on the bed.

"Your ex is an asshole who doesn't know how to get the best out of a woman."

Selina picked up the cream nightshirt that had dropped on the floor and walked over to the bed. She pried Bea's hands off her face and helped her put on the shirt.

"You are beautiful and sexy, and the success thing will come soon enough."

"I wish it would come now," her sis-in-law said. "I really wanted the role in the West End. I want to stay in London. But if I don't get one, I'll have to go back home. And everyone will know I wasn't successful."

"You need to stop worrying about what other people will think," Lina softened her voice. "There will be other roles, other auditions. Just hang in there."

Bea tipped over and lay down on her side.

"Is this why you're drinking so much?" Lina asked. "Because you didn't get through the auditions?"

Bea looked shamefaced. "I just saw the way everyone was at the club tonight, so happy and I got jealous because you left me out of the conversation with your friends. You and your friends were giggling and laughing so much I wanted to not hear the sounds."

"But you were also laughing and joking with Louisa."

"It's all a front. I felt like crying, and Louisa isn't happy that you got back together with Ben. But she said we had to keep up the front and make you three witches think we were having fun. I needed the drink for courage and to drown everything out."

"I'm sorry if you felt excluded. I didn't mean it that way. I thought you wanted to hang out with Louisa alone and you know I don't like her."

"Yeah, she doesn't like you either. Anyway, it's okay. I was just having a low moment. I'm fine now."

"Good." Selina stood. "Next time, though, remember alcohol is not the solution. In fact, it creates more problems. I see enough people coming in with alcohol-related illnesses at the hospital, and a lot of them are young."

"Not you as well." Bea groaned and turned her face into a pillow.

"I'm serious. There are men out there who take advantage of drunken women. And I know Ben won't be happy to leave you here if you don't promise to tone it down."

"All right. I promise I won't overdo it again."

Selina sighed. After all that counselling, she needed a drink.

"Right, get some sleep," she said in a light tone and with a smile, "and I'm not tucking you in or reading you a story, bitch."

Bea chuckled and pulled the cover over her body. "Witch," she said with a smile.

Selina laughed and headed for the door.

"Thank you." Beatrice smiled.

Selina nodded and shut the panel. Now she had another ally in the battle to win the hearts of her in-laws. Feeling happy with herself, she went in search of her husband.

Chapter Two

Selina withdrew a small bottle of water from the fridge in the kitchen and returned to Beatrice's room. After an unanswered knock on the door, she pushed it open.

"Bea."

All she got was a gentle snore as her sister in law turned over. Selina smiled. Ben had told her Bea couldn't be roused easily after a night out. She now had proof.

Leaving the bottle on the bedside table, she closed the door and headed for her own room.

In the bedroom, Selina tossed her sequined purse on her dressing table. She noted the opened sliding door leading to the balcony.

A warm breeze lifted the sheer voile, and it flapped gently. This late at night or relatively early in the morning, little noise came in from the outside. The scent of cigar floated in—a blend of tobacco and spice.

Sucking in a deep breath allowed the aroma to ground her in the present. Allowed her to shift focus from Beatrice to Benjamin.

Hand in hair, she unpinned the loose bun keeping her hair off her shoulders.

And froze.

Ben had instructed her to keep her shoes on. The implication? She shouldn't disturb her appearance without his permission.

Fumbling as she panicked, she reinserted the hairpin and patted her hair into place.

Phew! This wasn't the night to incur a demerit considering her husband's displeasure at Bea's drunkenness.

"Come to me," his low, seductive voice wafted in the breeze.

Heat unfurled in her core and her insides clenched. A month ago, she would've walked out there so fast in her eagerness to be with him.

Now, she stood still, shaky hand on her collar. Her bid to earn back the bracelet she'd tossed at him when she walked out on him. Lifting her other hand, she rubbed the empty space on her wrist as regret weighed on her shoulders.

Benjamin had walked into her life and changed her. He'd arrived quietly like the tide, yet forceful enough to impact her psyche. He'd earned the ultimate place in her thoughts, her heart. He had made her dreams come true.

The past couldn't be changed. The future could be fantastic if she could become the woman he desired. The woman he saw in her.

She needed to get things right. First time. Not by making mistakes.

Was he testing her with an incomplete instruction? Did he want her crawling on her hands and knees?

"Walk, Beauty." She heard the amusement in his voice and exhaled in relief. He must have sensed her hesitation. His uncanny ability to read her correctly always left her breathless.

Inhaling a deep gulp of air, she strutted across the bedroom floor, the hand-woven rug absorbing the taps from her pointed heels. The curl of rising smoke around Ben was his only identifying feature as she stepped onto the hard, tiled balcony. The red tip of the cigar glowed brightly when he puffed on the other end.

As her eyes adjusted to the gloom of the space only lit by stars and the little light filtering out from the bedroom, Ben sat in his usual spot. His suit jacket was off, leaving just his periwinkle blue silk shirt and midnight trousers.

She could just about make out the golden skin on his chest where the buttons of his shirt had been left undone.

That she wasn't drooling or climbing onto his lap was simply from sheer will power, waiting for his directive, not from composure. Inside she turned into a mass of anticipation. The only thing that kept her in check was Benjamin. His composure. His confidence. His presence. He anchored her with a mere look, a hand gesture. Even before he ever spoke.

That was the kind of relationship they had. When they started out, she never knew they would arrive at this point—with her trusting him enough to open her heart and soul to him, never mind her body.

But he took all she gave and treasured it, protected it with all that he was. And that was all she could ask of him.

Knowing this, she would do whatever it took to please him. To earn his trust again. She'd broken it when she'd tossed his bracelet at him. She knew that was why he hadn't given it back. He didn't trust that she wouldn't run after she met the rest of his family.

She had to prove to him that she could be trusted. One hundred percent.

"Sit on my lap." The glowing cigar settled in the ashtray on the table.

Wood creaked softly as he adjusted his weight.

Selina stepped forward and lowered her body on to his and then swivelled to tip her legs over the left arm of the chair. Ben drew his left hand over her thighs, his right one sliding up her back till it touched bare skin.

A shiver ran through her body.

"Are you cold?" he asked as he caressed her exposed shoulders.

"No."

In truth she warmed up nicely, heating up from the inside out and on the contact points with Ben's body.

"Good."

Applying a little pressure to her back, he tipped her forward. Relaxed lips grazed her neck and spine.

A soft moan left her lips, her breasts heavy with need.

His kisses continued her back, tender and rousing. But he didn't bother to unzip her dress like she hoped he would and reach the parts of her skin that were covered.

Her body's trembling increased, and she was close to begging him to show attention to other more intimate parts of her body when he gripped her nape and tugged her head back up.

His lips brushed the tips of her lips. His scent filled her nostrils—tobacco and spice. Safe and warm and aroused, the emotions churned inside of her. Was it possible for an aroma to make you feel secure, to remind you of the safety of home, of joy and laughter? That's what Benjamin's scent did to her. She moaned and opened her lips, inviting him to take and plunder.

He ignored her and carried on tracing the outline of her lips with nips and licks. She rocked her hips, clenching her thighs together to apply pressure to her clit.

Ben tugged her hair back, holding her body in place with the other hand.

"Be still, Beauty," he whispered against her lips before trailing those luscious lips down her chin. His wet tongue swiped her neck.

A long whimper resounded from her belly as her insides contracted, searching for something to fill it. Him.

But she knew nothing she did would hasten the process. He would only take her when he was ready. Any actions from her would only make him go slower.

She relaxed her body, going pliant in his arms, giving him what he wanted. Her compliance.

He licked and nipped the skin on her neck, lapping the line of her collar before tracing back up to her lips. This time he took her mouth in a kiss that was both crushing and tender. She succumbed to his lovemaking, taking what he gave and giving what he wanted. Lowering her eyelids, she couldn't hear anything except for the loud thumping of her heart mixed with harsh breathing.

He raised his head, breaking the kiss. She opened her eyes to find him staring at her. Even in the dark, his desire blazed like a furnace in their depths. Her breath caught in her throat.

The feeling was augmented as she felt the hardness of his arousal beneath her left bum cheek, separated by layers of silk. He'd worn the rigid erection for most of the night.

How did he manage to maintain such control when she was ready to burst? And it wasn't going to be her first orgasm of the night.

At the club, she'd been dancing with friends.

He'd sidled behind and pulled her into his arms.

"Watching you dance is just the sexiest thing," he whispered against her ear, warm air sensitizing her neck and cheek. "It makes me want to bury myself deep inside you so I can feel you moving all around me."

Lucky she had him to lean against. Her legs trembled and threatened to give way as her heart thundered. The band of his arm around her midsection held her upright.

Sure enough, the ridge of his erection nudged her back, and she rubbed her body against him, so turned on she was melting.

He manoeuvred her to a corner of the dance floor where they didn't have other clubbers bumping against them. Turning around, she faced him as he backed her up against the shiny black wall. In the dim lighting, he was roguish and overwhelming with his intensity. When he smiled, her heart melted along with her body.

Her husband had the power to protect anything in the safety of his strong arms and his world. He'd built a business around keeping people safe. In the time she'd known him, protecting her had become his top priority.

He also had the power to crush her. She'd packaged her heart and given it to him for safekeeping. She no longer feared him like she once did.

All this could change in South Africa. Was her heart safe?

The disturbing thought reared its head again.

"I'll wait till we get home so I can stay in you for as long as I want."

Her breathing picked up again.

"In the meantime, you're going to come all over my hand."

Here and now? In public? "Ben..." Her voice was husky as she struggled to get air into her lungs. She let her eyelids flutter shut. "I..."

She couldn't even articulate her thoughts. They'd vanished into the icy smoke of the dance floor as his hand trailed upward against her bare thigh, bunching the corner of her dress.

His rough palm settled on her left hip, inches from where she needed him most.

"Do you want me to stop?" Warm air fanned her cheek again, his lips so close to her skin, if she flinched, they would have contact.

She opened her eyes and stared up at him. His desire burned in his open gaze. For the briefest moment, there seemed to be a mask of torment over his features. The face of anguish. A cold shiver ran down her spine. She blinked, and it disappeared. There was no expectation or disappointment in his eyes. Just his need.

Had she imagined the darkness in his eyes? Or was it just the effect of the multicoloured lighting? Was she now hallucinating? She hadn't drunk enough alcohol to induce illusions, had she? She shook her head to clear her head.

"Say the word, Beauty."

The pad of his thumb stroked the tender outside edge of her thigh. She gasped as her body quickened to his touch.

As always, he was giving her a choice without prejudice. Like all their interactions, he wanted her willing—giving with her heart and mind.

Since he'd withheld the bracelet, she hadn't halted any of their play. Even with her heart hammering in her chest right now, she didn't want to stop this either. In fact, her entire body strung out like the wires of a guitar waiting for his fingers to strum it, waiting for him to play out a tune on her.

"No. Don't stop." She gushed out the words.

"Ask for my hand."

Heat scorched her face, and she turned her head away, staring blankly into the crowd of people dancing to a remixed version of *Blurred Lines* by Robin Thicke.

The grip on her thigh tightened for a heartbeat and loosened.

Afraid he would let her go, she blurted out the words. "Please, Benjamin, fuck me with your hand."

Arousal mounting, she swallowed hard and held her breath.

His fingers found their prize—her panty-less sex, waxed and wet and waiting for his caress. Benjamin loved her hairless and loved it even more when she wore no knickers.

"Good girl," he whispered against her neck.

Calloused digits worked her body, circling but not engaging her clit—the ultimate prize—keeping her on edge as pleasure coursed through her body.

His mouth played havoc on her face, neck and shoulders, brushing, licking, nipping her skin. Still, he didn't kiss her. And she died, yearned for his lips to crush hers, to taste him. She lifted her head, seeking contact with his lips.

Mistake. He ignored her lips. Instead, he slipped fingers inside her, filling her. Two? Three? He pumped them, and she keened, letting out a gasp.

"I'd love to hear you cry out my name, Beauty." He leaned down to speak in her ear. "But not right now. Unless you want an audience."

He had a wicked grin on when he lifted his head. She bit her lips as her cheeks heated again. Sweat trickled down her back despite the cold air coming out of air conditioning units.

As much as she loved what he was doing to her, she would die with mortification if anyone started watching them closely. Ben's broad back covered what they were up to, and it probably looked as if they were just talking. But a close inspection would reveal the difference. The thumping bass of the music matched her heart rate.

She needed to be set free. The pressure had built up so much that she was on the precipice. All it would take would be a brush of her clit, and she'd be over the edge.

"Come for me, Beauty." His voice was thick with lust as his thumb pressed down where she needed it most, and his fingers thrust in and out.

She shattered, biting down on her lip, so she didn't scream out loud, her body writhing out of control. He held her, not letting go until she was wrung out.

She opened her eyes when his hand slipped out of her body. She watched as he put the fingers in his mouth and sucked her juice off.

Oh boy. She has turned on all over again.

Then he kissed her for the first time that evening. He tasted of brandy, tobacco, and her musk. The music playing seemed to be coming from a distance as she responded to his kiss. It was *Safe with You* by Alex Metric. And she'd felt safe.

"We need to get out of here," he said, his voice thick with lust.

She couldn't help her happy smile as she headed to the ladies' room. Soon they'd bid their friends good night and headed home.

Benjamin's gentle squeeze of her arm brought her back to the present, and his intense gaze held hers. She couldn't wait to have him inside her. He brushed his lips against her forehead. Her skin tingled.

He tucked her shoulder into his chest and slowly caressed her back.

"How is Beatrice?" he asked. She heard his concern for his sister in his voice.

Her heart went out to him. The way he took care of the people around him showed how much he cared about them. He'd admitted to Selina how he felt responsible for Beatrice since their parents died.

"She's sleeping," she said. "She'll be fine. She just needs to sleep it off."

He puffed out a breath, lifting the strands of hair on her forehead.

"I'm worried about her. I've never known her to drink that much before."

She ran her fingers gently on the tense, unyielding muscles on his back. She always loved the feel of him when she could touch him.

"I talked to her. She just had an off moment because she didn't get the West End role."

He leaned back to look at her face.

"She did? Why didn't she say anything to me?"

"You're her big brother. You guys obviously haven't been talking."

Ben's chest heaved, and his sigh was filled with regret. "It's my fault. I should've paid more attention to her."

"Don't blame yourself."

She slid her right hand up his chest until she contacted bare skin.

Ben sucked in a sharp breath, and she smiled.

"I'm glad she talked to you." Sensuous lips curled upward as he smiled.

Her heart lightened at the humour on his face.

"For a while, I was worried the two of you wouldn't get on, especially after what happened the day she arrived."

"That's water under a bridge," Lina reassured him. "It was just a clash of personalities. But we understand each other a lot better now. And the truth is, we're similar in certain ways."

"How?"

"For starters, I see the same fear in her eyes that I had before I met you. And she covers it up with bravado and sarcasm."

"What has she got to be afraid of?" Ben's tone carried his displeasure as much as the frown creasing his forehead. "She has everything she could possibly want. In a couple of years, she'll have access to the cash in her trust fund. In the meantime, Leonard supplements whatever she earns from her acting, and when she's in London, I pay her expenses."

"Have you considered that it's not just about money?" Selina asked in a soothing tone. "What if she wants to be her own person, not depending on you or your uncle? What if she wants her independence?

"She can have it." Ben flinched as if she'd hit him, jaw stiffened, his expression offended. "I've never stopped her from doing what she wants to do or pursuing her acting career."

"I know you haven't, Ben. But she beats herself up because she's not as successful as your mother was."

"What?" Ben's eyes widened, and his entire body stilled, even his hand that had been caressing her back.

"She thinks everyone compares her to your mother and sees Bea as a failure."

The harsh sound of wood scraping stone filled the still air as Ben stood abruptly, lifting Lina with him.

Body tense, he lowered her into the chair before he strode down the balcony cursing into the night. She'd never seen him issue a litany of expletives unrestrained before.

Taken aback, she sat still, her shoulders and back aching with tension.

Why was Ben reacting so explosively to the mention of his mother? She wanted to ask questions but remained silent, waiting for him to talk in his own time.

Back muscles rippled as he raised his hand and scrubbed his scalp, obviously agitated. Wanting to go to him and soothe his restlessness but knowing it was best to leave him for now, she restrained herself from reaching out to him.

After a few minutes of pacing, he returned to face her, his appearance calmer.

"Please forgive my language," he said in a low, rough tone that hinted at inner turmoil. "I didn't mean to shock you."

"It's okay, Ben."

She stood up, and he returned to the leather armchair.

"Can you tell me why you were so distressed?" she asked when she folded her body back onto his lap, keeping her voice soft.

His chest pushed out as he drew in a long breath and puffed it back out.

"My mother was an addict. She died of a drug overdose."

Head rocked backwards with shock, she stared at him wide-eyed, and her heart broke.

"Oh, Ben." She turned her body and wrapped her arms around his torso, hugging him tightly. "I can't imagine what that feels like. I'm so sorry."

He tucked his head on her shoulders and held on to her body. Seconds ticked away. Perhaps minutes. She lost track of time. The only sounds came from their slow beating hearts, entwining breaths and the occasional rumble of cars driving across the Chelsea Bridge.

Eventually, he lifted his head and stared down at her face. Torment returned to his obsidian eyes.

For the first time in their relationship, she witnessed her husband in pain. Usually, he chased away the demons tormenting her and soothed her. Now, she wished to help him.

"Do you want to talk about it? I understand if you don't," she said, stroking his neck and shoulder in tentative brushes.

"I think I should tell you, especially since we'll be going to the house where it happened."

He dragged in a breath and turned his gaze toward the murky water of the River Thames, but his hand remained on her body, and she was glad for the contact.

"I loved my mother. She was beautiful and glamorous and as an actress, remarkably successful, having won a few awards and critical acclaim. As a boy, I remember travelling around the world with her sometimes. She would take me on location to some of the movie sets. It was exciting for me. She was always vibrant and full of life."

"But things changed after my father's death. She still seemed to be her old self on the exterior, but in her eyes, it was a different story. It was as if she had died too. When she passed on, it was reported in the press as heart failure. But I knew differently. My uncle had paid the coroner to omit the other part of his findings. Heart failure due to a drug overdose."

His forlorn sigh twisted her heart. Her chest ached at the sadness of his words.

"Beatrice was only a baby then so she didn't really know what had happened, except that Mama was gone. You can understand why I'm upset if she compares herself to our mother. While I want Bea to be successful, I never want her to end up the way Mama did. Never."

He stared at Lina, steely determination in his gaze.

"I understand, Ben," she said gently. "Bea is not your mother. I think you should let her stay in London for a little while longer. She has promised to behave herself."

Ben nodded. "I'll think about it."

He lowered his head and captured her lips in a tender kiss that knocked her out of breath. When he lifted his head, the wicked grin was back on his face, his torment replaced by desire.

"I'm such a lucky man."

She smiled in return, her heart filling out.

"You've been such a good girl, Beauty." He spoke in a low gravelly tone. "I'm so proud of all you've done, of your progress in the last three months."

He pulled the pin out of her hair, tossing it on the table. The mass of thick black curls tumbled around her shoulders and back. With his fingers, he combed the strands out, massaging her scalp gently as he went along.

Lust sparked to life in her belly.

"From the first time I saw you at Bar Atlantic, I knew you'd make a beautiful student." Warm, long fingers brushed her nape. Drawing air into suddenly tight lungs, she let her lashes flutter shut.

"Tutoring you in the art of submission has been such a joy." The quality of his voice—so deep, seductive, intoxicating. At times like this, his South African drawl filtered through.

His left hand stroked her knee and lower thigh but never travelled to where she needed him most. The combination of his words and his touch kept her on edge. And she was supposed to stay still?

Oh, God! She struggled to regulate her rapid, shallow breathing.

"Look at me," he whispered, warm air prickling her sensitive neck.

Her eyes flew open. Heat and openness gleamed in his grey gaze, snatching her breath away.

"Having you bend to my whim and knowing that you haven't lost the fire in your eyes, knowing that you've discovered an even greater zest for life makes all the ups and downs worthwhile."

Her heart swelled as she listened to his words. It hadn't been easy arriving at where they were, and it had been mainly due to his perseverance and patience that they'd made it. Her heart swelled with emotion, tears clogged her eyes.

"Thank you, Benjamin, for teaching me," she said through the choke in her throat.

He brushed his lips against her forehead. When he lifted his head, his lips were curled in a wolfish grin. The expression meant trouble. The best kind of situation for her.

"It has always been a pleasure," the tone of his voice was sinfully arousing, promising so much. "Now, it is time for you to move on to the next step."

"Next step?" Her curiosity spiked along with her apprehension. What did he mean by that? She'd thought they'd found a happy equilibrium at this point. He obviously didn't think so.

"Yes, you are ready. Stand for me."

Body quivering with excitement, she manoeuvred herself into doing his bidding. Nearly stumbling on her high heels, he held on to her thighs, stopping her from falling over, branding her flesh through the soft fabric. She straightened, holding her body still, waiting.

"Go and stand by the railing facing the water."

She did as he instructed with her heart pounding in her chest.

"Hold on to the top bar."

Puffing out breaths to calm her body, she wrapped her fingers on the round black cold metal.

"Spread your legs wide."

She was about to turn her head.

"No. No matter what happens, don't look back."

Chapter Three

This had to be a test of trust.

To stand still and not look back. When instincts screamed at Selina to find out what was going on behind her.

Senses heightened, Selina listened out, breath held, holding utterly still as her fingers gripped the railing tight.

"Good girl."

Approval. His words washed over her, settling on her skin like a warm blanket, comforting and safe. Exhaling, she relaxed a little as anticipation thrummed in her veins.

It was amazing how simple words from him could anchor her, excite her. From anyone else, those words might come out as patronizing and annoying. But from Benjamin, knowing that she'd pleased him was as arousing as if he'd stroked her sex.

Seconds ticked into minutes and all she could hear was the sound of her shallow breaths and the whoosh of blood in her ears.

Wood creaked. Did he just stand up? Goosebumps rose on her skin as his warmth engulfed her back. Rough palm swept the hair off her nape onto the other shoulder, and soft lips brushed where the hand left off.

His fingers stroked her back as the clasp holding the top half of her dress popped open. Tingles spread down her spine, her heart rate increased along with pulsing between her legs.

With a flick of his hand, the sleeveless silk slid down her body and pooled at her feet.

"Step out of it."

Lifting her right leg, she moved to the side, still holding on to the railing.

The water below shimmered with the yellow glow reflected from the lights on Chelsea Bridge.

From the corner of her eyes, she saw Benjamin lift the dress, shake it out and lay it over his chair.

Her back prickled once more as she felt his gaze burn her skin. She stood there wearing nothing but the pair of sparkly gold Jimmy Choo stilettos, fighting the urge to cover up as well as the urge to look back. Only one thing stopped her. Benjamin. And the knowledge that keeping still and doing his bidding pleased him.

Giving up control—to him, for him—gave her so much in return. Bountiful peace of mind for the first time in years. Unrestrained pleasure in abundance.

The gentle thud of leather against stone faded. He'd gone into their bedroom, she reasoned with certainty, refusing to turn to confirm her thought.

Drawing in a deep breath, she exhaled and stared at her surroundings. The water of the Thames lapped gently against the barriers. In the eastern horizon, past the old Battersea power station, beyond the London Eye, the sky tinted a dark grey indicating the approaching dawn.

For one moment, panic rose in her mind. She stood on her balcony as bare as the day she was born except for the ridiculously high-heeled shoes. Before long anybody going about their morning business would be able to see her in broad daylight. See her body. Her scarred body!

"You think you are better than us," the vitriolic words from long ago came back to haunt her. The men stood over her, eyes blazing with hatred.

"Do you think your body is too beautiful for people like us when other girls give themselves to us without a fight?"

Daggers glittered in the dim lamplights of the corrugated shack. The air, hot and thick with the scent of sweat and male musk. Harsh laughter rang out, mingling with her muffled screams as her body was held down and slashed. Pain, excruciating pain, lived in her. Sticky fluid dripped down, soaking the back of her torn dress. Blood, the metallic scent mixing with the already acrid smell of torture.

"You are ugly now," the last words she heard before she slipped into welcome darkness.

She squeezed her eyes shut, her grip on the railing tightening, her breath locked tight in her throat.

"Breathe through it." Warm hands stroked the back of her neck, shoulders and back. Just enough pressure to register and distract from her panic but still gentle enough to soothe.

She lifted her eyelids and sought out that eastern horizon again, images of hordes of people staring at her naked body superimposed in her mind.

"Soon they are going to see." Her voice sounded thin like a thread.

The hand on her nape tightened, and she turned her head in his direction but closed her eyes. She couldn't keep them open because he would see the fear in them, and she was ashamed of that fear. Despite everything he'd done to help her, she couldn't get rid of this fear of what other people thought of her body.

"Open your eyes."

She obeyed and looked up into his. There was no censure. Only curiosity.

"Who are they? And what are they going to see."

She was almost ashamed to speak the words out loud. But the look on his face said he wouldn't accept anything less. She swallowed.

"People on the street. They will see how ugly I am."

"I say you're beautiful—"

She shook her head, and the hand on her nape tightened.

"Are you calling me a liar, Selina?" This time his tone was low and full of reprimand, and her cheeks smarted.

"N—No, Benjamin," she stammered in a rush to clarify. "I was just referring to the people out there." *They don't see me as you do.*

"It seems I need to remind you whose body this is and refocus your mind."

He stepped away from her, and she missed his heat immediately. Her regret deepened. While he'd been watching her, she'd been fine. But the minute he stepped into the room, she'd allowed herself to panic. And now Ben was disappointed. This wasn't how she'd wanted them to end the day. She straightened her back, determined to take whatever reprimand he had for her.

He leaned over the table, and she realized he'd left the bag of toys there. He picked up an item that sparkled in the dim light. He held them up, and she saw the nipple clamps.

"Turn around."

"Benjamin, I—" With a heavy heart, she moved hesitantly, wanting to apologize first. Still, she faced him, her bum now against the cold railing.

"Do I need to remind you not to speak unless asked a question?" The fun man was gone, replaced by the strict master.

"No, Benjamin," she added after a couple of heartbeats. She was really screwing up. Although from the lack of expression on Ben's face, she wasn't sure how angry he was at her.

Without warning, thumb and forefinger covered her left nipple, and he pinched. Hard.

She cried out, blinking several times.

Usually, he would soothe the sharp ache by sucking on the tortured spot. Today he didn't, rolling the hardened nub before attaching the blunt clamp. She blinked again but didn't cry out.

"When you signed that agreement, you signed this body over to me."

He repeated the same torment on her right nipple, pinching them and rolling before attaching the clamps. She was ready this time, so it wasn't a shock to her system. Still, the bite of the clamps did their job, keeping her attention on the man standing before her.

"Every inch of the luscious curve and soft skin, every millimetre of scar and blemish belongs to me."

The way he said the words made it seem as if he was proud to have ownership of her scars and blemishes.

He went down on one knee and tapped her inner thigh. "Wider."

She shifted her legs further apart immediately, knowing that any hesitation would earn her even more punishment.

With one hand, he parted her lower lips, and other circled her clit before delving into her slit. Her nub swelled, throbbed, seeking his attention. When he removed his finger, it glimmered with her moisture. He reached across to the table and withdrew another item that glittered like the clamps.

Oh no! It was another clamp. And the way he stared at her clit, she knew exactly where he was going to apply it.

When he tugged at the hard button, she whimpered. He applied the clamp. She keened, tilting her head back, no longer caring who heard her cry or saw her as acute pain morphed into delicious pleasure. Her womb clenched, seeking something to fill it as the pressure on her clit mounted. Involuntarily, she rocked her hips.

"Tut. Tut. That's an extra ten minutes you're staying out here after I'm done with you. Every unauthorized movement earns you another five minutes each."

Damn! Selina held her body. She had no wish to rack up more "corner time."

He stood and stepped back, his gaze sweeping over her bare skin as if he scrutinized his handiwork. Reaching, he rummaged in the bag of devilish toys and withdrew a silver butt plug.

She sucked in a sharp breath. Nothing other than his finger had ever entered her there. What he held in his hand was hardly small. She opened her mouth to say something and clamped it shut.

The wicked glint in his eyes dared her to protest. Nothing less than a safe word would stop him.

She couldn't use it even if the size of the plug made her eyes water even before it had penetrated her behind.

"You see this." He angled the item in his hand so that it caught the light. On the flat end, something was engraved into it. She peered closer and read it.

B.M.

"Do you know what that means?" he asked.

"B and M are your initials," she stated.

"Exactly." His lips curled with amusement. She didn't understand why and she didn't dare to ask.

She watched as he picked up the tube of lube and slathered gel all over the plug.

"Turn around and offer me your arse."

Swallowing hard, she faced the water once again and held on tight to the bar. Keeping her legs spread wide, she tilted her hips back and up, opening and offering her bum like he demanded.

Rough fingers spread her cheeks. Then cold gel followed by metal nudged her pucker. Reflexively she clenched tight, her body rejecting the alien object.

He sighed. "You should relax, Selina. The sooner I get this into your lovely arse, the quicker we're done."

Yeah. She needed to remember that the dawn was fast approaching. It was early summer. She breathed in and out a few times and relaxed.

Benjamin worked the plug, in and out, gaining a few millimetres each time. She tried to concentrate on the undulations in the water instead of what he was doing to her. Still, every time she thought she'd reached a relaxed point, he pulled the chain linking the clamps, sharpening her focus when both pain and pleasure resurfaced.

After several minutes, the widest part of the plug pushed past the tight ring and filled her butt. She puffed air in and out of her mouth, letting her body get used to the new invasion and sensation.

She lost the heat from his body, and she didn't dare turn her head to see what he was doing this time.

"Now I have proof that this arse is mine." He tapped the plug and sensation vibrated through her body.

Oh. Now she understood his amusement. Her bum hole was now covered with his initials.

Arm and body caged her against the balcony rails. Rough fingers tugged at her swollen clit before spearing into her slit. Her knees jellied. If he hadn't been holding her up, she would have fallen to her knees.

"You are so wet." The gravelly tone of his voice added to the sensations driving her crazy. "For me. Mine."

With measured strokes, his long fingers fucked her sex, working her body as only he knew how. Breath restricted, she couldn't move with his arm braced around her body, his heat cocooning her. Lost in pleasure, she took all he gave. Like a good girl. *His* good girl.

"You have always belonged to me. It upsets me when you choose to disparage something so beautiful and precious to me."

Oh, God. She closed her eyes. She couldn't stand it anymore. She allowed her body to sway with his movements, giving in to the emotions he evoked within her. She needed an orgasm before she went mad. She was so close.

"You do not have permission to come." His voice held a harsh warning.

What? Her eyes flew open, and she bit her lower lip, letting the pain ground her. It had been ages, months since she was last denied an orgasm this close to release.

He withdrew his fingers, and she breathed a sigh of disappointment and relief. She wasn't sure how long she would've withheld from climaxing if he'd continued. The clank of his belt buckle and then the slide of his metallic zipper seemed to echo the thumping of her heart.

She wanted him. Yet, she knew this wouldn't be like their usual lovemaking.

"Have I not shown you how beautiful you are?" His voice had a dangerous, gravelly edge. Like a man pushed to his limit. She'd done this, forced him to lose his cool.

"Ben..." She trailed off, shutting her eyes tight. Regretful, the urge to rub her aching chest rose, but she couldn't let go of the railings. Couldn't disobey Ben.

Hands gripped her hips, and he yanked her backwards. In the same movement, he thrust into her soaked sex, filling her up. The breath was knocked out of her lungs, and pain flared at the point of brutal intrusion.

"Answer me," he growled. He withdrew, until just the broad head remained in the tight ring of her slick opening, allowed her to suck in much-needed air, and rammed into her.

Pleasure bloomed, replacing the initial shock and pain. She whimpered. What had he asked her? Thinking through the haze of lust felt like wading through treacle in her mind.

"You have, Benjamin." The words rushed out, and she sucked in another breath.

A slow withdrawal and a hard slam crashed her stomach against the cold metal. An ache spread out, travelled to her clit, and transformed into a decadent delight. A moan bubbled out of her mouth.

"Have I not given you pride of place in my home... in my heart?"

"You have," she could barely get the words out.

Despite his violent actions, her body responded, her arousal rising. She'd never thought she would take pleasure—a perverse enjoyment, mind you—from being manhandled.

She didn't care. Whatever he meted out, she deserved. Moreover, Benjamin would never hurt her. Not the lousy hurt anyway.

Arching her body to receive more of his impact, she closed her eyes. She moaned, relishing every slam, every jolt, every thrust, every ache. Her orgasm rose again, mini tremors clamping his dick. He stopped moving and yanked on the clamps. The sharp pain forestalled her climax and left her panting for air, sweat running down her face.

"Perhaps, you prefer to be treated like a pet...a plaything."

His grip on her thighs tightened as he rode her hard, her belly ramming into the metal railing in front with each thrust.

"To be used just for my pleasure. Is that what you want?"

Breathing harshly through a mouth that was suddenly dry, Selina managed to push the words out. "If...if it pleases you, Benjamin."

"You're damn right about that. This beautiful body is mine to do as I please and don't you ever disrespect it again."

Ben thrust into her several times, her pleasure building again. Just when she thought she would come. He withdrew, using his hand to finish himself off as warm cum coated her back and dripped down her thigh.

His heat deserted her body as he stepped away. From the corner of her eye, she saw him toss the handkerchief he used to wipe himself on the table. He straightened his clothes, packed up and closed the bag, entered the bedroom, and left her outside.

She didn't move even though her body screamed for fulfilment. Orgasm denial was one of the worse punishments Ben had ever used on her. But nothing hit its mark more than intimacy deprivation.

Ben knew how much she loved the moments when he held her after sex, loved the connection of when they were joined in post-coital bliss. This morning he hadn't even shared the intimacy of kissing her or coming inside her. As reprimands go, nothing else equalled its effectiveness.

Head bowed, her chin quivered, remorse a colossal lump stuck in her throat.

It rammed home how truly upset he was with her for going against something he'd warned her from doing. He hated it when she thought her body was ugly. She should've known better than to allow her fears to take over.

Now he'd left her outside with the sun slowly rising in the horizon. Anyone passing by across the river or on the bridge could see her. Bare. Vulnerable. Damaged. She couldn't dare think the 'U' word again in case she said it out loud.

She should move. Go inside. Cover up. Instead, her grip on the railing tightened. No rope or chain restrained her. She stood there by her own volition. For once, she wasn't worried about what those people would think. She didn't care about what they thought about her or her body.

The only person whose opinion truly mattered to her was inside their apartment, and she'd upset him. Tears pooled in her eyes, clouding her vision.

"You can come in now." His voice drifted out to her. "On your hands and knees."

She swiped her eyes with the back of her right hand and lowered her body to the cold tiles. Her legs were trembling so much she was glad she didn't have to walk.

However, the movement caused her breasts to sway, and the nipple clamps to bite. Breathing through the pain, she climbed over the threshold, padding into the room and glad when she stopped on the fluffy rug. She leaned back, bum on heels. The pressure on the anal plug made her wince, but it didn't hurt. Just uncomfortable. Alien.

Knees apart, she placed her palms on thighs and presented herself. But she was too ashamed to meet his gaze when he was so disappointed with her.

"Look at me," Benjamin instructed.

She lifted her head and found him sitting on the edge of the bed, his shoes off. His expression was a mix of sadness and something else she couldn't decipher.

"Do you understand why you're being punished?" he asked.

"Yes, Benjamin. I—" She swallowed the lump in her throat. "I had no right to say my body was ugly."

"This is not about your right to say what you want." He sighed, part annoyance, part resignation. "This is about you understanding that you have a beautiful body regardless of the scars. A beautiful, sexy body."

He stood and walked to the balcony door, pulling it shut, silencing the rumble of cars on the road.

"The savages that did that to you wanted you to feel inferior about your body, to feel ugly. And every time you look at your body that way, you let them win."

He shut his eyes and yanked on his hair.

"I won't let you do that to yourself. I love you too much. Do you understand me?" He walked back to the bed and sat on the edge again.

The tears returned. This time they ran down her face.

"Yes," she replied.

His callused thumb flicked the tears off her face.

"I understand, Benjamin. I'm sorry."

He stared at her for a few heartbeats before nodding.

"Go into the bathroom and clean up. Then come to bed. You have five minutes."

"Yes, Benjamin." She scrambled to do his bidding.

She ran into the bathroom and used a wet towel to wipe the semen dripping down her back and thighs. There wasn't enough time to have a shower which was what she would have preferred. But she didn't want to be late since Benjamin was timing her.

She used the toilet but didn't dislodge the plug. After washing her hands, she brushed her teeth and washed her face. She took one last look in the mirror, and the nipple clamps winked at her as if mocking her. Between the nipple and clit clamps and the plug her body was in a perpetual state of arousal.

She didn't have enough time to masturbate, which was probably what her husband intended when he only gave her five minutes to clean up—no time to finger herself and take the edge off. Squeezing her thighs together only increased the pressure on her back hole and on her clit but brought no relief. Puffing out a breath, she headed into the bedroom.

Ben was in bed already, naked under the sheets and reading a magazine with the small side lamp. She suppressed a groan as the bulges of his body outlined the sheets, especially the half-erect penis. How was she supposed to sleep next to him still highly turned on and with his instruments of torture still attached to her body?

Please let him take them off.

He seemed to have other plans. "Come here."

She stepped to his side of the bed.

He ghosted his fingers over her breasts.

She nearly arched into his touch, her need overwhelming her. It required iron will to resist moving.

"Are the clamps hurting?" he asked, gliding his fingers along the chain but not tugging.

Seeing an opportunity to get them off, she replied a little too enthusiastically. "Yes."

He quirked one eyebrow studying her face. "Let's try that again. Is the pain unbearable?"

She opened her mouth to respond. He raised his index finger to hush her.

"Before you answer, think about it carefully."

She clamped her mouth shut as his finger travelled down to her sex, and he played with her idly as he waited for her response.

"And?"

"No. The pain isn't unbearable," she admitted sullenly.

"Good. Lie on the bed and hold onto the bedpost."

She positioned her body at the foot of the bed as instructed. Ben rose to his knees.

"Brace yourself. This is going to hurt."

Her grip on the post tightened as Ben hovered above her. He clasped her breast with one hand and with the other unclamped the right nipple. The rush of blood to her numb nipple sent acute pain and endorphins firing through her body. She gritted her teeth, fighting the burn razing through her as he massaged her breast, spreading out the point of pain, so it wasn't focused on one end. A slight sheen of sweat coated her body.

He didn't warn her when he removed the other nipple clamp, and she screamed out as her body fevered. Instantly the pain transformed into pleasure. She realized her clit was engulfed in the warmth of Ben's mouth as he sucked, clamp and all. Her body arched off the bed, a flush of orgasm rushed at her.

"Ben, I need...please," she begged.

"Now." He unclipped the clit clamp. "Give it to me."

She came with a scream, the intensity of her orgasm making her pass out.

Chapter Four

Selina relaxed into her first-class seat, with Benjamin seated next to her on the flight to Cape Town. The apprehension about the trip had risen again and threatened to give her a headache.

What would the reception be from Benjamin's family? She already knew his uncle was not happy that they were married. Although they hadn't spoken about the man since her husband had revealed his past to her, she couldn't help the growing sense of doom pervading her mind.

Best not to think about it.

"Do you think Beatrice will be okay?" she asked absently.

"She will be now that she's in capable hands," Ben replied flicking through the in-flight magazine.

Benjamin had shocked both Selina and his sister yesterday when he'd invited Kenny Cruz over to their home. Kenny was a member of the Moss Star Security team. He was also the Bar Atlantic club owner. In certain circles, he was known as Master K, a strict practitioner of BDSM and a disciplinarian.

Benjamin was strict, but Master K was a whole other level. The dark-skinned giant of a man's presence demanded obedience. Selina didn't cower easily before men. However, she had to admit that she would never want to test the man's patience. She'd watched him wield a whip, and that was enough to give her cold sweats.

Two days ago, she'd come home from a quick trip down to the shops to find Kenny in their living room with Ben. She hadn't been expecting the man. Considering he was a part of Moss Star and a good friend of Ben's, there seemed nothing unusual. Until Ben had invited Beatrice into the room and explained the reason for Kenny's visit.

"Isn't Kenny a little bit of a drastic option. Christopher would've kept an eye on her."

"Yes, but she knows how to wrap Chris around her fingers. He spoils her like a kid sister. Beatrice needs a firm hand, and Kenny won't tolerate any misbehaviour from her."

Selina gasped. "You gave him permission to discipline her?" Beatrice was the same person who went bright red at the mention of spanking. "Your sister is as vanilla as they come."

"In which case, she'll behave herself if she doesn't want to find herself sprawled across his lap," Ben replied, his eyes sparkling with amusement.

Selina couldn't help pitying Beatrice. Ben's sister would really have to be on her best behaviour. And after her recent escapades, perhaps Kenny was precisely what the girl needed.

The rest of their flight went without event, and their plane taxied on the tarmac in the Cape Town airport. Carrying their bags in one hand, Ben held hers with his other hand until they were through customs. At the Arrivals lobby, they were met by a tall, blond-haired man built like a brick wall and outfitted in a dark maroon button-down shirt and blue denim.

"The prodigal son returns," the man said with a smirk spread across his Scandinavian features as he approached them.

"And you're still playing lapdog to Uncle Leonard I see," Benjamin said with a smile. But it didn't reach his eyes.

The man's expression hardened for a moment, and then he broke into a smile. "You're still as prickly as ever. *Welkom tuis.*" He extended his arm.

Benjamin released her to shake the man's hand. And then he tugged Selina close.

"It's good to see you again. This is my wife, Selina," Ben introduced her. "This is Lars Gottfried, an old friend."

"You always had an eye for pretty girls." The man studied her appreciatively before leaning in to kiss her cheek. "It's nice to finally meet you, Selina."

"Thank you." She smiled in return, taking her cue from Ben.

"The car is this way."

Still holding onto her, he nudged her to follow Lars to where the car was parked. Lars loaded the boot of the car as Ben helped her into the back seat.

Ben got into the front passenger seat, and Lars got into the driver's seat. The men started conversing in a guttural language she didn't understand but assumed was Afrikaans. She focused attention on the scenery since it was her first time in South Africa. The drive from the airport was pleasant, and Selina was glad to see that Cape Town was much like any other city with freeways, skyscrapers, and shopping malls.

After a while, the scenery changed, and it seemed they were heading out of town.

"Ben, I thought we were staying in the city," she asked out of curiosity.

Lars responded. "Ben's uncle spends most of his time at the ranch, so that's where we're headed."

"The ranch?" She hadn't known Ben's family owned a ranch. There were so many things she still didn't know.

"It's a cross between a game reserve and a farm out in the country," Ben replied, turning his head to smile at her. "But we call it the ranch out of fondness."

"Okay. How long to get there?"

"We'll be there in about two hours. Relax and take a nap. You didn't get much sleep on the flight. I'll wake you when we get there."

She knew an instruction when she heard one. Ben wasn't giving her the option to argue, and she certainly didn't want to disagree with him in front of his friend. She didn't know how much the man knew about the kind of relationship she had with her husband.

After her disastrous faux pas on Saturday morning, she certainly wasn't willing to incur Ben's wrath any time soon.

"Yes, Ben. Thank you."

He smiled at her, and she relaxed into the soft leather seat and closed her eyes.

The men continued their conversation, and soon she drifted off to sleep.

She awoke to find herself in Ben's arms as he scooped her up. She snuggled into him, thinking they were at their apartment in London and he was carrying her to bed. The sound of voices made her open her eyes.

Ben was walking up a flight of stairs. Another man, not Lars, dressed in white shirt and khaki trousers carried their luggage behind him.

"Welcome home, Master Benjamin."

Selina turned her head to see a dark-haired woman with blonde streaks dressed in black leather corset and trousers prostrate on the floor in the hallway.

What the hell was going on? Selina stiffened.

"Margo?" Ben asked, the tone of his voice and raised-brow expression conveying his surprise.

"At your service," the woman replied with an incline of her head.

Ben appeared dumbstruck as he contemplated the woman at his feet.

"Margo, I wasn't expecting to see you here at The Ranch."

"Master, where else would I be, but where you left me?" Margo didn't move, her body poised in elegant submission. No one watching could miss the slight uplift of her lips and the invitation in her emerald eyes.

Okay! Selina clenched her teeth, tired of the woman referring to Ben as Master. And what did she mean by "where you left me?" Had she drifted off to sleep and fallen down the rabbit hole or something?

"May I kiss your boots, Master?"

A monster, dark, green, and envious, reared its head within Selina. She sat up, ready to voice her protest.

"Go ahead," he replied before she could open her mouth, his grip on her body tightening.

Jealousy sliced through Selina as Margo lowered her lips onto Ben's tan leather Chelsea boots.

"Put me down, Ben," she said muttered through clenched teeth and wriggled in his arms.

"Be still, Lina." His tone was assured and low, just for her hearing. To Margo, he said more loudly, "On your feet."

The woman rose, her movement confident and gracefully lithe, like a cat.

Selina's skin flushed with warmth, her breath ragged and fast like she'd run a marathon as she eyed the woman suspiciously. It didn't help that she'd never been able to achieve that much grace rising from her knees.

At her full height, the biracial woman was even more glamorous, especially with the fuck-me leather stilettos she was wearing. Make-up, her hair swept back into a loose chignon and the leather collar with a D-ring around her throat.

"This is my wife, Selina."

The woman finally looked at Selina with a smile on her face. "It's nice to meet you."

She said it with as much cheeriness as a hotel receptionist greeting a guest. Selina couldn't tell if it was genuine or not.

"Thank you," she said in reply.

"Let me show you to your suite. Your luggage has already been taken up."

Ben nodded and the woman, swivelling, walked off.

"Ben, you can put me down now," Selina said, feeling embarrassed that Ben was still carrying her like a baby.

"Not yet," he replied and strode off behind Margo, who was about three strides ahead.

"Ben—"

He pinched her hard on the thigh. Selina gasped from the shock and pain and clamped her mouth shut.

Margo led the way up the sweeping, gilded staircase and down a hallway covered in paintings and sculptures. The house had the grandeur of a stately home and the opulence of a five-star resort.

At the end of the hallway, she opened a door and stepped back, allowing Ben to go in first.

The room was light and airy, and as Ben let Selina slide to her feet, she noticed the vaulted ceiling had a skylight, letting in sunlight and a view of clear, cerulean sky. Her breath hitched as her gaze took in the rest of the space.

The grandeur extended into the loft-like suite with its openness. Tan sofas and chairs at one end, an aluminium and granite-surfaced kitchen adjacent. At the other end, a Japanese style screen that hid what she assumed to be the sleeping area. Their suitcases stood against tall, dark wood cabinets. From the silhouette she could see through the screen, the bed must be massive and four-posted.

"Do you like it?"

She turned back to face Ben, whose eyes gleamed and a corner of his lips curled up.

"All I can say is wow...it is breath-taking. I wasn't expecting this."

Taking a step toward him, she clutched at his shirt and stood on her tiptoes.

"I'm glad you like it." His words fanned her face before their lips connected.

A chaste kiss—a gentle brush of soft lips, a tame nibble and a quick swipe of tongue that lingered but didn't delve further despite the invitation of her open mouth.

"What would you like me to do?"

Ben lifted his head and Selina saw Margo standing just inside the shut door, an expectant look in her eyes. She'd already forgotten about the woman.

"That'll be all, Margo," Ben said.

But the woman remained there. "Master?"

"Is there a problem?"

"It's just that I was assigned to serve you for the duration of your stay at The Ranch." Margo lifted her hands, revealing a brown leather leash.

"I appreciate your loyalty, Margo, but I don't need a slave." After a few heartbeats, he added. "I have Selina."

Take that, bitch. Selina eyed the woman balefully.

Margo looked disappointed and blinked several times as if at the point of tears over Ben's rejection. "But it never stopped you before, Master. Have I done something to offend you?"

Ben sighed. "No, Margo you haven't upset me."

In the blink of an eye, the woman was back on her knees, prostrated and pleading. "Don't send me away, please Master." There was a panicky edge to her plea; even Selina could sense her desperation.

Ben walked toward her. "Look at me," he commanded.

Margo lifted her head, her eyes wide with fright.

"What is going on?" He asked sternly.

Margo's gaze flicked to the floor, and she didn't say anything.

"Well, if you're not going to talk, you can leave now."

Margo's throat worked as she swallowed in apparent anxiety.

"If I don't convince you to let me serve you, I will be put into the box. And I don't want to go back in there, Master."

The box? What the hell was that? And why would anyone want to put Margo in it?

"Who will put you in the box, Margo?" Ben voiced Selina's thoughts.

This time the woman fidgeted with the leash in her hand, her gaze falling to the floor.

"Answer me." Ben stood stock still, his hand clenched behind his back.

"Uncle Leonard doesn't like being disobeyed. You know this." She looked up at Ben, her forehead creased in a frown.

Interesting that Margo addressed Ben's relative as 'Uncle Leonard'. Obviously, they weren't related, and the man wasn't as congenial as the moniker implied if she feared him.

Was Uncle Leonard really such a tyrant? Even after what her husband had said about him, she'd wanted to keep an open mind until she met him.

But putting Margo in the box—whatever that was—was mean, even if she hated the idea that Margo was offering her services to Ben.

"Why would he put you in the box, though?" Ben asked.

"He ordered I should be put in the box so I would understand what it would feel like if I disobeyed him."

"What? I'm going to talk to him. He can't do that."

"No! Please, don't tell him I complained. It will be worse for me." She lowered her forehead and palms to the floor. "Please, Master."

Ben heaved a sigh and walked over to the windows that overlooked the lush green manicured lawn.

Selina didn't envy Ben's position. Even she couldn't call it.

Was Margo sincere? Surely things wouldn't be as bad as she implied if Ben sent her away.

"You can stay as long as Selina agrees."

Selina gasped. "What?"

"If she stays, then she will be serving you as well. You will be her mistress."

Margo gasped.

Yeah. Selina felt the same shock down her spine.

"I can't. I'm not a Domme." She wasn't. In their kinky world, she was always the bottom. Selina loved it that way. She loved the freedom of not having control over anything including her own body. She certainly didn't want to oversee a hardboiled slave twenty-four-seven.

"You might not be a Domme, but you can do this." Ben stopped before her, lifting her chin up, so she was captured by his bright grey eyes.

"You're the deputy Chief Pharmacist in a busy public London hospital with several team members working with you. I know you can handle one female service slave."

True. She practically ran the pharmacy department, even if she was just the acting deputy. Anyway, if Ben believed she could do it, then she could.

But some things still bothered her about the whole set up.

She turned her head toward the woman still prostrate. "Before I can make a decision, I need to have all the facts."

Ben wouldn't lie to her, would he? She looked back up at Ben. He was studying her face.

"What do you need to know?"

"What exactly did Margo mean by 'where you left her' and why does she call you Master?"

Ben's hand dropped, but he didn't move from the spot, and he still held her gaze.

"It's a long story, but the short of it is that I trained Margo. She was my first slave. Before I left South Africa, I released her from her obligations to me. I expected her to move on. I didn't know she was still here. I promise you."

Selina nodded. She believed him.

"Okay. But what did she mean by 'it never stopped you before'?"

Ben sighed, his gaze flicking away as his hand ran through his hair, agitating the strands.

"While I was training Margo, I was also dating Siba."

"You were unfaithful to Margo?"

"No. The rules of The Ranch allow for multiple consenting partners. Margo knew and consented."

Ben's gaze returned to Margo.

Something about the woman's countenance had changed. Selina couldn't pinpoint it. Was she angry? She appeared cowered. Still, something was off.

"So, Margo do you consent to have Selina as your mistress?"

"If it is what Master wishes."

"You do realize that Ben doesn't own you anymore, Margo?" Selina asked, showing her growing irritation.

"But he does, Mistress, for as long as he is here."

"Fine. Whatever," Selina barked and stormed off toward the bedroom end of the open-plan suite.

She sat on the vast bed covered in crisp white cotton sheets and a thin chocolate silk duvet. Sitting on the edge, she crossed her arms and puffed out a breath. The corners of her head throbbed with the beginning of a headache.

She heard footsteps before Ben's heat, and spice surrounded her as the mattress dipped and he sat beside her. She opened her eyes when he lifted her onto his lap so that her back was against his chest.

"I'm sorry if the whole situation is giving you a headache," he said and rubbed her temple gently.

"How do you know I have a headache?" she turned to look at his face.

"The lines on your forehead are a dead giveaway. Whenever I see them, I know you're overworking that brain of yours." He placed a soft kiss to her brow before turning her around so he could continue his massage.

"Don't worry about Margo. I will take care of her. I shouldn't have put the responsibility of making the decision on your shoulders."

"What are you going to do? I don't like the idea of her being here, but I don't want her punishment on my conscience either."

"I think we could use her being here to our advantage."

Ben's fingers trailed down to her neck, and he pushed the strands of hair that had escaped her ponytail hairband. He worked the kink out of her neck and shoulders with his magic fingers. A moan of pleasure escaped her lips, her headache slowly being replaced by a different kind of throbbing south of her navel.

"How do you mean?" she asked, her voice now husky with need.

"I have to understand what's going on here. Knowing my uncle, this place could soon turn into a nest of vipers if we're not careful. Keeping Margo with us will keep her loyal to us, and I assure you, we are probably going to need all the help we can get."

"Your uncle is really that bad?"

"You don't know the half of it. But don't worry."

He nibbled her neck and right shoulder while his hand slipped under her dress. He pulled her panties down.

"Be good and take that off. You won't need it for the duration of our stay."

She leaned forward and pushed the item down and lifted her leg to pull it off. Used to not wearing lingerie when Ben was around, she'd been surprised he'd allowed her to wear one for the duration of their flight from London to South Africa.

He patted her bare sex and her inner walls clenched. She wanted him inside her and whimpered in response.

"Margo, come here."

"Yes, Master." A few seconds later, the woman stood beside the screen.

"Kneel down in front of Selina."

The woman complied, lowering her body, so her head came up just above Selina's knees.

"Lift your dress and spread your legs, Lina. Show our slave your pretty pussy." He gave her shoulder an open-mouthed kiss and then sucked hard. Pleasure shot straight to her clit.

Selina's breath hitched, her heart racing. "Ben, I—"

"Do it," he said in the low, dominant voice that brooked no challenge.

Selina swallowed. "Yes, Benjamin."

She spread her legs either side of Ben's thighs and lifted her bum as she pulled the hem of her dress to settle around her waist.

"Describe what you see, Margo."

The woman licked her lips as she stared at Selina with open hunger, her green eyes glittering.

"She's beautiful, brown and pink, like chocolate and strawberry swirl."

Selina flushed with heat, her insides contracting widely. So turned on, she never believed having another woman watch her bared like this could be arousing. Especially since she couldn't even decide if she liked the woman or not.

Her state of arousal had more to do with Ben's dominance and less about Margo's presence. Surely. She bit her bottom lip, suppressing a moan as he squeezed her breasts, covered in a lace bra and cotton dress.

"Lina, use both hands to open yourself for me."

For me. For him. Yes. She sat spread apart, exposed, for him. The knowledge empowered her, freed her from her disturbing thought. Reaching down, Selina did as he instructed, cold air from the open window teasing her sex.

"How is she looking, Margo?"

"She is the prettiest lotus bud covered in morning dew." Margo swiped her pink tongue over her glossy lips. "Can I taste her, Master?"

"Can she taste you, Lina?"

What? She had to think hard to process Ben's words. She'd never been intimate with another woman. But the way her body burned; she didn't care who got her off if Ben controlled it all.

"Yes," her voice was so guttural it didn't sound like hers.

"Go ahead, but no hands. Selina, guide her head and set the pace the way you want it.

Margo scuttled forward.

But Selina hesitated to touch her. She'd never done this before.

Usually, when Ben ate her, her hands were either tied up or clutching something else. She'd never held anyone's head against her sex.

Ben lifted her left hand and guided it to Margo's head, making her grip where it was bunched up in the loose bun. With his hand still on hers, he pulled Margo's head down until her mouth settled on Selina's clit.

"Work your magic, Margo. Show Lina how good you are with your mouth."

The woman attacked her sex. By Jove she did, lips sucking her clit, tongue swirling around her labia and slit, teeth nipping the plump lower lips.

Selina whimpered, her hips arching, gyrating as she ground against Margo's face. At the same time, Benjamin teased and plucked her nipples and kissed the sensitive skin on her neck. Soon all she felt was sensations, mindless in her rising pleasure as she moaned and writhed, her hand on Margo's head tightening.

"You may come at will, Lina."

His permission opened the dam. Her orgasm rushed in a feverish flood from her toe tips to the crown of her head, and she screamed.

When she came to, Margo was still between her legs and Selina tried to push her away from her sensitive clit. Ben held her down.

"Lap up every last drop, Margo."

The woman eventually lifted her head, a satisfied smile on her face, like she'd gotten what she'd wanted.

As she lay limp and replete in Ben's arms, Selina couldn't understand it because the woman had given her pleasure and received nothing in return. She should be unfulfilled.

Unless this was what Margo had wanted all along. Then it clicked. Margo took pleasure in Ben's dominance, even if she wasn't sexually fulfilled.

Another reason to hate the damn woman.

"Give me the leash."

Margo picked it up from where she'd dropped it on the floor and presented it to Ben in her open palms.

He took it. "Do you promise to serve Selina and I loyally for the duration of our stay at The Ranch, to execute your duties promptly and without questions?"

"Yes, Master. My word is my bond."

"Then I promise you my protection and care for the duration of our stay here. My word is my bond."

He hooked one end of the long extendable leash onto the D-ring on Margo's collar. Shifting Selina onto the bed, he stood and attached the other end of the leash to the post at the foot of the bed.

"Show your appreciation, Margo."

"Thank you, Master," she said and shifted on her knees to kiss his boots.

Despite still floating in post-climactic bliss, Selina's unease rose. She would need a whole different mindset before she would fully accept Ben taking on Margo.

As if reading her mind, he spoke to her. "Margo is a fulltime service slave. She cannot go anywhere nor do anything without my permission. Even her bathroom time requires that I grant permission. Do you understand, Lina?"

"Yes, but..." Selina bit her lip.

"But what. Say what's on your mind."

Selina eyed the woman before looking back at Benjamin. "Does that mean you're going to sleep with her?"

"Margo will sleep on the futon at the foot of the bed unless you invite her to our bed."

"Okay, but that's not what I meant."

"Then say what you mean, Lina."

She puffed out a breath. "Are you going to have sex with her?"

"Do you want me to have sex with Margo?"

"No... I don't know." Selina had never been so confused.

A part of her wanted to watch Ben with another woman. Yet another side of her baulked at the idea.

Ben was her husband. They were monogamous, weren't they? One man, one woman and all that.

"Then I won't until you're certain. But that doesn't mean I won't tell her to fuck you or vice versa." His eyes gleamed wickedly.

"Oh," was all she could say as her cheeks heated up, trying to picture how two women could fuck each other.

"Do you have any other questions?"

"What are her hard limits?" She remembered all the questions Ben had asked her when they'd started their relationship. Didn't they apply in a Master-slave relationship too?

"Margo, tell us your hard limits."

"I'm a house slave. I have no hard limits," she replied.

"Nonsense. You are my slave for the next two weeks. State your limits."

Margo sighed. "No blood."

"Is that all? So, you're happy with knife play, wax play, sensory deprivation, public display, humiliation, caging—"

"No!" Margo swallowed, her eyes wide. "Not confined or dark spaces."

"I thought as much." He stared at her as if thinking. "So, what are your soft limits?"

"I love pain, Master as long as it doesn't draw blood."

"Yes, I remember. You were quite a pain slut."

Great. Selina rolled her eyes heavenward. Another thing the woman did better than she did. Selina was no masochist and had only learned to enjoy a little pain with pleasure.

"What's your safe word?"

"Jelly babies."

"Good. I remember that too. Selina and I are going to freshen up. You can unpack our bags and put the clothes away."

"Yes, Master," Margo replied and focused on the luggage.

Benjamin tugged Selina's hand, and she followed him into a massive bathroom with the bath sunk into the floor Jacuzzi-style and a separate alcove with an unenclosed walk-in shower unit. The walls and floor were covered in light limestone slabs that reflected the sunlight coming in from the expansive windows overlooking large mountains in the distance.

She turned to find Ben staring at her, his expression intense and his trousers sporting a huge bulge. Feet spread apart, his hands lowered his zipper silently.

She understood the unspoken command. Out of breath, she rushed to obey it.

Chapter Five

Benjamin strode down the hallway. On his right side, Selina walked alongside him dress in a coral strapless asymmetrical sundress he'd chosen. He held onto her hand. It trembled slightly. He knew she was nervous about meeting his uncle. And frankly, after the reception they'd had so far, he couldn't blame her.

For someone who was brought up in a vanilla world, the practices of his "family" would seem bizarre and outlandish.

But like the brave woman she was, she tackled her fears with bravado, only voicing them privately to him.

And as always, he would do whatever it took to take that fear away from her. And one of those fears had been Margo, who currently walked a step behind him on the left side, the leash slack in his hand. He hadn't welcomed the idea of having a slave, even if temporarily. He'd walked away from that lifestyle when he left his hometown to live in the UK. He didn't welcome being thrust back into it by the machinations of his uncle.

Personally, he would've left the woman in their suite. But to play along with his uncle's plans, he'd brought Margo along for his meeting with the old man. He wanted to watch the old man's reaction when he saw Margo being led at the end of a leash by Ben. Especially with Selina beside him.

A quick glance over at Selina and he caught her eyeing the other woman. But there was no malice in her expression. The way she watched Margo with her lips parted slightly and the pulse at the base of her next jumping, she was aroused.

Was she remembering the feel of Margo's lips on her pussy? He would bet she was wet under the flare of her dress. His erection throbbed to life in his trousers.

Watching Margo eat Selina up had turned his half-awake arousal into hard rock. He'd relished Selina blowing him in the bathroom, naked and on her knees, so much that he came with a roar all over her face.

Then he thought about the anal plug lodged inside her, jostling each time she moved, preparing her for him. He'd made her wear one every day since Saturday. Before the end of this trip, he would take her where no other man had been before.

Now he was ready to take her against the nearest flat surface.

Movement at the corner of his eyes reminded him this was hardly the time. The bodyguard posted outside his uncle's annexe of The Ranch estate pushed the door open as Ben nodded to him.

As soon as he walked into the house, the scents—tobacco spice, leather, and wood—all mixed together to take him down memory lane. Familiar and yet disconcerting, almost.

The living room hadn't changed from what he remembered. Worn brown leather sofas faced each other with a low, square dark wood table in the middle. On the walls hung the heads of trophies his uncle had hunted. Persian rugs covered the marble floor tiles, and the wind flapped the edges of the pulled back curtains on the wide windows overlooking the Stellenbosch Mountains.

He used to call this home. Now it reminded him off all the things he'd left behind, both good and bad.

The ladies walked in behind him, and he ushered them to the sofa. He waited for Selina to sit down and he sank onto the couch beside her.

"It's so intimidating in here with all the animal heads hanging on the wall," Selina whispered to him.

Ben smiled wryly. "I think that's the effect Leonard was going for." He placed his hand on her nape and caressed her bare, tense skin until she relaxed into his touch.

Margo settled on the floor, sitting back on her heels where she knelt. He placed the leash on the sofa next to him.

The door at the end of the room opened, and out walked his uncle. The wooden cane he leaned on tapped on the hard floor, and he'd lost a little weight. But it was still the old man he knew—greying blond hair and trimmed beard and moustache on a weathered face, tall and stocky, a giant of a man. Ben used to refer to him fondly as 'the Viking' when he was a boy.

A smile curled the man's lips as Ben stood from his seat. He was glad to see the man well despite everything that had happened between them, and he took a step toward him.

"It's good to see you, Uncle," Ben said, stretching out his hand.

The man stared at this hand and then up at his face. "Is that the best you can do, boy, after so many years?" he asked in a deadpan expression that was designed to unsettle those who didn't know Leonard well enough.

Uncle opened his arms, and Ben smiled as he stepped into the man's tight embrace.

"It is good to see you, son," Leonard said in a low voice that sounded choked.

Did the old man really miss him that much? Ben pulled back to stare at his face, but he couldn't read his blank expression.

"Gaan jy die jong dame te stel?" Leonard said in Afrikaans.

"Of course." Ben turned to find Selina standing behind him. He stretched out his right hand, and she took it and moved to stand beside him.

"This is my wife, Selina." He placed his hands on her shoulders and stood behind her. "Selina, this is Uncle Leonard."

"It's good to finally meet you, sir," she said with a smile on her face and curtsied.

His uncle scrutinized Selina from head to toes. "I can see why you chose her. She is beautiful, and at least she has some manners. That's always good."

Ben quirked his eyebrow, and his uncle laughed. "Come. Inge has prepared a feast and set it up outside. It's a beautiful day, and we should make the most of the mild weather before the temperature drops."

He turned around and walked toward the door.

"And Margo you can come along too. I'm in a good mood today. The prodigal son has returned, so let's celebrate."

Ben turned to Margo who still knelt where he'd left her by the sofa. He inclined his head, and Margo stood and followed them out into the garden.

A table covered in white cloth was set up under the shade, with six places set. Uncle sat at the end and waved his hand. In the old days, Ben would sit at the other end of the table. He wondered if that still applied and decided to test it. He pulled out a chair.

Inge came out, smiling. She was Leonard's long-term partner and fulltime sub. She'd aged gracefully, and the smile and hug she gave him were very motherly.

"It's good to have you home, Ben," she said after she exchanged pleasantries with Selina.

Ben pulled out the chair beside his uncle, and Inge sat down as Lars strolled in. Knowing that Lars was going to eat with them, he pulled out a seat next to Inge for Margo and then went around. Lars pulled out a seat for Selina who sat the other side of Uncle. But by the time Ben could get to the chair next to her, Lars pulled it out.

Ben eyed Lars, who just smiled at him. He settled opposite his uncle. He hated leaving Selina between Leonard and Lars. But there wasn't much he could do without making a fuss.

"You are back in your rightful place, son," his uncle said.

Ben nodded and met Selina's gaze, asking her with the raise of his brow if she was all right. She inclined her head in assent, and he relaxed.

Over lunch they chatted easily, catching up on what had been happening in Stellenbosch and South Africa for the past few years. He saw Selina visibly relax as Inge and Margo suggested all the different sites they could visit, including the local wineries.

Just when Ben thought the afternoon would go smoothly, Uncle's next words had him on edge.

"Tell me, girl. Why has Benjamin not collared you?"

Selina snuck a quick glance at him, and he shook his head while holding her gaze, wondering what she would say. She bit her lip before turning back to the old man.

"I don't want to be collared," she replied.

Ben's heart sank. She'd just given his uncle some ammunition to use against her.

"Pardon me, but I thought you were his submissive."

"I am, but it's not a 24/7 arrangement."

Leonard nodded and looked across at Ben. "It seems London has turned you *sagte*."

Ben clenched his fists as he fought not to rise to Leonard's bait.

"Well, girl. Over here, a submissive knows her place and is collared," the man said as he nodded towards the two women on his right.

"Margo wears a collar showing she's a house slave, a property of The Ranch and Inge here—" he reached out and stroked the woman's silver collar that looked like a standard necklace but with a silver lock as a pendant "—wears a collar that shows she belongs to me."

He upturned his palm and Inge place a kiss on it.

"They both wear their collars proudly because they are proud to be identified as Moss property."

Ben didn't like where this was headed. "Uncle, what Selina meant—"

Leonard held up his hand. "Do not interrupt me, boy. She was quite clear about her position on wearing your collar."

He turned back to Selina. "If you do not want to wear Benjamin's collar, then you do not deserve to be a Moss. Perhaps Lars can teach you a thing or two about submission."

"What? No way." Ben pushed back his chair.

"House rules. Any submissive without an owner's collar is available for any Dominant to play with. You should know this. It's your rule."

Shit. He'd forgotten about that. He'd created the damn rule that was now biting him in the ass.

"My rules and I can bend them. Nobody touches Selina."

Lars shook his head. "It won't work, Ben. Remember Cordelia?"

Shit. Shit. Shit. His past was really smacking him in the face this afternoon. As a brash young man, he'd done some stupid things and playing with Cordelia, who Lars had a thing for in those days, was one of them.

But she'd been uncollared and had been staying at the resort to discover her kinky side. Lars had been infatuated with her and Ben had lusted after her. Call it teenage hormones.

"Cordelia was a long time ago. You can't use that against me now."

Lars stood but kept his hand on Selina's shoulder. "Payback is a bitch, isn't it?"

Ben growled.

"Enough, both of you," Leonard said, cutting into the testosterone explosion. "Ben, you have two choices. Put her on the next plane out of here or collar her. Otherwise, Lars has my permission to do as he pleases with her. You have until tomorrow morning."

Ben glared at Lars as he walked over to Selina and pulled her up.

"If anyone touches her, they will have me to deal with." And he stormed out with Selina in tow.

"What the hell was all that about?" Selina asked as soon as they got back into the suite.

"That—" Ben pointed at the door they'd just walked through "—was my life. The life I walked away from. The life I didn't want you to see. That was the way I grew up, brash, hedonistic, a narcissist. I could do whatever I wanted. Take whomever I wanted."

He stopped pacing and faced her. She looked shocked at his outburst.

"This whole fucking mess is my doing—the resort, the rules. I fucking created a monster. And I thought it would just die when I walked away. Now, look at it."

He waved his hands, feeling almost despondent.

"Ben, I don't understand what you're saying." She stood stock-still.

"I mean that The Ranch is my creation. What you see, I designed. Sure, this place has always existed in some form for hundreds of years, but it was just a family home. Moss's family home. But later I turned it into a holiday destination for the perverted."

He ran a hand through his hair, needing to dispel the rancorous energy coursing through his veins.

"I took Margo, who was a sweet girl, and turned her into a raving pain slut who would do anything for the lash of a whip."

"I can't imagine Margo ever being a sweet girl," Selina's tone was a matter of fact.

"Perhaps sweet isn't the word. But I'm the one who made her the woman she is today. And Cordelia. I knew Lars was in love with her, but she had a hot body, and I had to have her. So, I took her. That's the kind of man I am."

"No. You are not that man," Selina bit out. "Yes, you did some bad things in the past. But you were no more than a boy. It can be written off as youthful folly. I forgive you, Ben. You need to forgive yourself."

"How can I forgive myself when even Lars hasn't forgiven me? He will have you as revenge for Cordelia if I don't stop him."

"I'm sure he wasn't serious. He was probably just trying to goad you."

Ben gave a bark of laughter. "You don't know him. Why do you think he's joking?"

"For starters, I'm a grown woman capable of making my own choices. I will not be bartered like a chattel."

He did laugh this time, but there was no humour in the harsh sound.

"You don't get it, do you? The normal rules do not apply at The Ranch. In here, Ranch rules apply. You came here as a submissive, my submissive, even if you're not wearing my collar." He waved a hand at her neck, turning his face away. His gut churned at the idea there was no physical evidence she belonged to him. "You can't stay here."

"You're not really going to put me on the next plane back to London? I don't want to leave."

He looked at her sideways. Her forehead puckered with frown lines.

"You still don't get it. I will commit murder rather than have anyone touch you without my permission." He screwed up his face, his insides churning like he was possessed by a beast. "Hang on, you want him to fuck you, is that it?"

"No!"

"Tell me the truth. You imagined him being inside you."

She bit her lip and look downward. He took a step in her direction.

"Selina?" he growled.

"Yes," she said in a low voice, out of breath.

"And it turned you on."

She bit her lip and squeezed her eyes shut, her chest rising and falling rapidly.

The jealous beast reared its ugly head inside him, dark and dangerous.

"Strip and present yourself."

Her eyes flew open wide as she tried to read him. "Now!"

Flinching, she pulled the dress over her head and folded it onto a table. Then she kicked off her sandals and put it beside the table. Lowering onto her knees, she spread her thighs wide, pushed out her chest and folded her hands behind her back.

He nearly groaned out loud at the sight of her uncovered, and he was thankful he'd changed into a loose pair of linen trousers.

"Show me your pussy."

Hesitantly, she reached down and spread her lower lips. As he suspected, she glistened like the early morning sun reflected on the Eerste River.

"You are wet."

She hung her head forward, her mass of dark curls covering her face.

"I'm sorry. I don't know what came over me. It was just one moment when the two of you were arguing, and I pictured the two of you dominating me. I'm sorry and ashamed of myself. If you decide to put me on that plane back, I'll go. It's probably for the best," she rambled in a strained voice.

Hearing her honesty unravelled him. He exhaled a shuddering breath and lowered his shaking body onto the sofa. *What am I doing?* They'd only been here a day, and this whole place was messing with his head. Again.

"Come here," his voice sounded like he was sawing wood, his throat dry.

She stood and walked over to him. He patted his lap, and she lowered her body onto him. He held her chin with his thumb and forefinger and stared into her brown eyes. Remorse reflected at him. His chest tightened, and he rested his forehead against hers.

"I never want you to be ashamed of your desires," he said through a raw throat as he fought to maintain his composure, to be the man she needed. "But I want you to always be honest with me about them."

He sighed. *What am I saying?* The man in him wanted her to only desire him. He wanted to be the sole person fulfilling her needs. But he also had to accept that she had a thing for multiple partners. Christopher had already warned him about that.

"I'm sorry. I just didn't want you getting more upset when you were so adamant you didn't want Lars touching me." She leaned into his body, and he welcomed her warmth and scent, wrapping his arms around her torso.

"I know. I'm sorry too. It was a shock to have him touch you out of the blue. And I should have warned you that my uncle would try to bait you. I let them lull me into a false sense of security."

"What are you going to do now? I guess I better start packing my bags."

"You can pack your bags and mine. We are going to stay in another hotel. They won't be able to get their hands on you as long as you are not here."

"You shouldn't have to do that, Ben. That's going to look very odd to people. This is your home. Your family home. I can't let you become the gossip of your town."

"And I can't let you fly back to London even before you've had time to see the rest of Stellenbosch or South Africa. And remember we're supposed to stop over at Freetown on the way back to pick up your brother."

"True. I guess I could go to Freetown instead of London."

"No. I'm not letting you go there alone."

"In that case, there's only one thing for it. You have to collar me."

Ben froze.

"What are you talking about? You just said you didn't want to be collared."

"Your uncle has a point. I've been looking at the whole collaring thing the wrong way. Okay, maybe in London I wouldn't want to walk around with a collar around my neck. People wouldn't understand especially in the kind of environment I work. But here, it is the accepted norm. I am proud to belong to you, Benjamin and I don't mind everyone knowing it."

The corners of his lips lifted. He couldn't believe what he was hearing. Would it take his uncle's intervention to get Selina to wear his collar willingly?

"Selina, don't joke about this."

"I'm not joking. I want to wear it if you think I'm suitable."

"Of course, you are suitable. But you realize, once I put a collar on you, it stays on for the duration of our trip. It means you become a submissive, twenty-four hours of the day, seven days a week."

She bit her lower lip and nodded. "I understand."

He exhaled. His heart was pounding so hard.

Chapter Six

"You know you don't have to kneel for me when Ben isn't around," Selina said three days later as she sat on the sofa drinking lemon tea with Margo. The woman had practically been her shadow since they'd arrived.

Selina fiddled with the leather play collar around her neck. It was padded underneath and made from soft leather, making it exceptionally comfortable to wear for long periods.

Benjamin had put it on her the night they'd arrived, in the presence of his family.

There seemed to be satisfaction all round that she was wearing a collar. His uncle had nodded in approval as she knelt in a black corset and short skirt before the little group for the collaring.

The last few days had passed without more drama. Ben had taken her to visit one of the local wineries for a tasting, and they'd also bought some wines. She was excited to see the way they made the expensive wines she and Ben drank in London. She hadn't realized they'd been made in his hometown.

"I'm so used to being on my knees I don't even have to think about doing it," Margo said as she rose and settled on the sofa opposite.

"I can imagine," Selina replied, taking a sip as she mused. The past few days had been a shock to her body continually being used, and mostly on her knees.

She loved being dominated by Benjamin, and to be honest, he wasn't a hard man to please. But she couldn't imagine what it would feel like to be Margo, available to any dominant who came along.

"I don't know how you do it? How do you keep safe? How do you trust that the Dom you play with will not hurt you?"

"I'm a house slave. The Ranch protects me. There are security cameras in every playroom, and the team ensures everyone is safe."

"But what about in the suites. Like in here. If Ben was mean and hurtful, they wouldn't be able to stop him."

"There are also cameras in all the suites."

"What? In here?"

"Yes." Margo nodded with a smirk.

Selina's cup clattered to the floor and smashed.

People were watching her. Even now. They'd seen her naked. Seen the scars on her body.

"Are you okay?" Margo knelt on the floor, picking up the pieces of bone china.

"Where is Ben? I need to talk to him."

"He is in a meeting with Uncle and Lars."

She sat up abruptly. "I need to get out of here."

"Master's instructions were clear. We were not to leave the apartment until his return."

"I don't care."

Selina walked over to where her sandals lay and put them on. She picked up her cardigan and put it on over her dress.

At the door, she turned back to Margo, who had deposited their cups in the sink and cleared out the broken pieces.

"Are you coming?"

"You do realize we'll both be punished for this?"

"Are you afraid of a little punishment?" Selina eyed the woman.

"No. In fact, I'm well overdue for some caning," Margo said as she put on her shoes.

Selina winced. "You really do like pain. None of that for me, thank you."

"Eh, news flash. The whole point of punishment is that you don't enjoy it."

"Not for me. No caning, No whipping. I can just about cope with a flogger or paddle, but that doesn't hurt as much."

"You mean Master Benjamin has never used a whip on you?"

Selina shook her head.

"You don't know what you're missing."

"I'll take your word for it. Let's get out of here."

***

"In a few days Selina and I are going to Freetown to pick up her brother and then we're going back to London," Ben said, sitting in Leonard's den.

"Your life is not in London. It is here," his uncle replied. "There's nothing that you get in London you can't have here. Plus, there is the business."

"I have my own business now, and we're doing quite well."

"Yes, I know. I've been keeping a tab on you."

Ben shrugged. He didn't expect anything less from the man.

"But I'm not going to be around here forever. You are going to have to take over soon."

"I don't want any part of the business."

"It is Moss Enterprises. Your heritage. You are in line to take over."

"Why me? Lars is as much a son to you as I am. And he's been here running the operations."

"Lars is a good man. But he isn't you. He isn't my blood. You are."

The way his uncle said that should have clued him up on what was coming next, but nothing prepared him for it.

"I know you see me like a son and you are my father's brother but seriously, give this to Lars. He deserves it much more than I do. And I'm sure he wants it a lot more than I do."

"Lars may deserve it, but you are entitled to it. It is yours."

"For heaven's sake, Uncle. Have you not been listening to me? I don't want it. Why can't you understand? I have a different life now, and I want different things. I want to settle down. Selina makes me happy, and I want to make a family with her. Not here—"

"No. You cannot make babies with that girl. I forbid it."

"You forbid it?" Ben shook his head as he stared, mouth agape at the man, and stood. "I think you must be going senile if you think you can control my life. I give you respect because, at one point in my life, I looked upon you as a father. I came here out of the regard I once had for you. But do not insult my wife or me. You have no right to do that."

"I have every right to do as I please because I made you."

"What did you say?"

"You are my son."

Ben staggered backwards as if he'd been punched in the stomach. The old man had finally lost his mind.

"I know you think of me as a son, but you are not my father. My dad, your brother, died in a car crash years ago. Remember?"

Leonard stared straight at him, not blinking. "The man you called Dad was not the one who sired you. I did."

"No." He shook his head. That would mean that Leonard had an affair with his mother. "No. It can't be. You're trying to screw with my head. This is low even for you, Leonard." He used the man's given name, suddenly sickened that someone he'd respected so much would be this devious. "I know you want me to stay, but you don't have to make up stories."

"You think it's a story?" The man glared at him and reached into a drawer on the desk in front of him. He pulled out a leather-bound notepad and tossed it at the table. "Well, you don't believe me. Perhaps you will believe your mother."

Ben eyed the notepad. "What is that?"

"Your mother's journal. Take it. Read it." The man stood and took his walking stick. He leaned on it more than usual as he plodded to the window, turning his back on Ben, dismissing him.

Ben unclenched his fists, snatched the journal, and stormed out of the office. He would be damned if he was going to read it in the man's presence.

Back in the suite, he tossed the book on the coffee table and paced up and down a couple of times before he discovered that Selina and Margo were not there. He picked up the phone by the kitchen wall and dialled reception.

"This is Benjamin," he spoke when the girl at the desk picked up. "Have you seen my wife or Margo?"

"They both left the premises a while ago, Sir."

"When they return—" he thought for a moment "—send them to the dungeon immediately."

What were the two women up to that they would blatantly disobey his instructions to wait for him? He'd planned to take them out for the day after his meeting with his uncle. He hadn't designed for it to drag on. Regardless, they should have been patient and waited.

Now, it didn't seem like he would go out anyway. Not with the journal sitting on the table daring him to open it, to find the secrets within.

He eyed it malevolently.

He remembered the journal. It had been very private to his mother. She used to love writing in it, and when she finished, she would lock it away in the safe in her bedroom.

He'd been tempted to break into the safe and read it. His respect for his mother and her privacy had stopped him. When she'd died, he'd looked for the journal, but it hadn't been among her personal items after the funeral. Now he knew why.

The back of his eyeballs hurt and a lump formed in his throat. He'd loved her so much.

Her mother had worshipped his dad. He remembered all the stories she'd told him about the sort of man he'd been, good and loving.

Now Leonard was telling him that what he knew about his mother and his father were lies. There was a straightforward way to prove the man wrong.

He eyed the journal.

What if the contents had been changed? It wasn't beyond the man's capabilities to produce a fake journal and claim it belonged to Ben's mother.

Ben picked it up and first examined the leather of the cover. The nicks and scratches he remembered from his mother's old journal were evident. The leather was old and worn.

He lifted it and closed his eyes, sniffing. The faint scent of Chanel No5, his mother's perfume and an underlying fragrance he linked with his mother floated into his nostrils.

He pictured his mother, reclining on a chaise lounge, in a floppy sun hat and dark sunglasses that reminded him of Audrey Hepburn in Breakfast at Tiffany's. She would smile at him as he approached after school and give him a big squeeze before pouring him a glass of homemade lemonade.

And then she would chat with him about his day while locking the journal back into her safe.

Once he'd asked her if he could see what she wrote in it and she'd smiled brightly and replied, "Not yet, Ben. You wouldn't understand. When you're grown up and a man, then you can read it."

And he'd prayed to grow up quickly. That wish had come unexpectedly, as he'd grown up fast after she died.

But growing up hadn't meant maturity. Just the right to do whatever he pleased when he wanted.

He held the journal to his chest as if was hugging his mother, hoping to divine the mysteries it hid without having to open it. As a boy, he'd been eager to read its content. Now a man, his heart heavy and stomach twisted, he struggled to bring himself to open it.

What was he so afraid of?

The implications. If Leonard was telling the truth, then Ben's life as he'd known it had all been based on falsities. His values and belief, his family, and his life—what made him a man.

He'd never procrastinated over anything. Yet one little book was threatening to turn him inside out.

He sucked in a deep breath, unclasped the binder, and started reading.

***

Selina and Margo spent the day window shopping at the local shops and then had a late lunch in one of the cafes. After they strolled through a park to the river.

They were talking and laughing when they bumped into each other, and Margo kissed Selina. She tasted of the strawberries and wine, which she'd had at lunch. After the initial shock, Selina pulled back, breaking the kiss.

"What was that for?" Selina asked with a frown.

"I wanted to find out what your lips tasted like," replied Margo. "I've been dying to kiss you since the other day."

Selina blushed and looked away, embarrassed.

"I'm sorry. I didn't mean to make you uncomfortable."

"It's okay. It's just...just that I've never been with a woman before you. Never kissed a girl."

"Oh, really." Margo looked surprised. "Then, I'm really sorry. When Master Benjamin was here, he used to love getting his women to make out. He and Master Christopher used to make quite a pair."

She paused to stare at the steady flow of water along the river.

"I'm surprised he hasn't introduced you to his orgies. You must be special." She gave a wry smile. "I better get you back to the Ranch before he thinks I'm leading you astray."

Margo turned and walked back the way they came.

"Wait up," Selina said and caught her arm. "Look, I'm sorry. I didn't mean to be abrupt earlier. I liked kissing you. But I would rather do it with Ben's permission. That way, I don't feel as if I'm cheating on him."

"You two are monogamous?"

"Yes. Well, when we're in the UK. But for the time we're here we've agreed to explore a few other things. But we can't interact sexually with others without each other's knowledge."

"No problem. So, if he gives his permission, I can kiss you?" Margo traced a finger down Selina's cheek. A tingle ran down her spine.

"Yes. I guess so."

"Good." Margo met her gaze and intense heat flared in her emerald eyes. "Because I'm looking forward to fucking you."

Selina's cheeks burned. "Sorry. I hope you don't mind me asking a foolish question, but how does a girl fuck a girl?"

Margo laughed. "It's not foolish at all. With my tongue—" she wagged her tongue and did a fucking action with her two middle fingers "—fingers and of course, the good old strap-on."

Selina's eyes widened.

"I look forward to initiating you. I promise I'll be gentle." And Margo laughed some more.

"So why are you not in a relationship? Surely you want your own man or woman." Selina asked in the car on the way back to the Ranch.

"Why settle for one when I can have my pick of any man or woman that takes my fancy." Margo shrugged.

"Don't you get tired of it all? Surely everyone wants someone who cares about them enough to give up all else."

"I did once. A long time ago." Margo had a melancholic glaze in her eyes. "But the person didn't feel the same way about me."

"I'm so sorry. That must have hurt. Is the person still around? Maybe they'll change their mind if you tell him how you feel."

"I doubt if that's going to work."

"Why not?"

"The person is Benjamin."

"Oh," Selina said and looked out of the passenger side window, unsure of what else to say to Margo. To find out the woman had been in love with her husband was disturbing.

"Look. It's water under the bridge. I was just a kid, and he was my first Dom. Teenage crush, that's all. I've moved on, and Benjamin never looked at me that way. Not the way he looks at you. And he's not going to start now. So, don't worry about it. I'm definitely not going back there."

Selina nodded. "Okay. But if he wanted to have sex with you, would you want to?"

"I doubt that'll happen." Margo dismissed with the wave of a hand.

"What if he did?" Selina insisted.

Margo parked the car in the carport and put the handbrake on before turning to face Selina and meeting her gaze.

"Since you arrived, with his permission, I've watched him fuck you, while stuffed with toys. I've brought myself off. I've even sucked you and watched you blow him. But in that time, he's never touched me sexually."

Margo reached across and squeezed Selina's shoulder.

"And he never will unless you tell him to. He cares about your feelings. Something he never did with any other person."

"If I say yes, you will?"

"Hell, yeah. A man who packs as much heat between his legs as he doesn't come around often."

Selina blushed. She really had to get used to the directness of these people.

Margo laughed and opened the car door. "Come on. It's time to face the music."

At the reception lobby, the man behind the counter stopped them. "I have a message from Master Benjamin. You are both to go straight to the medieval room as soon as you return."

"Thank you," Margo said and turned to a frowning Selina with a smile. "We're in trouble."

"Uh, oh." Selina covered her mouth with her hand as Margo led her down the hall.

Windowless and with exposed brown bricks and stone flooring, the medieval room was the least welcoming of all the playrooms. Chains hung from pulley systems attached to the high ceiling. A St. Andrews cross stood against one wall. Benches and tables and another wall with tools of torture on display—whips, floggers, paddles, canes, all made from different materials, leather, wood, rubber. There were drawer units below, and she didn't dare imagine what was in them.

Margo picked up a note pad on the table and read it out loud.

"Take all your clothes off and kneel. Both of you. Master Benjamin."

"No. He didn't write that."

"He did. Here." Margo handed over the note pad.

Selina read the note clearly written in Ben's masculine handwriting. There was no mistaking his instructions. Her heart jolted, her breathing choppy as panic rose.

She shook her head.

"What's the matter?"

"Ben knows I can't be naked in front of other people."

"You can't? Why?" Margo was already taking her shoes off. She placed them under the table before pulling her jumper over her head, revealing her black lace bra.

Selina envied the confident way she could undress without minding that someone else watched her.

"I just don't. I've never been naked before anyone else but Ben."

"That's true. I've never seen you totally naked. You always sleep in a teddy—panty-less, mind you. But still...his instruction was clear to me. This time I think he wants everything off."

Margo pulled off her trousers. Underneath she had a black thong. She folded her clothed neatly and placed them on the table.

"Look. If you really don't want to get naked, you can always use your safe word. But you better be sure about it because the alternative could be a lot worse."

What could be worse than having whoever was watching the camera feed seeing her scarred body? Seeing how repulsive she was.

Ben's infuriated image from the other night in London loomed large in her head. The night she'd described her body as ugly.

She closed her eyes and sucked in a ragged breath.

His punishment had been a lot worse—the pain of orgasm denial and loss from intimacy deprivation returned—and he'd still left her outside naked for the world to see. She never wanted to anger him like that or suffer those consequences again.

Opening her eyes, she puffed out a breath and with shaky hands took her clothes off.

Margo eyed her. "You changed your mind."

Selina nodded. "There are worse things than being naked."

She turned her back to Margo as she took the rest of her clothes off and folded them onto the table. Then she slowly turned around watching for Margo's reaction to her scars, trying to avoid being in full-frontal view of the camera. She trembled.

"Honey, you are beautiful regardless of those scars," Margo said. Even though there was a hint of sadness in her voice, her sincerity was evident in her eyes.

"You really think so?"

"Of course, I do. And the most important person is Master Benjamin. He loves you as you are, so stop worrying."

"But what about the people watching?"

"Hell, they don't matter. Now, we better get on our knees before Master gets in here."

They both lowered themselves.

"Damn. This floor is hard, and the room is cold."

Margo laughed. "Welcome to the dungeon."

Chapter Seven

The hissing sound of the door indicated that someone had opened it. Selina's heart raced off, thundering in her chest. Both she and Margo knelt with their backs to the door so they couldn't take a sneak peek to see who was there. And she didn't dare lift her head up from her position.

The smack of leather against stone indicated the person was moving, coming closer and her apprehension level spiked up. What if it wasn't Benjamin? Who else would dare to go into a room he'd already booked for his subs?

Shit.

Suddenly, she wished she was facing the other way. She wasn't good at this and panic rose from her stomach like a worm, wriggling its way to her throat.

She swallowed hard trying to quell it. She wouldn't disrupt her pose and disappoint Benjamin. No matter how long she had to stay in this uncomfortable position.

How long had they been there? There was no clock in the room that she could see. At least not from her position.

"So, the two naughty girls are eager for their punishments, I see."

Selina gasped. This wasn't Ben. She recognized the heavy male South African accent as Lars.

Black leather boots and trousers came into her line of vision and stopped.

Her heart thumped against her chest.

Did Benjamin know that Lars was in here? He'd sworn he wouldn't let Lars touch her. So, what was going on?

She wanted to raise her head and ask, but she didn't know Lars well enough to push her luck. She took her cue from Margo by tilting her eyes in the woman's direction.

The woman kept perfectly still. Margo always had a perfect pose and never fidgeted.

Unlike Selina.

Lars stood in front of her silently, as if waiting for something. He hadn't asked a question so she couldn't speak. Was he testing her? Seeing if she would slip up? Even more reason she couldn't. Ben would be disappointed anyway.

After what seemed like hours but was probably just seconds, he stepped away.

"So, Margo, tell me who is responsible for disobeying your master's instructions."

"It was my fault, Sir. I took Selina out to the shops."

"Is that so?"

What? What was Margo doing? Selina had been the one who suggested going out in the first place. If she hadn't, Margo wouldn't have driven her to the shops.

"May I speak, Sir," Selina said, hoping the man would give her audience.

"Speak."

"Sir, I was the one who wanted to go out. Margo only accompanied me so I would be safe."

"Look at me when you're speaking."

Selina lifted her head. Feeling self-conscious, she didn't raise her upper body although she felt awkward looking up at tall Lars from that angle. His face seemed miles away.

"And why would you disobey Benjamin's instructions?"

She squeezed her face in a frown. "I found out something which upset me, and I wanted to talk to Sir Benjamin, but he wasn't available. I decided to go out to clear my head."

"And what was it that upset you?"

"I would rather discuss it with him. Is he coming soon, Sir?"

"I'm the one asking the questions, Selina." He crossed his arms over his chest and raised one blond eyebrow.

"I'm sorry, Sir."

"Apology accepted." He took off his shirt and flung it over the back of a chair. "What is your safe word?"

She swallowed her gasp. She'd always thought Ben to be as beautiful as a Greek god, but he was nowhere near as golden as Lars. Lars reminded her of the Viking god, Thor. The British winter didn't allow anyone to keep a tan for longer. And Ben's was purely from the outdoors and so was Lars.

"Scars," she said.

"Good."

She swallowed again as she caught herself staring. She shouldn't be looking at Lars that way. Ben had already made it clear he wouldn't be giving his permission for Lars to touch her.

But the man was here, apparently with Ben's blessings if he was going to administer their punishment on Ben's behalf. How much leeway had Ben given him?

He walked over to the wall of implements and picked out a cane from the shelf and whipped it as if testing it. The sound zipped through the air right through Selina's body, and she shuddered.

Let him not choose that one.

"Selina, go over to the spanking table and position yourself." He zipped the cane through the air again.

Her eyes widened, her arousal replaced by apprehension. She froze on the spot even though her brain shut down. For one thing, moving would mean revealing all her body to Lars, never mind that people were watching her through the camera. But they were faceless and nameless, and she could imagine they didn't exist.

Lars, on the other hand, was flesh and bone in front of her. There was no way she could do this. Not without Benjamin. The sight and sound of the cane raised goosebumps on her flesh.

"What are you waiting for?"

"Sir, I can't."

Where was Ben? Was he so mad about her disobedience that he would do this? Send someone else in his place. It was probable common practice over here. But she wasn't used to doing this without Ben's presence. He was her anchor and safety net.

"You can't stand? Margo, help her up."

Margo rose from the floor.

"No!" She didn't know when the scream left her. "Scars!" For the first time in months, she yelled her safe word and started sobbing. "I need Benjamin. Please, Sir."

"Don't touch her," she heard Lars say to Margo.

She stayed prostrate on the floor and sobbed. Knowing she'd failed Ben. But also knowing unequivocally that she needed Ben to play. No one else could replace him. She didn't trust anyone else like she trusted him.

Moments later, Ben was on the floor beside her.

"Hey, Beauty." He lifted her and wrapped himself around her before settling onto the nearby bed. He let her cry, just holding her tightly and gently massaging her back in a circular motion. His warmth, his scent, his body, a safe harbour that finally settled her nerves.

"Tell me why you panicked," he said in a low voice.

"You weren't here," she murmured into his shirt.

His knuckle pressed under her chin, and she had to lift her head to scrutinise his face. He didn't appear angry or disappointed. Curious, perhaps.

"What did you say?" he asked.

She exhaled. "I panicked because you weren't here."

"Do you trust me?"

"Yes?"

"Do you trust that I will always protect you?"

"Yes, of course, Benjamin." She fidgeted with his shirt, feeling guilty now.

"Did you understand that Lars was here on my behalf, that he had my permission to be here?"

"Not at first. But eventually, yes, I did."

"Then you should've known that he wouldn't do anything I wouldn't have wanted him to do."

She frowned.

"Yes," she said with hesitation. "I knew that, but he was waving the cane, and he asked me to go over to the spanking bench. He was going to cane me."

"And?"

She looked up at him, and he looked annoyed. She frowned again. Had he really asked Lars to cane her?

"I'm sorry, Benjamin."

"Since you used your safe word, I have to find an alternative punishment suitable for you. Are you feeling better?" He was all business now.

"Yes, Benjamin."

"Kneel on the bed between my legs."

She scooted off his lap, knowing he wouldn't take any arguments, grateful that he'd come to her when she'd safe-worded. Now he was here she felt safe and able to cope with whatever was going to happen.

When she turned around Lars was strapping Margo to the St Andrew Cross. They'd been there all along, and she'd thought they'd left Ben and her alone in the room.

Lars wasn't looking at her as she climbed back onto the bed and knelt as Ben instructed. He spoke to Margo in low guttural Afrikaans. There was something about the way they interacted with each other; Selina could swear there was some tension.

Perhaps it was her heightened imagination, creating illusions that didn't exist.

"Lars is going to cane Margo, and you're going to count them out."

Oh no! That meant she had to watch and concentrate. She always cringed when they watched anyone receiving corporal punishment. She would find it hard to focus.

"You should pay attention. For every count you miss, is an hour away from orgasm you get. And when I eventually fuck you, it will be to an audience."

Huh? An audience? How many people? How was she going to do this when she was terrible at it?

"Pay attention," he said in a low voice before saying louder for Lars's attention. "Ready when you are, Lars."

Lars looked in their direction and nodded.

Selina wished she could hide. She pulled her hands to cover her stomach. Ben held her hands onto her thighs, keeping her and her scars exposed. Her heart thundered.

Lars didn't even seem to notice. If he did, his expression didn't change. He appeared to be in a zone of his own. He picked up a wooden paddle which he used to tap Margo's skin all over her back. She understood what he was doing. He was warming the skin up, preparing it for the sharper sting of something else.

The cane.

All the while, Margo just made small moaning noises, as if she was enjoying it.

Lars put the implement down and picked up the cane. He flipped it through the air and Selina flinched, closing her eyes. Then she opened them in a panic. Had she missed a count?

Phew. Luckily, that had been just a test. Lars stood behind Margo, to the side. At the same time, Ben's fingertips marched down her belly towards her centre like little soldiers. Her breath hitched when he stopped at the apex.

The first lash landed in the middle of Margo's right bum. At the same time, Ben's finger slid between her lower lips.

"One," she said in a breathless voice.

The second cane landed just under the first one. Margo swayed in her cuffs, the links jingling. Ben's finger did a slow circle around her clit. She bit her lip.

"Two."

Three and four came close together, and she counted them out. Concentrating was difficult with Ben's fingers playing with her folds.

Her body got wet. But because he didn't engage her clit or sink into her slit, she managed to maintain the needed focus. Just about.

Red stripes began to colour Margo's back.

At number ten, Lars paused and admired his handiwork. Ben's fingers plunged into her wet opening. Caught by surprise, she moaned out loud and gyrated her hips. He withdrew and slammed back in, fucking her with vigour. She couldn't stop her moans or her hips gyrating as her pleasure climbed and the wet sound of his fingers slamming into her filled the air.

He stopped, pressing the heel of his palm against her clit. She whimpered.

"You are not permitted to come," he said in a husky voice to her ear. "You've missed two counts already."

She opened her eyes and saw the cane landing on Margo's lower back. Lars was now using his left hand. Poor Margo. An ambidextrous Lars won't be getting tired anytime soon. And it looked like he meant to mark every part of her back with red stripes.

"That was number thirteen." Ben's words whispered against her sensitive neck.

"Thirteen," Selina counted as she panted.

"Good you could join us again, Selina," Lars said with a smirk spread across his face.

Ben continued ministrations, alternating between fucking, and teasing her and always keeping her away from a much-needed orgasm. She managed to concentrate and count out until it got to thirty.

Margo couldn't stand as Lars released her from the cuffs, her body covered in red welts and sweat. With glassy eyes, she appeared spaced out, although there was a hint of a smile on her face.

Lars wrapped a blanket around her, placed on his lap and gave her water from a plastic bottle.

Selina watched, amazed to see such a tender moment from two people she'd come to associate with hardcore BDSM. Margo didn't look like the kind of person who would want anyone to cuddle her. But here Selina had the proof.

The two of them seemed to be in a world of their own as Lars spoke to Margo in Afrikaans.

"He is going to fuck her," Ben said in a distant voice, his hand covering Selina's mound but not teasing anymore. "We can go unless you want to watch them."

Cheeks heating, Selina turned to face Ben, her body primed for sex. Hadn't he said he would fuck her to an audience?

Seeing his shadowed expression and it dawned on her. Something was off with him. He would usually just make the decision, and the Ben she knew would stay and watch or bring her off in the process. He didn't seem to be there, although he was physically present.

Abruptly he stood and dug into his trouser pocket. He withdrew Margo's leash and walked towards where Margo straightened off Lars lap. As soon as she saw him, she prostrated.

"Master Benjamin," Margo said.

"On your feet, Margo," Ben said. "I am your Master no more. I rescind all rights and responsibilities towards you. You are free to choose your new Master."

"May I ask why...Sir?" She hesitated as if debating how to address him.

Ben smiled. "It has been fun getting reacquainted this past week, but I believe this is for the best. I hope you understand."

"I do. Thank you, Sir."

"You are welcome." He handed the leash to her. "I think there might be someone interested in taking up the role of your master. I hope you'll be on your best behaviour for him."

For the first time, Selina saw Margo smile almost shyly. "I'll try."

Ben laughed before turning to Lars. "I won't tell you to be gentle with her because she probably won't like it. But take care of her."

Lars nodded but didn't say anything.

Ben walked back to where Selina still knelt on the bed. He scooped her up without saying a word and headed for the door. Lars tossed him a blanket which he used to cover her.

Selina was grateful to be in his arms but somehow sad that she wouldn't see more of Margo in their suite any longer. She wondered why Ben made the decision to let her go.

Ben didn't say anything and Selina was simply happy to have the hardness of his body and his warmth. Back in the suite, he settled her on his lap and just held her. Ben ordered dinner, and they sat and ate and watched the sun go down with only the terrace lights in the semi-darkness.

In her heart, she knew something was wrong but fear stopped her from raising the topic. Had she really messed up by safe-wording? Was he still upset because she'd disobeyed his order by leaving The Ranch premises with Margo?

The whole point of discipline was to wipe the slate clean of a demerit. To start afresh. Ben had never been one to bear a grudge. Once they discussed the issue and he meted out punishment, her transgression would be nullified.

So, it couldn't be the reason for his withdrawn mood.

That night he loved her and fucked her in equal measures. One moment he bound her hands to the bedpost. He fucked her hard and fast from behind while holding her head down, leaving them slick with sweat and juices. Another they were wrapped up in each other, grinding slowly or cuddling, with the brisk night air cooling their hot skins.

Before she fell asleep, the following words from him stuck in her mind.

"I can't always be around to hold your hand physically. But you must trust that wherever I am that I'll always work to keep you safe, even if I'm not present."

And she slept, knowing he would always be with her.

The next morning he woke her with his head between her legs and she was screaming her first orgasm when he buried his thick length inside her, her legs pushed all the way back so that her knees touched her shoulders.

"Hold onto the back of your knees," he said.

He rammed into her so deeply, she felt as if he would nail her to the bed. She was open and vulnerable, the way she loved to be with him. Each thrust permeating every fibre of her body.

She loved this Benjamin. He was beautiful in his masculinity, in his dominance, in his control. Her body didn't know any other way to respond to him but in submission.

"Whom do you belong to, Beauty?" He groaned.

"You, Benjamin."

He lowered his head and gave her a bruising kiss. Pulling out, he flipped her onto her hands and knees. Then he rammed in, all the way to the hilt.

She came with an almighty shout. He didn't wait for her to land as he fucked her hard, using her body even as her pleasure rose again.

His hands tightened on her hips when she finally heard him grunt and thrust himself to oblivion. They both collapsed on the bed, their bodies slick with sweat. He didn't put his weight on her and supported himself on his elbows and lower arms. Then he rolled to the side as he caught his breath.

"I love you, Lina," he whispered against her shoulder and kissed the flesh.

His declaration always knocked her breath out, making her own reply breathless. "I love you, Ben."

She smiled, content and happy in the moment, her body sated and aching because of the hard way he'd taken her several times last night and this morning. A knock on the door had her moaning.

"Who could that be at this hour?" It was early although she couldn't be bothered to check the time.

Ben rolled out of bed and pulled on his trouser. "That'll be Margo."

Margo?

"I thought you released her."

Ben tossed a bathrobe onto the bed. "I did. She volunteered to come and help us pack."

Huh? Selina pushed her body onto her elbows and got to her knees.

Ben had already disappeared behind the screen as he walked over to the front door.

"Ben, what's going on?"

"Good morning, Sir," she heard Margo's chirpy voice. "I brought the dry cleaning."

"Morning, Margo. Selina is in bed," Ben said.

Selina pushed her arms through the bathrobe sleeves and tied the sash before stepping around the screen and waving at Margo. "Hi, Margo. Thanks for collecting the laundry."

"You're welcome," Margo said as she sashayed over and lowered the packs of cellophane-wrapped clothes on the bed.

"I love the well-fucked look you've got on," Margo said in a low, conspiratorial voice.

Selina's cheeks heated up.

"I could say the same thing about you," she remarked.

"I'd tell you all about it, but Sir wants me to pack your bags, and you know how much of a slave driver he is," she said in a Chinese whisper.

"I heard that." Ben laughed. He pulled Selina, so her back was moulded into his chest. "It's shower time."

His warm breath against her exposed neck awakened all her nerve endings.

She followed him into the bathroom. "Where are we going?"

"I'm taking you away from here. I need some time alone with you," he said ominously before kissing her.

Shower time was hot and sensual and long. By the time they finished, Margo had packed their bags and was sorting out breakfast. They dressed quickly and settled down to enjoy the meal that Margo had prepared.

When they headed out, Uncle Leonard and Inge came to bid them farewell. Lars drove them to Cape Town. They spent the day sightseeing. The next day they flew out to Port Elizabeth and spent a day there before flying up to Durban and then Bloemfontein.

Five days after they left Stellenbosch, they were in Johannesburg.

"South Africa is amazing and beautiful," Selina said as they relaxed in the hotel suite. "I wish we had more time to see all of it. We'll come back, won't we?"

"Yes." Ben cleared up the tray of food they'd been eating and left it for housekeeping to pick up. When he returned, his expression was blank. "We need to talk."

"Oh-kay."

With a grave expression, he sat on the sofa opposite and faced her. "I'm not going back to London with you."

Her heart stopped, and her head lightened.

"There are some things I need to do here. I won't be returning to London for a while. I'm not sure how long."

This can't be happening. She'd known things were off for days now. Since the day they left Stellenbosch. But this?

"Are you breaking up with me?" She blinked several times, trying to stop the tears building up behind her eyes from falling.

"What are you talking about?"

"Is it something I've done? I don't understand what's going on, Ben?"

He was beside her on the sofa in the blink of an eye, holding onto her hands.

"Selina, look at me."

She lifted her gaze from where he held her hands. His serious expression made her breath catch, and his eyes showed his concern.

"We are not breaking up."

"Promise?" She struggled to speak, lost for words.

"I promise you with all that I am. We are not breaking up. You belong to me and I to you. I'm not about to let you go."

Her shoulders slumped in relief at his welcome words, and her hands trembled. "Then, what's going on? And don't tell me nothing because I know something is wrong."

His sigh hung in the air, heavy and forlorn.

"Yes, something is wrong."

She waited for him to tell her the rest, her heart thumping against her chest, her lungs tight as she struggled to breathe normally.

"You know how I told you about my father dying when I was a boy."

"Yes, you mentioned he had a car crash."

"Well, it turns out he wasn't my father...at least not my biological father."

"Really?" Selina frowned. "If he wasn't your father then who is?"

Ben shook his head. "Uncle Leonard."

Selina's mouth dropped open, her eyes wide, and her hands slack as shock raced through her.

"You're not kidding, are you?"

"No. I found out a week ago."

No wonder he'd been so closed off. His world had turned upside down.

"Oh. My. God." She covered her mouth with her hand. She didn't even know how to respond to this news. Was it a thing of joy or sorrow? She studied her husband's face, but he had his inscrutable mask on, and she couldn't read him.

"Ben, how did you find out? Why are you just finding out now?"

"Uncle Leonard told me. I didn't believe him. Then, he gave me my mother's old journal. I read it."

He stood up and walked to the window, staring out sightlessly. He looked so lost as if unsure of himself. Uncertain of how to take the new development.

Her throat ached; her shoulders heavy in sympathy for him. After a while of stony silence, Selina went to him. She wrapped her arms around his torso, offering him comfort from behind.

"My uncle and my mother had been lovers before she married my father. He wanted to make her his fulltime slave. She didn't want the lifestyle even though she loved him. She chose to marry his brother instead. My uncle never forgave her for it and never left her alone. Even after she was married, he returned to coerce her into a relationship." Ben sucked in a ragged breath, tremors raging through his body.

Selina tightened her grip around him, wanting him to know she'd be here for him no matter what.

"You know I have memories of him visiting us. We lived in Johannesburg. My father—the man I knew as Papa—worked here. All that time Leonard had been having an affair with my mother. And she had seemingly been unable to stop it." Ben's voice sounded strained, angry. His muscles tensed beneath her touch.

"You couldn't have known," she said in a soothing voice.

"They hid it from everyone, although Mama wrote about it in her journal. Apparently, they'd found out I wasn't my father's son because I had been in the hospital for a sports injury requiring a blood transfusion. After being tested, my blood hadn't matched Papa's. Uncle had volunteered and tested, and it had been a match. Afterwards, my father and Leonard had argued. My father left in anger and crashed the car the same day."

The pain, in his words, lanced through her. "I'm so sorry, Ben."

"You know, after my father died, Leonard became a father figure in my life. I respected and admired him as one. He saw me through tough teenage years. He practically took care of my mother, me, and Beatrice as if we were his own. And now I find out that we were really his. And everything I'd ever known and valued had been based on lies."

Grabbing her hands, he pried them wide as he swivelled.

"The man that I am is based on those things that I thought I knew. Now, I'm not sure about anything. I don't know who I am anymore." He rubbed the back of his neck as the skin bunched around his eyes.

She recognized the anguish in his voice. She'd been there before and felt the despair he was going through now. He'd replaced her suffering with hope, taken her mistrust and given her confidence.

"I know who you are, Ben." She gripped his arms, making him look into her eyes so he could see the sincerity of her words. "You are a good man, strong and steadfast, generous and caring. You gave me back my life, gave me the confidence to walk in the light when I had been living in shadows with fear. You are the man that I love, and I trust you, implicitly."

Both his palms settled either side of her face, and he tilted her head up, pinning her with his intense gaze.

"I love you too, Selina. This is exactly the reason I must do this. I don't want to be in a situation where I break your trust. It's taken us a long time to get to this point. I am not going to jeopardize it because of the way I'm feeling now. I'm furious. Hurting. I want to lash out. Or go back to being the narcissistic person who didn't give a shit about anyone. And I'm afraid I'm going to take it out on you."

He blew out a harsh breath. "If I do that, you will leave me and then who will I be? Nobody."

"I know you are hurting, Ben. What kind of person would I be if I left you when you needed me most? We can work this out. Together."

"Please, Lina. Give me some time to work this through. I want to be the man you need, the man you can rely on. I'm not that person right now. My head is all over the place. This break will be good for you and me."

"You and I being on different continents is not good. How can I be there for you when I'm not able to see you," she said in a flat, monotone voice as sadness seeped into her bones.

"You'll be fine. We'll be fine. Trust me." His tone lightened, the corner of his mouth lifting. "Just think about it like those times when I have to travel for work."

"But you're usually only away for days, and I know when you'll be returning."

"I'll try and make this separation as short as possible. I promise you we will keep in touch every day and the time will fly. And when I get back to

London, I want us to start working on making our own family."

"Family? You mean babies." Breathless, she gulped air and coughed." You want us to—" She frowned, a dark cloud looming over her.

"You want to have children, don't you?" he asked, worry lines etched deep on his forehead.

"I do. But what if I can't."

"Of course, you can. You're a healthy woman."

She bit her lip, worried that she wasn't woman enough to bear his offspring. "The attack messed me up both inside and out."

His jaw tightened visibly, and he pulled her into a tight hug. Head pressed against his chest, she heard the rhythmic beat of his heart, matching the thumping of hers.

"Don't worry about it," he said when he leaned back. "There are other options to explore as well, so we'll cross the bridge when we get to it."

She hoped it was as easy as that, but she couldn't help thinking there was more bothering Ben.

"Is your uncle...father—"

"Don't call him that, he might have made me, but he's not my father." Ben clenched his fists by his side.

Selina nodded. She could understand his attitude. "Did you tell Leonard about wanting us to have a family? Is he all right about it?"

She hadn't forgotten that the man was all about pure races. Any babies Selina and Ben had wouldn't be black or white. They'd be the combination of both, the best of them.

"Don't worry about what he said. It's not important."

"It's important to me. I want to know what my father-in-law thinks about us making babies, Ben."

"Fine," he bit out in frustration. "He thinks you're only good for one thing and that isn't bearing my children."

Selina closed her eyes tight, fighting back the tears. Her chest hurt. Her throat dry. After everything she did to try and fit in at The Ranch and to make Leonard like her, he still only saw her skin colour. Was that really the sum of who she was? A girl with brown skin?

"What did I ever do to that man? Why is he so mean?" Her voice sounded small, and for the first time since their trip to South Africa, she wished she hadn't come here.

Ben growled and folded her into his arms again. "This is why I need you in London, away from his poison. So that I can take care of business on this end and make sure he never hurts you again."

"But what about you, Ben? Who will be taking care of you? I know how manipulative that man can be from first-hand experience. Who's going to be there for you at the end of the day when you need to unwind?"

"We've got the phone. I'll call you all the time, and we can talk through any issues."

She nodded and smiled. "And will we be having any more phone sex like the day Beatrice arrived?"

"There'll be plenty of those. I can access the cameras in the apartment from my laptop anywhere in the world."

She had a full grin now. "Then I guess it won't be too bad."

He lifted his arm and glanced at his watch and pulled out his phone from his pocket, typing quickly on the screen.

"The downside is that I'm going to miss your birthday," he said.

"Well, that's okay as long as you make it up to me."

"That I plan to do starting from now."

"Now?"

A knock at the door had her looking in that direction.

"Yes." He pressed soft lips against her forehead before walking over to the door, a mischievous glint in his eyes. He opened it and her breath caught in her throat.

"Chris!" she shouted and ran across to hug the tall man with dark hair and blue eyes that had just crossed the threshold of their hotel suite. He dropped the black overnight bag he was carrying when their bodies collided. "What are you doing here?"

She leaned back to look up at his handsome face with features carved out of the Crimean Mountains.

"Good to see you too, sweetheart," Chris said with a laugh and put his arm around her shoulders as they walked further into the suite.

"Seriously, what's going on? I thought you were in London." She said, staring from Chris to her husband.

"I was—"

"He was in London, but I asked him to come here as a surprise for you," Ben said and walked to stand behind her. He swept her hair off one shoulder.

"A surprise for me?"

"You know how I said I would be making up for not being at your birthday next week? Well, this is your first birthday present. There will be more to come."

"Birthday present?" She loved seeing Chris again after two weeks of not seeing him. He was one of her closest male friends and Ben's best friend. So yes, it was good to see him, but she didn't understand how that was a birthday present.

"You know how you once told him you would love to be with more than one man at a time," Ben's words whispered against her sensitive neck.

Her breath caught in her throat, and her heart pounded. "Yes."

"And your confession to me last week about Lars finally got me to take action. We are about to fulfil that fantasy for you."

"You are?" she could barely get the words out of her suddenly constricted throat as her heart thundered and her cheeks heated up.

"I told you once we used to be a double act and I would never think about sharing you with anyone else but him. Would you like that?"

"Yes, Benjamin."

"Good girl."

Across from her Chris's eyes brightened and his lips curled in a sexy smile.

Chapter Eight

Selina couldn't believe it. Something she'd fantasized about for a long time was finally going to happen. She was going to have two men who meant more to her than anybody else.

She turned around to face Ben. Her husband stood tall, magnificent, her Greek god. He tilted her back around so that she now met Chris, the Slavic god with his dark features.

Chris lowered his tall, muscular body to one of the sofas in front of her while Ben settled his warm fingers on her shoulders. Slowly he massaged her skin in a long line from the juncture of her neck to her arms. She inhaled a deep breath, her body relaxing under his touch.

"That's it, Lina. Relax and let us take care of you."

Her body sighed at Chris's words. His tone had a deep lulling quality, and the strength in their depth could soothe her worries.

"Yes, Sir." She didn't know when the words slipped out. They just did. Naturally, as if she'd always said them.

Through her drooping lashes, she saw Chris exchange a glance with Ben, his lips curled in amusement.

Before she came to South Africa, she hadn't addressed either man with that term.

"Beauty has decided to embrace her submissive side more openly." She didn't miss the amusement in Ben's low voice as the skin on her neck prickled with the warmth of his breath. "And I welcome it."

"So do I," Chris said. "The Ranch always has that effect on people, they always embrace their true nature after a spell there."

He was correct.

The Ranch had been a shock to the system. It had changed her for the better.

Hands covered her breast, squeezing through the fabric of her clothes before Ben pinched her nipples. Body arched, she pushed into his hands, seeking more as her bum connected with the hard rock bulge in his trousers.

In front of her, Chris's gaze stayed on her, watching her body's response to Ben's ministrations, one pink tongue darting out to lick lush lips. At the same time, his arms stretched across the back of the sofa, his thighs relaxed and spread apart in a very masculine pose. She couldn't miss the very male tent in his jeans.

Desire watered her mouth, and she imagined going down on her knees and letting him take her mouth while Ben took her from behind.

"Remind us of your safe word, Beauty." Ben's voice was rough in her ears.

"Scars."

Gosh, she was already breathless, and they hadn't even done anything yet.

"This isn't going to be a heavy session," Ben said.

"I'm going to rope you," Chris said, sitting up.

She sighed. She wanted that very much.

"And I'm going to flog your bum."

Her breath hitched, and her eyes widened.

"Not as a punishment," Ben added. "Chris and I will enjoy having you submitting to whatever we want. And I know you'll enjoy it too."

His fingers squeezed her right bum cheek, and her insides contracted.

"And when you're ready, we'll fuck you."

I'm ready now she wanted to shout as her juices ran down her thigh. She was so horny she didn't really care what they did to her. Soon.

Ben's hands pushed the straps of her top down her arm, exposing her breasts. Cold air kissed her skin, pebbling her nipples. No matter how often her husband's manly hands roamed her body, she never got enough. She always craved more. Like she did now as his firm fingers slid under her ribs and cupped a plump breast each.

"Push your clothes down for me."

For a few heartbeats, Selina hesitated with the realization that she would be naked before Chris for the first time. Yes, they'd had sex before, but she'd never been bared before him.

Chris sat on the sofa watching her every move, perhaps wondering if she would obey her husband's instruction. Behind her, Ben said nothing, just squeezing her breasts and nibbling the skin on her neck as if he already knew her response.

She loved both men in different ways. Chris, as a friend who had always stood by her. He'd known she needed the intensity that Ben provided and had been happy to stand aside for his friend. For that, she would always love him.

And Ben was the man who saw beyond the barriers she'd put up. He'd done what no other man could do. Stripping her bare and exposing her true self and loving her regardless of her darkness and damage. She would love him till the day she died. And she needed to show him as much.

Hooking her trembling fingers into her top, she pulled it down along with her skirt, past the indented curve of her waist and hips. After that point, they fell to pool at her feet.

She kept her gaze on Chris, watching his response. There was no flinch of disgust. Instead, his smile broadened. He rubbed hands along his thigh, which drew her attention back to the bulge in his jeans. It seemed to have become enormous.

Her eyes widened as she glanced back at his face. The expression there was of pure hunger.

"Step out."

She lifted one leg to the side and moved across, abandoning her clothes in a pile.

Her breathing quickened, her heart thumping against her chest. Both men desired her, scars, and all. After the attack, she'd never thought she would live through a moment like this, even though she'd fantasized about it. A part of her had always wanted the double validation, of two men desiring her totally.

"Isn't she beautiful?" Ben asked, warm air from his deep voice feathering her shoulder.

"Absolutely." The awe in Chris's voice matched her husband's. He stood and scooped her clothes off the floor, tossing them on one of the sofas before walking over to where he'd abandoned his overnight bag. "And she'll look stunning wrapped up in our rope."

"Well done," Ben whispered against her cheek.

With one hand tugging the knot holding her hair so that her face was turned to the side, he covered her lips with his, his hunger apparent in his kiss. Pure ecstasy zinged in her veins. The palm of the other hand covered her mound, fingers slipping between the swollen lips.

"She is so eager," Ben said as he raised his fingers covered in her essence. He placed them against her mouth. Her scent filled the air.

She opened and sucked them in, tasting her musk. Eyes closed, she moaned out loud, rocking back her hips and rubbing against Ben's.

"Do you want to come?" The low growl of his voice only helped to raise her arousal to another level.

"Yes...please, Sir."

"When she's this good, she deserves a reward for her trust and submission," Ben said.

"And I'm happy to give her what she deserves. Spread your legs."

Hands wrapped around her hips. She opened her eyes to find Chris on his knees. He tapped the inside of her thigh, and she shifted her legs wide apart. Her body flushed with heat, the hammering of her heart loud to her ears.

Without preamble, Chris lifted her right leg, hooked it over his left shoulder and dived into her sex with his mouth. She'd forgotten how masterful he was with his sinful tongue.

Between his decadent actions and Benjamin's masculine body behind her, his hands strumming pleasurable torture to her breasts, she soon became ready to crest the wave of ecstasy.

Two dominant men working her body at the same time. She would die and go to heaven as they pinched, pulled, and prodded her sensitive areas. Pain and pleasure melded into flames of desire burning in her veins.

"You're not going to come again until we're both inside you, Lina," Ben said. "Make this count."

"Oh!" She let out one never-ending scream of pleasure, her body rocking back and forth as she came. Again, and again. They didn't let up until they rang the third orgasm out of her and she was slumped against Ben.

The sound of a zipper made her open her eyes. Chris pulled out a beautiful ruby silk coiled rope from the bag. It was still wrapped in the maker's box and logo, implying that it had never been used.

"I ordered this to be designed especially for today, and Chris picked it up on his way here."

"It's beautiful," she said, her voice choked. "Thank you."

Of all Ben's kinks, the Shibari bonds were her favourite. It was also her kink. She loved the sensual feeling when he tried out new patterns on her body. The rope was in her favourite colour. Her wedding dress had been in the same hue.

"You are welcome," he said. "Can you stand?"

"Yes, Sir."

Stepping back, Ben released her body. She lost his warmth and strength and wanted to shift backwards but knew better. She had to remain still. A shiver ran down her spine with cold and anticipation. She was so ready for what both men had in store for her.

"Are you ready?" Chris asked.

"Yes," she breathed out.

Chris removed the packaging, unfurling the rope. Then he draped it around her shoulder. She'd always loved red tones, and this ruby complimented her dark skin brilliantly. Her husband understood her so well. She had to blink a few times to stop tears of happiness dripping from her eyes.

Chris knotted the rope at her throat and made a chain of knots to the apex between her thighs. The rope dangled from her neck like a beautiful long necklace.

"Lift your hands to the sides."

She obeyed.

At her back, Ben caressed her skin as he moved his hands across to settle in front. He looped a separate piece of rope, passing it through the knots Chris had already made and then pulling them around to her back to form the shape of a kite.

He wrapped a few more pieces of rope around her the same way, repeating the pattern until her torso was covered in the gorgeous, knotted rope the shape of diamonds. Each point of rope contact felt like fingers massaging her. Between her legs, it felt like tongues licking her skin. Where the knot rubbed her clit, it felt like teeth nipping. Flames of desire lapped her body, and she nearly went mad from keeping still. A little bit more friction and she could come.

"Oh, God!" she moaned, remembering she couldn't come again until they were both inside her as Ben had said.

The diabolic grin on Chris's face confirmed her thought, and she knew Ben, behind her, was sporting the same smirk. They would make her wait for it this time.

Chris tugged the rope, pulling it between her legs. It scraped her sex as Ben attached it to the network of strings on her back and it nestled in the cleft of her bum.

Her breath hitched. Any movement and one knot tugged her clit while the rope pressed against her back opening like a finger. She panted, fighting hard not to detonate.

"She is stunning."

She couldn't miss the masculinity in Chris's voice nor the admiration and lust in Ben's eyes as both men circled her, admiring their handiwork. Ben walked over to the full-length mirror covering the wardrobe at the other end of the suite.

"Come here," he said. "Come and see how beautiful you are."

She took a step and suppressed a moan as the knots teased her clit and bum. With each step, the pressure increased, exciting her. If she squeezed her thighs, she was sure she would come. But she couldn't, knowing she had to wait and yet hovering at the edge of pure bliss. Her brain had already turned to mush. All she wanted—needed, was to come. The sooner they both fucked her, the better.

She stopped in front of the mirror and closed her eyes as she tried to calm her body.

"How do you feel?" Chris's deep voice reached out to her from behind.

"Good. Too good," she said, breathing hard. "I feel as if you're both caressing my body as if you're licking my sex. Yet neither of you are touching me. I need to come."

There was an edge of frustration in her voice.

Chris chuckled, and she felt his heat on her back, but he didn't touch her.

"No coming, Lina. Not yet."

"Open your eyes."

She did and stared at her body. Her heart skipped a beat and her breath caught in her throat. The intricate crisscross of rope all over her body looked like they had dressed her in rubies. Even the scars on her stomach looked like they were part of the design. She felt beautiful. Tears misted her eyes.

"Thank you, Sirs," she said, catching Ben's heated gaze and then Chris's in the mirror.

"Without the rope, you are beautiful, Lina," Chris said and kissed her neck.

"We just wanted you to see how beautiful you are both inside and out," her husband said.

She nodded, unable to speak as she realized for the first time in ten years that it was true. The fear she had felt, the self-disgust, all melted away. She would never doubt her husband again when he called her beautiful.

Chris tugged her back, and she followed him, the delicious torture of ropes resuming. "Kneel on the chair facing the back."

She climbed onto the single-seater upholstered armchair counterpart to the sofa and gripped the low back. Chris pulled his t-shirt off, revealing a torso of stiff muscles and fine black hair tapering into his trousers. She licked her lips, and he pulled at the buckle of his brown belt, undoing it.

Distracted by Chris, she didn't see Ben disappearing into the wardrobe until he came out with his black leather bag. He'd pulled his shirt off too. And she was reminded that she had the attention of two stunningly good-looking men, each wanting her.

Ben's hand was his leather flogger with long suede leather tails in black and red. Heart racing, her mouth dropped open. Fear shot through her body. He'd been serious about flogging her. She took a steady breath.

The truth was, she almost didn't care what they did to her. She was already at the point where she just didn't want them to stop.

"Keep your eyes on me," Chris said.

She obeyed.

He'd unclasped the buttons on his fly, and the edges of his jeans dangled, exposing black briefs stretched out by a huge bulge. Her mouth watered as he stepped close and pulled out his hard erection, the blunt head already beaded with pre-cum. She stared at it in awe. Euphoria spiked through her.

Chris stepped in front of her and laced his hands through her hair.

"Open wide, Lina." He placed the tip of his cock against her lips, and she opened her mouth. With a long, drawn-out stroke, she swirled her tongue around the head and sensitive underside of him. His denseness widened her lips, and his masculine taste coated her tongue. Having Chris in her mouth felt sinfully indulgent as a guttural, sexy sound filled the quiet hotel suite.

Cool strips of leather feathered her bare bottom, reminding her of Ben who stood behind her.

With her ample ass high in the air and nothing to cover herself, feelings of vulnerability mixed with pure decadence washed through her.

He caressed in circles along her skin and took his time going back and forth from one globe to another. His hand grabbed the rope that ran along her ass and sex, and she nearly came with a jolt.

She needed to beg again, but it was impossible to talk with Chris's cock stuffed in her mouth, and his hands in her hair, holding him all the way to the back of her mouth. Selina relaxed her throat and made her best attempt to swallow against his flesh.

"Fuck!" His hands tightened in her hair and the muscles in his body visibly tensed. "She's going to make me come."

It seemed like a lifetime ago since she'd rung that kind of response from Chris and her chest bloomed with pride. A stinging thud across her bottom fired an intense arc of pain from her backside to her clit. It hurt, in a terrific way, and she wanted him to do it again.

A deep ache built in her womb, her inner muscles contracting greedily. She needed Ben inside her too. Another blow from the flogger landed on the other side of her bum, making her cry out, her mouth tightening around Chris's length. An orgasm rose, pleasure razed through her until she thought she was set alight. Ben loosened the rope around her sex, and it dropped away to bring her some relief.

"Oh yes, Lina, suck my cock."

Encouraged by his urgent and unrestrained words, she carried out his instructions giving him the best blow she could. Hands gripped her thighs, spread her apart. With a slow thrust, Ben plunged deep into her aching, dripping pussy. Filled and stretched at both ends, she cried out. Ben pulled out to his tip. Christ thrust in, pushing his cock a little deeper into her throat. When he withdrew, Ben rammed into her pussy.

Both men carried on, increasing their actions to an almost frenzied pace. Experiencing both usually restrained men, act with such reckless abandon was a heady drug in her veins. Desperation to push them both over the edge flowed through her body. She tightened her mouth around Chris's dick as she clamped on Ben's cock in her pussy at the same pace they fucked her.

"Oh. Fuck!" Chris's words came out clipped as if she was torturing him before hot semen blasted her tongue. She'd done that to him, and she didn't let go, sucking every drop of his release.

"Do you want to come, Lina?"

It took her a few seconds to understand Chris's question. With Ben pounding into her, building such intensity, her brain only focused on one thing. Her need to come.

"Please." Mouth free from Chris's cock, she begged.

"Please what?" Chris demanded.

Her body bucked with every stroke, and she was lost in arousal. Fingers touched her breasts, her back...everywhere.

"Please, I need to come!" she screamed out to them, so desperate now. A finger pressed against her clit and her body exploded, fracturing her into tiny bits of light and pleasure as her body rocketed against them in spasms. Her legs and arms weakened, unable to support her any longer. She slumped against the sofa.

Ben gripped her hips and pounded into her until he roared his release and covered her body with his.

Chapter Nine

Ben leaned over the sofa chair, his arms braced against the back, mindful of putting his weight on Selina. Her head laid on her hands, tendrils of hair covered her face so he couldn't see her expression.

His heart hammered into his ribs, even as his chest tightened. Brushing back hair plastered onto her shoulder, he pressed his lips against her skin and tasted her saltiness.

Their bodies remained merged, heat and sweat making the contact slick, both their bodies rising and falling in concert as they caught their breaths.

After he'd sucked much-needed oxygen back into his body and regained enough strength to move, he slid his partly sated cock out of her. He scooped her into his arms as he sat on the armchair.

She snuggled into his arms, attempted to bury her face between the crook of his arm and chest. But he needed to see her face. Brushing her dark tresses out of the way, he tilted her head back by pulling her hair.

Drops of moisture beaded her lashes. Were those just sweat drops or had she been crying?

The clamp around his chest tightened.

"Lina, are you okay?" His voice was roughened by his concern for her.

Knowing it would be her first time of volunteering to be with two men at the same time, they'd tried to take it easy and go slow. But he'd been unable to maintain his restraint once he'd entered her hot, slick pussy. God, she'd clamped around him hungrily, and he'd lost himself, and all thoughts of taking her slow had flown out of his mind.

More moisture beaded her lashes, dropped down her cheeks and he knew for sure she was crying.

"Beauty, did we hurt you?" He leaned in, kissed the tears. "Talk to me."

She opened her caramel eyes and stared up at him. "You didn't hurt me."

Chris lowered his body beside the chair and squatted at eye level to them. "Then, what's wrong, Selina?" he asked as he passed a bottle of water he'd retrieved from the fridge. "If we've done something wrong just say and we'll fix it. If you want me to leave, I'll go. No worries."

Selina turned her head around so she could look at Chris. "You've both done nothing wrong. It's quite the opposite, in fact. And I don't want you to leave, Chris. At least I hope not yet."

She turned her gaze to Ben, and his heart thudded loudly. He saw the plea in her eyes.

"Do you want more...more of both of us? Is that what you're saying?" Ben asked. He'd agonized for a long time over setting up this scene, wanting it to be perfect for her.

But the trauma she'd gone through had always played on his mind. He'd wondered how she would cope with having more than one pair of male hands on her body for a prolonged period.

"Yes, please." She lowered her lashes as she smiled. "I want more of both of you. You've both given me something I didn't think I could have. The last time men stood over me, wanting to use my body, I ended up with these."

She looked down at the scars covering her lower ribs and abdomen.

Ben's grip on her back tightened momentarily.

"Now, I have the confidence of knowing that two men want me and the reassurance that I can give my body to both of you and trust that you will not brutalize it even if I say no. No amount of psychotherapy ever gave me that reassurance."

Ben closed his eyes and sucked in a breath, pulling her into his chest. He wanted to say so much to her, but the words failed him right now.

"Lina, Ben loves you more than anything else in this world," his friend spoke, and Ben was glad for his intervention. "And I love you, not as Ben does, but in my own way. We would never do anything to hurt you. Even if Ben isn't around, I will always take care of you. You should know that."

"I know that now," Selina responded. "Thank you."

"You are welcome."

"Here. Drink some water." Ben opened the cap of the bottle and tipped the top onto Selina's lips.

She opened her mouth and drank, her throat muscles rippling as she swallowed.

His half-mast erection stirred and throbbed.

"I'm going to run that massive sunken bath. Should be big enough for all three of us," Chris said as he headed toward the bathroom.

Ben used the moment of privacy to survey Selina. "Are you really okay? You don't have to continue if you don't want to."

"I do, Ben. I really love having Chris here. Having both of you here." She bit her lower lip. "But I'm worried about you. Do *you* want Chris here? I mean you were so adamant when we first got to The Ranch that you didn't want anyone else touching me. I'm worried about what you really think about me having sex with your friend."

"Lina, you need to stop worrying right now." Ben scolded. "For starters, this is your birthday present. If you don't want it, you can say no. Secondly, after the graceful way you coped with everything I threw at you while we were at The Ranch, you deserve this little reward."

He palmed her face and held it so she could stare into his face.

"You may be the sub in this relationship, but you have to realize that you own my heart. I will do anything for you. Anything. And if having Chris here makes you happy, then it makes me happy too. Got it?"

"Got it. Thank you, Ben. I love you so much."

"I love you too, Beauty. More than you could ever know." She was his everything, and he would do whatever it took to please and keep her.

Chris strode out and headed in their direction, his jeans slung low on his hips. "I'm going to get Selina ready for the bath while Ben orders some room service. She's going to need the food before we're done with her."

Ben chuckled as Chris scooped Selina into his arms and she gasped.

"I'm enjoying having two men pampering and fussing over me." Selina's warm laughter filled the air.

"Enjoy the pampering because we're going to work your body very hard too," Ben said over his shoulders as he reached for the phone.

"I'm looking forward to it," she teased back from the bathroom door.

Smiling and happy, Ben ordered the food, going for the entrée and dessert options and skipping the main courses. Selina wouldn't want anything heavy since they'd had a big lunch earlier.

Once his order was confirmed, and he told them the time to bring it, he returned the phone handset to the cradle and shucked his trousers, tossing them over the arm of the sofa. Keeping his boxer briefs on, he ambled to the ensuite.

Grey limestone covered the four walls, with matching slabs on the floor. His-and-hers sinks occupied one wall and at the far end stood a shower enclosure large enough for a handful of people. Next to the door stood a chrome rack with fluffy white towels made from Egyptian cotton. Chris's jeans hung from a metal hook next to the frame.

In the large sunken tub filled with water, white bubbles and red rose petals, Selina sat in the middle. Her hair pinned in a pile on her crown, her head tipped forward as Chris caressed her neck and shoulders with gentle strokes of his fingers. The soft purring noises coming from her heated the blood in his veins.

Crossing his arms over his chest, Ben leaned against the door jamb and watched them. He never thought he'd invite anyone else to participate in fulfilling Selina's sexual fantasies. He'd always seen it as his responsibility.

When he'd first met her, he'd been consumed with claiming her and gaining her submission. The thought of sharing her with anyone else would have sent him into a jealous rage.

Yet here he was, observing his best friend massage his wife's body as if they had always been lovers. His stomach hardened, and his breath quickened.

Of course, they had been lovers a year ago. However, not since he'd married Selina.

On their wedding night, Selina had offered Chris a quickie after Ben had stuffed a vibrator into her pussy and kept her mad with arousal during the party.

Chris had revealed her proposition, as a good friend should and Selina had earned a spanking that night for her misdemeanour. She'd hadn't propositioned Chris or anyone else since. They'd remained monogamous.

He hadn't ever contemplated taking another woman. Not even when Margo had offered her services. While he'd been so turned on watching the two women play, he never made any direct sexual contact with Margo. And he never would with any other woman. Not without Selina's permission.

The truth was, he would happily live the rest of his life without anyone else, if he got to fuck Selina any time he wanted.

Considering there was a time when the idea of monogamy didn't appeal to him, this came as a great shock. He hadn't wanted monogamy with Margo, Siba or Cordelia. And yet he couldn't think of living any other way with Selina.

"Are you going to join us, Sir?" his wife's sultry voice pulled him out of his reverie.

Her luscious lips curled in an inviting smile, and her eyes sparkled. His dick hardened painfully.

"Try keeping me away." He pushed down his underwear, kicking it to the corner before stepping up to the bath.

With a grin on his face, Chris leaned back, making room for him. "No one will dare."

Ben chuckled at his friend's teasing and lowered his body in so he could face Selina.

Curling his fingers around her nape, he pulled her in for a gentle kiss. She tasted of Selina and tangy sweetness.

"You smell so good," he said, breathing the scent on her skin.

She gave a half-gasp, half giggle. "I think it's the fragrance from the bath crystals."

"Whatever it is, it makes me want to eat you up." He continued nipping and licking his way down her neck to her left shoulder.

"Talking about food," Chris said and rose out of the bubbles. "I'm going to set up the buffet."

"Buffet?" Selina asked, raising her head to look at his friend who stepped out of the bath and trailed water and bubbles over the thick floor mat.

Chris pulled a towel off the nearby rack, dried his body, and wrapped it around his hips. "Yes, Lina. You're on the menu."

He winked and strode out and shut the door, giving them privacy once more. Another reason they worked well together. His friend understood him.

Selina's breath hitched, and her pupils dilated. "What does he mean?"

"You'll find out soon enough," Ben replied as he tipped her head back so her body curved up and he could get to her chocolate tipped succulent breasts.

As always, any form of breast play had her writhing and panting in his arms. She canted her hips, rubbing up against his hard dick. With the slippery water, she wouldn't get much friction unless he pushed her down tight.

He didn't. Instead, he kept her on edge, taking the swells of each breast into his mouth in turn and sucking, kneading the tautened nipples.

"More...please, Ben."

"More what?"

"I—I need more of you. I need you inside me. I need to come, Sir. Please." Frustration coated her plea.

Lips curved in a devious smile, he stared into her lust-glazed eyes. He wanted to push her and see if she would bite. "You sure need a lot of things, and you'll get all of them in good time."

"Grrr."

"Did you just bare your teeth at me?"

She pouted her lips. "I'm sorry, Sir."

"I will accept your apology once you get your spanking. Lean over the bath."

"Sir?"

"Don't make me repeat myself."

Before he finished the statement, she stood and gripped the edge of the tub. Supine and compliant, she offered the globes of her ass, water and suds dripping from her glistening body.

Kneeling behind her, he reached across and grabbed hold of each yielding cheek, squeezed, and parted them. She moaned and curved her spine downward, offering more of her bum. The star winked at him, and he groaned.

Leaning forward, he swiped his tongue over it. She squirmed in response.

"I'm going to fuck you here tonight." He pressed his right forefinger to her opening, using the mix of saliva and soapy water to work his way to his first knuckle.

"Yes. Fuck me now."

He withdrew his finger and landed his palm to her right cheek in a hard spank.

She yelped, and he grinned.

"Good to know you want me there. But I wasn't asking for your permission, and you don't dictate what happens when."

"Yes, Sir." Her head tipped down in a cowered gesture.

He gave her five more hard swats in quick succession, alternating the sides. Apart from the jolting body, she didn't cry out again and took her chastisement with quiet grace.

Another sign of the progress she'd made since they started their kink journey together. His chest swelled with pride. While he enforced the discipline that was a part of their relationship dynamic, his previous sadistic tendencies had become muted since Selina. She didn't enjoy pain the way masochists did. There was no joy in inflicting pain on her because it only acted as a trigger for her past trauma.

Stepping out of the tub, he grabbed a towel, dried, and threw it around his waist before taking another for Selina.

"Step out of the bath." He opened the bath sheet.

She obeyed and still didn't meet his gaze. With tender care, he dried her body off and dropped the towel on the floor. Then he tangled his fingers into her hair and tugged back.

"I'm sorry, Ben," she said in a subdued voice and shut her eyes. "I didn't mean to mess up after you've gone to so much trouble for me."

"Look at me," he said, keeping his voice low.

Lash lifted, she stared at him with remorse.

"You didn't mess up. You reacted exactly the way I wanted you to."

"I did?"

"Mmhm." He nodded. "I test you because I want to. You've been to The Ranch, and we've pushed your usual limits back. I know your boundaries. Moreover, you've been so well behaved lately. I haven't spanked you in a while. You were well overdue."

"I was." Her face lit up in a beautiful smile. "Thank you, Sir."

"You are welcome." He leaned forward and gave her a bruising kiss.

Chapter Ten

Two days later, Selina twisted her hair and wrung out the excess water before stepping out of the shower enclosure and picking up a towel from the rack.

Her languid body cried out for more sleep, her sex and bum ached sinfully and deliciously. Rest would have to wait.

Wrapping her damp, wet hair with a clean towel, she lifted her head and stared at her reflection in the mirror above the sink.

The woman who stared back at her had an almost delirious smile on her face, her eyes bright and lips tilted upward.

Memories assaulted her. Chris's arrival at their hotel room in Johannesburg. The way both men had fed, loved, and used her body in equal measures.

Her skin tingled as she remembered how they'd spread her out on the low coffee table made of solid dark wood and had proceeded to lay out the food on her body. Every part had a piece of entrée on it—mouth, chest, stomach, arms, thighs. They'd eaten the meal from her bare body with hands and mouths; fish sushi, beef teriyaki, bruschetta, calamari. Tongues swiping, lips sucking, fingers smearing, each touch raising her awareness, torturing her as they kept her hovering over an elusive orgasm.

Until Ben ate his dessert from her pussy.

Oh, God! Her insides clenched tight, her clit throbbing to life. She gripped the edge of the sink and rubbed her thighs together to relieve the pressure but only seemed to make it worse.

She needed her husband. Right now.

He, however, was in South Africa and she was in Sierra Leone, having arrived last night with Chris. He'd checked them in and settled her into her room before going to his. It was back to business as usual; despite the intimacy they had shared in the hotel room in Johannesburg. Despite the fact, his dick had been in her sex while Ben had taken her ass. Together they had fucked her so thoroughly. Stuffed in both holes, the sensation had triggered a mind-blowing orgasm that she had passed out at the end of.

Now her legs trembled. She walked out of the bath and sat on the bed to catch her breath.

The men had been amazing. Ben had been fantastic. Cleaning her up afterwards, making sure she had enough water to drink and then spooning her for the rest of the night. She'd slept for most of the night and the next morning. Had only found out Chris would be accompanying her to Freetown when she'd been getting ready for the trip.

On their arrival last night, she hadn't seen much of the city she'd last seen ten years ago and was hoping to make up for it today. Most importantly, she would be seeing Kaya, her brother, whom she hadn't seen in as long.

Suddenly excited about the prospect, she reached for the mobile phone she'd discarded on the bed after her phone conversation with Ben this morning. She scrolled through her contacts and found Kaya's number. The phone rang twice before someone picked it up.

"Hello?" A young male voice she recognized asked.

"Kaya, it's so good to be finally speaking to you," Selina replied, unable to hide her excitement.

"Is this you, Selina?" her brother asked, his Sierra Leonean accent strong.

"Yes. Guess what. I'm in Freetown."

"Really? You are in this city? That is wonderful." His voice rose, matching the anticipation she felt, his words rushed. "When am I going to see you? Where are you staying?"

"I'm here with a friend, and we're staying at a hotel. He's gone out, and I'm waiting for him to come back so we can come out to see you."

"How about if I come to you? Can I come to your hotel?"

Chris had been adamant about her not going out without him, although she didn't understand why. She'd grown up in Sierra Leone. And despite the war, things had returned to normal. Life had moved on. The country was being rebuilt from what she could see of it from her hotel window. The hotel was on a quiet residential street lined with green leafy trees, so she couldn't see much.

Inside her room, the décor was white walls and light wood and clean furnishings. The air was fresh and crisp. There was no reason she couldn't relax and enjoy her environment.

Anyway, even if she couldn't go out, there was no reason Kaya couldn't come to her.

"Of course, you can," she said and reached for the hotel literature on the wooden desk. "Let me give you the address."

She told him the name and the address, reading it out from the brochure.

"I think I know where that is," Kaya said. "I'm going to get ready and come over."

"That's good. See you soon."

As soon as she put the phone down, Selina ordered breakfast and got dressed. She would explain to Chris when he returned that Kaya had decided to come to them instead.

Not seeing her kid brother for many years, and only communicating via phone and internet, meant she couldn't wait to see the boy she'd thought had died with her parents. She'd only found out last year that he had lived.

Shoulders slumped, she dipped her chin to her chest as guilt swamped her and she swallowed a lump in her throat.

The full story of where Kaya had been all this while was still shrouded in darkness. Her brother refused to discuss it on the phone, and Selina didn't want to push him. But now they would see each other again, perhaps he would trust her enough to tell her the horrors he'd suffered. Because she was sure, he had suffered too, just as much as she had.

She would take him away from all that. His visa to travel to the United Kingdom had been confirmed. He would make the trip back to London with Selina and Christopher and live with her in Ben's apartment. He'd go to college and perhaps university like all other boys his age.

Soon the past would remain in the past.

Room service turned up, and she enjoyed her continental breakfast of croissants and scrambled eggs. She was having a sip of her apple juice when her phone rang.

"Sister," Kaya said when she answered her phone. "I've had an accident and—"

"What? Are you injured? What happened?" The words rushed out in a breathless jumble as she pictured the horrible scene of Kaya bloodied and stuck in a smashed car. The medical system here wasn't the same as the one in the UK. Did they have an ambulance service? She couldn't remember. "Do you need a doctor?"

"No. No. I'm not injured. Another car hit mine, but it's not that bad. Just a big dent on the car. I'm not going to be able to come to you."

"I'm coming over to you. Tell me where you are."

"Are you sure? You don't have to. I can come once everything is sorted out here."

"Nonsense. I want to see you and make sure you are all right for myself."

"Okay. I'm close to Mends Street Market. You can ask for a taxi at the front desk of the hotel, and it will bring you here."

"I'll be there as soon as I can," she said and hung up.

Despite the fact he said he was okay, she still worried. Her brother had a knack of being dismissive about things. He might have sustained an injury, and he didn't want to tell her. She would make sure he got medical attention. At the least, she had first-aid training.

She grabbed her handbag and headed down to reception. The girl at the desk arranged for a car to take her to the Market square.

When she arrived, the sights and sounds and bustle of the market overwhelmed her. A rainbow of fruits and vegetables, textiles, and wares. She inhaled the scent of spices mixed with food being prepared.

People milled about, bartering with market women for wares.

She called her brother to find out where he was, and a face in the crowd caught her attention. She stared in that direction and blinked, but it wasn't there.

Her mind must be playing tricks.

"Where are you, Kaya?"

"I'm parked over at the petrol station. If you tell me where you are, I can walk to you."

Selina stared around her. The red cursive lettering on a white background drew her attention. "I'm in front of a shop, Diaka Textiles. See you soon."

She switched off her phone, and a prickling sensation made her turn around. The face was there again. This time he stood before her.

Her eyes bulged, unblinking. She shook her head, not believing what she saw. But the man hadn't moved. He stood before her flesh and bone, dressed in a dark suit made from the expensive shiny material. Real.

"Hello, wife." This voice, she would never forget it. The one that sold her into sexual slavery. The voice of her first husband. He dared to still refer to her as 'wife'?

She opened her mouth, only emitting a silent scream. She gasped for air, her lungs feeling tight. Terror coiled around her body, suffocating her like a deadly python. The nightmare she thought she'd escaped replayed itself in her mind repeatedly.

"It's good to see you again," he said with a devilish smile and strode towards her with confident steps.

Turn around! Run! Her mind screamed. Yet she couldn't move her leaden legs, and she felt as if she was stuck in sinking sands.

"Don't come closer," she managed to spit out. Her hands trembled, and she clenched them against her bag, hanging off her shoulders.

"But I have been searching for you for so long. This is going to be quite a reunion," the man said as he continued coming towards her.

"N—" A cool damp cloth covered her face, and someone grabbed her from behind. Panicked, she sucked in breath harshly. Bad idea. Fumes filled her nostrils as she struggled against the muscular arm caging her. The last face she saw was Tony's hovering above hers as she blacked out.

***

Ben stood by the window in his father's office, gazing out at the mountains in the distance. God, he still had to get used to referring to Leonard as his father. The man had been in a great mood since he'd returned from Johannesburg.

Unfortunately, Ben's mood hadn't improved. He missed Selina. He'd spoken to her last night and this morning, and just hearing her voice had been great, but not enough. He had to conclude his business here so he could go to her.

But they were going through the Moss business documents. Apparently, he would be inheriting everything in the eventuality of Leonard's death. The fact remained; he didn't want any of it. But it didn't hurt to understand what there was at least for Beatrice's sake, whom he would pass most things off to.

He pulled his vibrating phone out of his back pocket. His best friend's name flashed on the screen.

He'd been expecting a call from Chris, so he answered it without thinking.

"She's gone."

Ben's spine stiffened, cold dread sliding down his back. Panic laced Chris's calm words. They'd been friends too long for preambles when the shit hit the fan and could read each other.

But Ben still asked, "Who's gone?" as if asking would change the outcome.

He needed certainty.

"Selina is not at the hotel. She's missing."

His hands turned clammy and sweat beaded his forehead. "Shit!"

Spinning around, he walked to the opposite wall. "What happened? She knows she's not supposed to go out without you."

He wanted to believe she'd just gone out without telling Chris. That she would be back any moment now. Because if it was anything different... He shook his head. He couldn't bear to think about it.

"I had to meet with our contact in Freetown this morning. When I came back, I checked on her. When there was no reply, I let myself into her room, only to find she'd gone out. Her bags are still here, but her phone and purse are missing. The hotel receptionist said he booked her a car to take her to Mend Street Market. I've called her several times. Her phone is switched off. I decided to let you know immediately. I'm going to head out there and search for her."

Benjamin read the subtext to Chris's words. Foreboding sat like boulders in his stomach.

Selina wouldn't leave the hotel without telling Chris. When Ben had spoken to her earlier, she hadn't said anything about going out. She'd only been excited to see her brother.

"The only reason she would leave the hotel would be for Kaya. I'm going to send you his mobile phone number. She's probably gone to meet him and forgot to call." He hoped that was the case. "I'll be flying out to Freetown as soon as I can get it arranged."

"We will find her," Chris said emphatically.

"We will." He hung up and turned around to face his father and Lars. "Something's come up, and I'm going to Freetown."

"What about what we're doing here?" Leonard asked.

"This will have to wait. Selina is more important." Ben said as he headed to the door.

"Selina is where she belongs."

Ben's hand froze on the handle of the door. "What did you say?"

He turned around to find Leonard studying him. Sometimes he couldn't decide if he loved or hated his father. The old man had made him, given him what he'd thought he'd needed as a boy. And yet if Ben allowed, Leonard could break him. Could destroy the things that had come to mean the world to Ben.

"Selina is where she belongs. With her husband," Leonard said in a slow, deliberate manner as if he'd just said the sky was blue, a shrug lifting his shoulders. "You did know she was married before you met her. She's gone back to him."

"No!" Shoulder muscles knotted, Ben balled his fists and strode toward his father's desk. He didn't want to imagine what the old man had done. But the sinking feeling in his stomach didn't go away as the man held his gaze. Lips pulled back, Ben barred gritted teeth. "How do you know? What did you do?"

"He wanted her back, and I told him where to find her."

"Fuck!" Ben roared as he charged his father. Lars rammed into him from the side, knocking him into the wall and smashing a framed photograph that had been hanging there.

"Calm down, Ben," Lars said in an out of breath voice.

"You want me to calm down," Ben shouted as he punched the wall before pointing at Leonard. "He sold my wife back to her ex, and you want me to calm down? She belongs to me. Mine. No one touches her. I mean no one!"

Selina's ex had sold her out. Now she would think Ben had done the same thing to her. Never. He had to get to her. Before it was too late.

Ben drew in a ragged breath and shoved back. "Let go of me," he hissed.

Lars released him and stepped back, but he didn't give him room to manoeuvre toward Leonard.

"Let me tell you something." He gripped the edge of the table and glared at Leonard. "If anything happens to her, if one hair on her head is harmed, I will come back here and make you pay."

"Benjamin, you forget whom you're talking to. I'm your father."

"In which case, I have your ruthless blood running through me, and I don't have any problem eliminating anyone who messes with what is mine. Selina belongs to me. You either accept it or be willing to pay the price."

The shocked expression on Leonard's face didn't sway him as he swivelled and stormed out of the office.

Chapter Eleven

Selina's head hurt, her body seemed heavy, and sweat trickled down her back from the heat.

Had she switched off the air-conditioning unit in the hotel suite?

She tried to move her limbs to adjust her body and found she couldn't move them.

Her eyes flew open, and her gaze swept the room. This wasn't her hotel room. It was a nice enough room, with cream walls, a clean bed, and a dark wardrobe in the corner. But it felt like the room in a house rather than a hotel.

Panic rose in her throat. Where was she? How had she gotten here?

Her hands and feet were tied to the bedposts with raffia rope. It wasn't at all like the soft and silky Shibari bonds Ben used on her. These were rough and hurt, and she could barely move her hands or feet in any direction. There was nothing pleasant about it.

Who would do this to her?

She remembered leaving her hotel to meet Kaya. Kaya! Where was he? She'd gone to the market to meet him. Instead, she'd seen...

Oh no!

Tony! She'd seen him in the market. He'd stood in front of her and said her name before the world had been blanketed in darkness.

The door creak and she tilted her head in its direction.

Think of the devil. A cold shiver ran down her spine as she studied the man who walked in the door. A man she hadn't seen in ten years until today.

Her ex-husband.

The last time she'd seen him, she'd been dragged away by fierce-looking militia with guns and machetes. He'd been a young man, handsome, and arrogant.

He didn't look much different now. He was dressed in a flashy suit, a white shirt with tailored burgundy jacket and trousers. His hair was cropped close, and his features were sharper.

"Good. You're awake," he said, his voice as cold as his dark eyes.

"Wh—what am I doing here, Tony?" She couldn't believe her heavy tongue worked in her dry mouth. She was sure he could hear her heart thumping in her chest.

"I'm sorry about the situation, Selina. But I wanted to be sure you were safe."

"By tying me up?" she asked sarcastically.

"I was under the impression you liked that sort of thing," he said with a leer on his face.

Her face flamed at his implication. How did he know that? "Well, I don't like it now. And you still haven't told me what I'm doing here."

"This is my house, and you're my guest. I'm hoping to get reacquainted with you. It's been a long time."

"There's no reacquainting to be done. You sold me out, Tony. You abandoned me. I don't want to be anywhere near you."

"Come come, Selina. That was a long time ago, at a challenging time for our country. We've all reconciled and forgiven each other. We had a great life ahead of us. We can have it again."

His clammy hand touched the bare skin of her arm, and she flinched.

"You abandoned me when I needed you, Tony. You promised to love and protect me. But at the first sign of trouble, you left me. You let them hurt me. I'm not ready to forgive you."

"But you will, which is why you are here." He settled on a seat next to her bed.

"How did you know I was coming to Freetown?"

"Who else? Your Mr Moss?"

"Ben? You're lying." She bit back with disdain.

"I don't need to lie. I have details of the email he sent with your flight and hotel details." He dug in his jacket and pulled out a sheet of paper which he held close to her face. The email address looked like Ben's.

But that couldn't be right, could it? Ben would never sell her out. Something else had to be going on.

"He was very keen to have us reacquainted. As you can read, he sees no future with you as he resettles to life in South Africa."

"There are some things I need to do here. I won't be returning to London for a while. I'm not sure how long."

A knot formed in her belly and bile rose in her throat as she remembered Ben's words from two days ago. Had he planned it this way all along? Had he lied to her when he said they belonged together? That they were going to make a family?

She closed her smarting eyes. She'd told him there was a possibility she couldn't have children. Had he changed his mind because of that?

No. Not Ben. Not after everything he'd done for her. He wouldn't build her up just to crush her back down. He just wouldn't.

"I don't believe you." She lifted her head and glared at Tony. "Unlike you, Benjamin will never sell me out. He will never let me go." She punctuated the last four words for emphasis.

"It's your choice, but it seems to me he's the one that has been lying to you. At least with me, you know what you're getting. The question to you is, do you know Mr Moss as well as you think you do." He paused as if for effect. "For example, did you know that he was in Sierra Leone ten years ago?"

"Of course, I do." She rolled her eyes, staring at the white ceiling.

"Okay. So, you know that he supplied the guns and knives that destroyed our wedding and our lives?"

"What? No." She shook her head.

Ben's uncle was a weapons dealer. But those guns could've come from anyone.

"I've got the proof of that too." He dug in his pocket and produced a photograph of young men in camouflage, a mix of white and black men. The image of the men who attacked her was forever imprinted in her mind. Two of them stared back at her from the printed image in Tony's hand.

Squirming, she glanced away and swallowed down the panic rising in her throat.

"Look closely at the white men and tell me if you recognize any of them?"

She turned her face and stared at the picture. The men were young, one with blond hair, another with brown hair, and a third with black hair. Younger versions of Christopher and Benjamin. Her heart stopped, her mouth dropped open, and nausea made her light-headed.

They stood with the men who'd brutalized her body.

They'd been in the camp at the time of the attack.

Had Ben supplied the weapons? Had he been there when the men sliced her skin into ribbons? Had he stood there and watched them?

No! She couldn't believe that. If he'd known the girls in the camp were being raped, surely Ben would've done something to stop it? He and Chris wouldn't have turned a blind eye. Not the men she knew. The men she trusted with her life.

Then again, she'd trusted Tony once, and he'd disappointed her. Ben could be the same.

But everything she knew about him said he was a different man. In her heart, she felt he had changed.

She wished she could see him, to ask him questions and watch for his answers. He always told her the truth, didn't he?

He wouldn't sell her out to Tony. They had wonderful days and had made plans. They were going to start a family when they got back to London.

That's if she ever got out of here.

He would come for her. Chris would know she was missing and inform Ben. They would look for and find her. She had to believe it.

"Ben did some bad things when he was a young man." She tilted her chin and met Tony's amused gaze. He had to be testing her to see if she would break. "But he is an incredibly good man now, and he will find me. I advise you to return me to my hotel room. I promise I won't tell anybody you took me. I'll just say I went to look for my brother and got lost."

"I see you're still delusional. Nobody is coming for you. Get used to it." Tony stood and went to the door. "I will send something to drink and eat, and if you behave yourself, I'll get them to loosen the ropes. But don't get any ideas. This is now your new home."

He walked out, leaving her in the darkening room.

Selina hissed in frustration.

***

She must have fallen asleep because she jolted awake to the sound of a thud like somebody had hit a hard surface. The room lay in darkness, the whole place quiet as if there had been a power outage.

Earlier, someone had brought her a drink which she'd managed to sip through a straw. She'd asked to use the toilet and had been led into an adjacent bathroom. The burly man stood just outside the open door, and she hadn't had the time or opportunity to look out and survey her surroundings.

The door to her room opened, and light beamed through as Tony rushed in, followed by the same burly man from earlier. The man pulled out a knife and Selina screamed.

Tony clamped her mouth shut. "You better keep your mouth shut or I'll shut it for you."

The man cut away her bonds. Tony yanked her off the bed, clamped arms across her chest, and dragged her from the room, down a dimly lit corridor.

Frightened, her body trembled.

The man in front opened a door at the end and collapsed on the floor.

Something cold and metallic pressed against her temple. She froze, stifling a scream. Her heart nearly punched a hole through her chest. She blinked rapidly, sweat dripping down her face and back.

"Don't come any closer or I will shoot her," Tony said in a menacing voice.

Selina's eyes and mouth widened as she looked up. Two men dressed in black clothing stepped out of the shadows, raised guns glinting in the low light.

"You have nowhere to run, Kana. Let her go, and we can all walk away. No harm done." Ben's voice was cold and dangerous. It rippled through the room.

He'd come for her. A soft gasp escaped Selina's mouth, and she slumped against Tony in relief at hearing Ben's voice, only to stiffen instantly as the metal from the gun dug into her temple.

Oh, God! Fear spiked through her again. Three men with guns stood around her. The last time men had surrounded her with weapons, they'd taken her away and hurt her.

This situation was different, though.

She knew these three men very well, intimately.

And yet one held a gun to her head while the other two pointed guns in her direction. She sent up a silent prayer that the men she loved would get out of here alive.

"No harm done?" Tony bit out in a harsh tone. "You invaded my house and killed my men."

"You abducted my wife. I'd say we're even." She'd never heard Ben so menacing before. He was like a different man. Someone dark and deadly. Someone who could kill without remorse.

"Your wife? She was mine first."

"You gave her up. She belongs to me now." Ben met her gaze, and despite the hardness of his voice, there was brief warmth and reassurance in his eyes. He told her everything would be all right.

"Don't think that because I let you rescue her the last time, it's going to happen again."

Rescue her? What did Tony mean by that? Confusion superseded her fear. She bit her lips and narrowed her gaze as she watched Ben.

He remained rigidly poised. Another glance at him showed he'd moved from his original position. However, she hadn't even seen any movement from him. Neither had she seen Chris moved. Although he remained silent, Ben's partner stood a few feet away from where she thought she'd seen them at first.

Were they circling, getting closer? Searching for the best angle to shoot from?

"Selina trusts me. She knows I will do whatever it takes to keep her safe. Which is why when I say the word, she takes the position."

He gave her an almost imperceptible nod, and she knew he was giving her a direct order.

How was she supposed to 'take the position'?

Tony held a gun to her head and gripped her around the shoulders.

Still, she trusted Ben to know what he was doing and to protect her.

"Really?" Tony said arrogantly, his arm around her loosening a little as he focused the gun on Ben. "When she spends time with me, she'll also learn to obey my every command."

"You won't ever get that chance again," Ben said. "Now!"

Selina knew a command when she heard it. Letting her head drop, she relaxed her body, letting her knees give way. Her sudden movement must have caught Tony unawares. He tried to tighten his grip to stop her downward motion, but couldn't get a hold on her sweat-slicked shoulders. A gunshot rang out, blasting loud in her ears. Then, she heard a thud as her body and Tony's tumbled down to the cold floor at the same time.

Curled into a ball, she hugged her knees and shut her eyes, her body trembling, her ears ringing. A calloused hand gripped her shoulder, and she jerked, kicking out.

"Selina, it's me," Ben's husky voice penetrated her despair.

She opened her eyes. He crouched beside her, his gaze filled with worry.

"Are you hurt?" He turned her over, checking her out.

"No," she whispered when she found her voice in her dry throat. "What about you? You were shot."

She remembered the gunshot. Tony's gun.

"I'm fine," he replied as he scooped her into his arms, holding her tight.

Sucking in a deep breath, she let his spicy scent ground her and chase her terror away." I knew you would come for me." Her throat was so dry she could barely get the words out.

Ben leaned back, tilted her head up with his fingers. "What did you say?"

She met his intense gaze. In the dark, it was a mix of relief, affection, and dark desire. She sucked in a ragged breath, tried to quell the rush of adrenaline and fear in her veins.

"Tony said you told him where to find me," her voice trembled, matching her shaky smile.

"I never did—"

She lifted her hand to his lips, cutting him off. It felt so good to feel his soft lips against her skin.

"I didn't believe him. I knew you would come for me. I knew you were not like him. I trust you."

Ben closed his eyes. His body shuddered as he sucked in a breath. When he opened his eyes, tears misted them.

"Thank you for trusting me." His voice was husky with emotion. "More than anything else I've asked of you, your trust is the one thing I have craved beyond measure. Knowing that you trusted me even when things seemed to show the opposite makes me even more determined never to let you down."

Selina's nodded, warmth spreading in her chest. "More than anyone else in my life, you've earned my trust, and I know you will never break it."

"I won't." He pressed his lips against her forehead.

"We have to leave now." She turned to see Chris standing over Tony's prone body.

"Is he dead?" Silly question to ask since blood and mush oozed from a hole in the man's head, but the words slipped out in a numb tone. She had loved Tony once. She'd been attracted to his swagger and arrogance. Perhaps she'd been seduced by the cash he used to flash on gifts for her. The naïve girl had died on the grimy floor in that shack as the militia took their turns maiming her body. Now she felt nothing for him. Not even sorrow at his demise.

"Yes," Ben said and turned her away from the dead man. "Did you find her things?"

Chris lifted his hands, showing Selina's bag, and the other held a laptop. "Her phone is in the purse, and I checked the room out. Nothing else of hers. I found Kana's laptop. We must go now. This place is set to blow in ten minutes."

Flinching, Selina's mouth dropped open as she swivelled to look at Ben. "Blow? You are blowing up the place?"

He had a grim expression. "We can't leave any traces of you for the police to find and neither can we leave any traces that we've been here."

He lifted her as he stood.

"But—"

"Selina, it's for the best. There are dead men all over this house. It is best if the finger points elsewhere when the police investigate."

Swallowing, she nodded.

He was right.

They could be arrested and put in jail.

Ben had killed her ex, even if the man had abducted her, and she was complicit.

Ben held her hand as they headed down the corridor, Chris leading the way. At the door, she stopped. Ben bumped into her.

"What's the matter?"

"We can't leave without my brother. You have to find him."

"We found him already," Ben said. "He's outside in the car. He told us where to find you."

Chris led the way again, gun still drawn as if he expected more trouble. "Stay behind me, Selina."

She did, while Ben brought up the rear. They got outside, and there was an eerie silence, perhaps due to the lateness of the hour. Outside the gate, Chris flashed a small torchlight, and a large SUV rolled up without its headlight on.

"Get in," Ben said after he opened the back door.

She stepped inside and saw her brother sitting in the back seat. They hugged each other.

Ben got in the car beside her and Chris got in the front seat.

She didn't recognize the driver.

"I'm so glad you're okay. I was worried about you," she said to Kaya, relief at seeing his unharmed flooding her body

"I'm sorry," Kaya said in a distraught voice and twisted his hands together in an agitated manner on his lap.

Seeing him upset, unsettled Selina. She wrapped her fingers around her brother's wiry arms, hoping to reassure him. He looked so different from the boy she remembered. He'd grown into a young man, tall and filled out with lean, boyish muscles.

Still, he remained her kid brother.

"There's nothing for you to be sorry about," Selina said in a soothing voice. "Tony was the one who abducted me. You had nothing to do with it."

"If you hadn't left the hotel," Kaya's voice sounded small. "If you hadn't come to the market, he wouldn't have taken you. That was my fault."

A yellow streetlight illuminated her brother's face briefly. Selina recognized the expression of shame in his averted gaze. Her body tensed and anger welled in her veins. Her ex-husband had nearly destroyed their lives again. She wouldn't let him hurt them anymore.

"Trust me." She shook Kaya's arms. He turned to look at her. In the darkness, she couldn't see his full expression. "Tony would've found another way to get to me. It wasn't your fault. You've got to believe it."

"Tony is not going to hurt anybody else ever again," Ben said as he put his arm around Selina's shoulders. "You are both safe now, and that's what's important."

Kaya sighed and nodded. "Thank you."

Glad for her husband's intervention, Selina relaxed back into his arms as they drove them to their destination. They whizzed down quiet streets, and she didn't recognize the neighbourhood in the dark except that the houses were behind high brick walls and metal security gates. They seemed to be avoiding the major roads.

She'd assumed they were going back to the hotel she'd stayed in upon her arrival. But they pulled into what looked like a residential home in a gated suburb.

Security let them in, and the car stopped in front of a grand mansion. A man stood at the entrance.

"We're going to freshen up and then head for the airport. Our flight leaves for London in four hours."

"But my bag, all my stuff, is still at the hotel."

"Chris moved your things when you went missing. You'll find everything you need here."

Outside the house, the man greeted them and led them inside. As Ben had said, her suitcase was in one of the bedrooms.

"Try and relax before we have to head out again. I'll take care of Kaya," Chris said before shutting the door and leaving Selina and Ben alone.

As soon as the door shut, Ben had her against the wall and kissed her. Relief and passion. Desire and need. All mixed in that kiss, a brutal claiming. Hers wasn't a quiet surrender, but an all-out open-hearted relinquishing of control and allowing him to take possession. Knowing that she would never call anywhere home but in his arms.

He ate at her lips as if she was succour. She understood the craving, with all the adrenaline stored in her body needing to dissipate. She wanted to get under his skin and have him get under hers.

His hands tore at her clothes, taking a break from the kissing to yank the top over her head. She palmed his groin and the hot, hard bulge pulsed in her hands.

He groaned and buried his head in her shoulder. She tilted her head, giving more room as he nipped and licked the side of her neck up to her ear.

Her core clenched, seeking him and feeling empty as his hand massaged her breast. Her clit throbbed and she cried out.

"Ben, I need you."

She gripped his arms, one braced against the wall, the other twisting her nipple as he sucked her earlobe. A pulse of electricity razed through her body, and she canted her hips, rubbing up against his bulge.

He swore and lifted her around the waist, pivoting and walking away from the wall. He released her, and she landed on the soft covering of the bed as he covered her body with his. He resumed kissing her while his hands tugged at her skirt, pulling it down. She lifted her hips, aiding the progress. Before long, she was bare under him, open to his touch. Aching for him.

His fingers caressed her clit, making her burn, clench, ache, cry out his name.

"Ben, please."

"Please, what?" He lifted his head, watching her as if he wanted to eat her up.

"I need to come."

"Not without me, Beauty," his voice was deep and husky. "I need to be buried deep inside you. I need to feel you in every nerve...every fibre of my body."

He leaned back onto his knees and pulled his t-shirt off, revealing his tanned torso and honed abs. Her mouth watered, and her heart drummed against her chest. There was beauty in masculinity and Ben represented it in all the rippling muscles on display.

He shucked his trousers, his usual tidy discipline discarded. His grey eyes smouldered with heat, holding her captive as he settled back between her thighs.

"I need to feel you in my very soul."

Gripping her hips, his tip brushed her slit. With one thrust he was in, banging her against the headboard.

"Oh, God." She cried out as pain mixed with pleasure. She bowed off the bed, lifting her hips, needing more of him.

And he fed her, pulling out to the tip, and slamming into her again, his balls against her bum.

"Ben..." She panted.

"Tell me what you need."

"More." She clenched around him. "I need more."

He slid out and rammed in. "Is this—" Out and in. "—what you need?"

"Yes," she cried out. She was so close. A fire burned in her core, her insides clenching around him.

Ben lifted her leg over his shoulder and pistoned in and out harder, one hand squeezing her breast.

"Come for me, Lina." He tugged her nipple hard.

She screamed as the fever took her over. He didn't let up until finally he growled her name, slammed into her one last time, and came in shudders after her.

She must have dozed off because she woke with a start, frightened to the core thinking she was back in the room in Tony's house.

"You're in a safe place, Lina," Ben said in a gentle voice as his arm got tighter around her, his fingers stroking her skin. "He won't hurt you ever again."

She sucked in a deep breath and relaxed back into his body. Yes, she was safe with Ben. He'd rescued her.

Again?

She turned her head up so she could see his face as he lay beside her in the bed, their bodies now covered with a sheet as an air-conditioning unit kept the room fresh.

"He said you'd rescued me before. What did he mean?"

Ben met her gaze and held it. She was grateful he wasn't going to hide the truth from her. His fingers stroked her cheek and neck tenderly, matching the look in his eyes.

"I told you we'd been in Sierra Leone. The mission had been simple. Deliver a shipment of ammunition to the rebel group. We did that easy enough. But what I hadn't been prepared for was the dehumanization I witnessed. What the militia did, especially to young boys and girls. That got to me, and I wasn't going to just turn my back and walk away. So, Chris and I planned the rescue and freed a bunch of young girls and women from the camp after drugging and incapacitating the men of the militia."

Selina frowned. "You rescued me? I was told I was rescued by the Nigerian peacekeeping ECOMOG army."

The ECOMOG troops were multilateral armed forces established by the Economic Community of West African States to work together, especially during a period of regional military strife. The Nigerian army formed the backbone, but there were also troops from Ghana, Guinea, Sierra Leone, and other West African countries. During the war in Sierra Leone, the intervention of ECOMOG troops had saved countless civilian lives, including hers.

"Well, we weren't supposed to be in Sierra Leone and didn't want to answer any questions, so we delivered the escapees to the Nigerian army peacekeeping team. That's how we met Kenny. He was the Lieutenant leading a troop of men who were stationed in the area. They helped us execute the safe delivery of the captives. We made sure everyone was given the help they needed, and then we left. It was reported as a successful rescue by the ECOMOG peacekeeping force, and that suited me fine."

"Did you know it was me in London? All this time?"

"No. I didn't. Not until you told me what happened to you and I started thinking about it. I hired an investigator and got Kenny to make some inquiries. He'd found your ex and made the connection. Tony had become the local crime kingpin, with a hand in everything from arms dealing with Boko Haram in Northern Nigeria to human trafficking to MUJWA jihadists in Mali. That was partly why I didn't want you to come here alone. I didn't want you to be on your own in case you met your ex again."

"You saved my life. Twice." Adoration for him left her breathless, her body tingling and temperature rising.

"No, Beauty. You saved my life. If I hadn't come to Sierra Leone and seen what I'd seen, I never would have changed. I would never have become the man I am today. You opened my eyes to a life beyond my own selfish desires. I am a better man because of you."

His words warmed her heart. She'd never saved anyone's life before, beyond dispensing drugs that helped make people better. Her own way of giving back. Now finding out that Ben thought she'd saved his life was like the cherry on top of a lovely cake.

"We saved each other." For the first time in ten years, she felt as if her scars were no longer festering, but were now healing. She was going to be all right. No more lurking in the shadows, hiding who she was.

"We did. I love you, Lina."

"I know. And I love you, Ben."

This time she kissed him, her hand braced against his head.

"I can't seem to get enough of you this morning," she said.

"In which case, we can have a shower quickie before we have to go catch our flight. I want to be in the air when the news about Tony breaks."

He stood and tugged her up from the bed. She followed him, understanding the urgency. She wouldn't be fully relaxed until they were all back in London.

Epilogue

Ben slid off the stool. They were back in Bar Atlantic, and it was a month after their return from Africa. This time only a handful of his and Selina's friends were here. It was strictly a private affair.

On one of the sofas, Juan sat next to his wife, Noni. There was a gentle bump on her belly, her pregnancy now beginning to show.

A smile played on Ben's lips. Soon he looked forward to seeing Selina blooming with his baby growing inside her. They had started working on it as Selina had stopped taking her contraceptive pills.

Nervously, he patted the medium-sized box on the bar counter. As much as the idea of being a father gave him joy, given the recent incidents in South Africa, he wondered if he would make a good father. He certainly never wanted to put his children through the pain his parents had put him through.

With Selina by his side, he would be the best husband and father. Their African trip had solidified his love for her. And to top it off, she had agreed to give herself to him, no holds barred. Body, heart, and soul.

Today, finally, she would accept him as her Master, with their friends to bear witness.

Today, though she would kneel at his feet before everyone, he would accept her submissiveness and raise her above all else. He would show them his devotion to her and her only.

"Can I see what you bought?" Kenny stepped up to him. The man had been very reserved after Beatrice returned to South Africa a few weeks previously.

Ben could swear something passed between his friend and his sister. But he wouldn't bring it up unless than man wanted to talk about it.

Ben would return to South Africa soon. He had unfinished business with his father.

He opened the medium-sized box revealing the bespoke jewel-encrusted collar he's had made. It was designed like a choker with a large ruby and smaller diamonds. Instead of a standard clasp, it had a gold padlock with his initials engraved onto it.

"Wow," Kenny said. "That must have cost a small mortgage."

Ben laughed. "She is worth it."

It wasn't a twenty-four-hour collar. It was a symbol of devotion she could wear during their playtime or when they went out together. For every day, he would return the bracelet he'd given her on their wedding night to its rightful place on her wrist. She had earned it back. And it would make him both proud and humbled to see her wearing it every day. Of course, he had added other charms to it. A ruby heart and a silver padlock.

Chris approached with a grin on his face and clutched Ben's shoulder. "Are you ready?"

"You bet I am." Ben smiled in return as the door leading to the back offices opened, and Lora stepped out first, followed by Selina.

A lump formed in his throat and his heart thundered. She was dressed in a ruby corset and a short black layered-chiffon skirt, her dark hair swept up in an elegant bun. He'd selected her outfit. The sight of her took his breath away.

God, I love her. And he was about to declare it to the world.

A smile lit up her face as she walked towards him. With grace, she lowered her body onto her knees in front of him and tilted her head forward, baring her nape where the lock of the collar would caress the top vertebra. Two words sprang into his mind.

Mine. Forever.

From the author:

Thank you for reading The Ben & Selina Trilogy. Please leave a review on the site of purchase. To find out about my upcoming book releases and giveaways, sign up for <u>my newsletter</u>.

Visit: www.kirutaye.com

I would also love to connect with you on social media. You can find me on <u>Facebook</u>, <u>Twitter</u> and <u>Instagram</u>.

OTHER BOOKS BY LOVE AFRICA PRESS

A Place Called Happiness by Diana Anyango
One More Night by Rosemary Okafor
Love Happens Eventually by Feyi Aina
Fine Scotch by Emem Bassey
Bad Santa by Kiru Taye

CONNECT WITH US

Facebook.com/LoveAfricaPress
Twitter.com/LoveAfricaPress
Instagram.com/LoveAfricaPress

SIGN UP TO OUR NEWSLETTER
https://www.loveafricapress.com/newsletter

www.ingramcontent.com/pod-product-compliance
Lightning Source LLC
Chambersburg PA
CBHW050750190726
48285CB00005B/1607